Stone Garden

ALSO BY MOLLY MOYNAHAN

Parting Is All We Know of Heaven

Stone Garden

MOLLY MOYNAHAN

wm

WILLIAM MORROW
An Imprint of HarperCollins*Publishers*

This is a work of fiction. The characters, incidents, and dialogues are products of the author's imagination and are not to be construed as real. Any resemblance to actual persons, living or dead, is entirely coincidental.

HarperCollins books may be purchased for educational, business, or sales promotional use. For information please write: Special Markets Department, HarperCollins Publishers Inc., 10 East 53rd Street, New York, NY 10022.

FIRST EDITION

Designed by Cassandra J. Pappas

Printed on acid-free paper

Library of Congress Cataloging-in-Publication Data
Moynahan, Molly.
Stone garden / Molly Moynahan.—1st ed.
p. cm.
ISBN 0-06-054426-0
1. Loss (Psychology)—Fiction. 2. Grief—Fiction. I. Title.
PS3563.O965S765 2003
813'.54—dc21
2003041204

'This book is dedicated to
Lucas Joseph Moynahan Helliker, the light of my life.
I will feed you tea and oranges . . .
"thank you, Miss Nesbit."

ACKNOWLEDGMENTS

Thank you to Jane Gelfman for always telling me the truth and giving me the dream after this long sleep. And Cathy who said I could be a diva now. And to Carolyn Marino and Jennifer Civiletto, an editorial team spun from pure gold.

Thank you to my mother for her unflagging belief in my writing, and to my father for giving me his support, his genes, and some of his brilliant connections.

Thank you to Judith Ruhana, the best boss I've ever had in my life, colleagues at ETHS—Nancy, Rodney, Carol, Janet.

Thank you to all the teenagers I have taught who let me listen to their passion and learn some of their mysterious ways.

Thank you to Brian and Robin, Jamie, Truda, and Steve and Linda. Friends who frequently tell me my life is ridiculous.

Thank you to Timo Goodrich, renaissance iron worker, kind man, amazing father, graceful friend.

Stone Garden

One

THE POETS HAD COME BEFORE. We listened to their poems politely, wondering how it must seem to them, being bused out of prison to visit a bunch of high school students to tell them about poetry. Except it wasn't like that. You never heard any of these guys discussing nuance or meter or any of those terms our English teachers try to make us remember even though they're boring and useless.

The prisoners never talked about poetry at all. They talked about prison. They talked about how it felt once you heard all the doors locking behind you, how it no longer mattered who you were or what you'd done or whether your lawyer was some big shot. They said *fuck*. They said *shit* and *asshole* and *butt-fucked*. It was like all the rules were suspended when the poets came. Our headmaster, Duncan Farley, stood at the side of the stage and smiled. Smiled and smiled in his white duck pants, brown deck shoes, and paisley bow ties. His face was the same face he had when the little boys from the American Boys Choir came at Christmas and sang "Ave Maria," their voices so high and sweet they made your teeth hurt. He scanned the auditorium searching for kids who weren't paying attention. As soon as he caught their eyes he'd gesture toward the poets and wink. Duncan Farley was a major winker.

The poets said stuff like "Listen, you spoiled motherfuckers—don't do anything stupid. You'll end up like us—locked up, fucked up, somebody's bitch with nothin' to look forward to but your momma comin' to visit and you sittin' there crying till you can't take it anymore and you cut your throat." They paced back and forth like the fake wrestlers on the WWF, trying to convince us we were about to lose everything.

But kids like us didn't end up in jail. There was rehab, loony bins, and special schools for anyone who might get violent. We were tutored, braced, immunized, counseled, and medicated. Our counselors would write notes for us describing our symptoms in the most glowing terms, convincing everyone that our lack of direction and respect for authority and our general laziness were the result of adolescent angst and unrecognized brilliance. If we performed poorly on standardized tests, special academic support was just a phone call away. Many of my friends had personal trainers and their own private therapists. We took SAT prep classes, we consulted nutritionists, we gave ourselves Myers-Briggs personality quizzes and told our teachers the reason we couldn't meet deadlines was that we were wired in a unique way. The stuff the prisoners told us didn't register. We were spoiled rotten and didn't have a clue.

And then they read their poems. Poems about sunsets, rainy days, and kittens. Bad poems our teachers would have marked up with "cliché," "mixed metaphor," "stale image," "???."

Really corny rhymes about their mothers. But mainly it was food. Endless stanzas about food: mangoes, grapes, fatback, steak, peas, corn, cucumbers, lemons, spaghetti, ham, apple pie, turkey. There weren't even metaphors in these poems, just point-blank descriptions of favorite meals. They could have published a cookbook.

Some of the poets seemed proud of how they ended up in jail. One guy read a poem about cutting someone's throat, and then he looked up at us and said: "I did that."

Since I'd started high school, I had seen these poets five times. Christmas vacation was over and the poets were back. Some of the parents decided the poets were a bad thing. A petition to stop their program was circulated that had the following statement attached:

Prison poets would be a wonderful asset to a nonprivate, less selective institution than Millstone Country Day. The life experiences these individuals describe, while inspiring, are irrelevant to the experiences of MCD's population. The school would be far better served by a series of lectures given by CEOs, successful entrepreneurs, and famous artists, all of whom exist in the current alumni pool.

My mother found the petition hilarious. "What about Leopold and Loeb?" she asked my father. "What about Graham Steadforth's son being arrested for running a gambling and prostitution club? And Lizzie Macklin's daughter who sold drugs?"

My father looked over his bifocals and frowned. "You can't argue that students from Millstone frequently end up in the slammer."

My mother looked disgusted. "Of course they don't," she said. "Their parents hire famous criminal lawyers to dispute speeding tickets and pay off judges. It's black and Hispanic children that end up doing time."

This was their normal routine. Mom was "down with the people" and Dad pretended to be a snob.

"Nevertheless," my father said, removing his glasses slowly. "While Leopold and Loeb introduced the concept of Ivy League psychopaths, most senseless murders are committed by southern drifters. Mainly men in their twenties who hail from Texas."

Sometimes I wonder whether people realize how stupid their habits are. Take the glasses thing. My father had twenty different ways to take them off.

"And live in trailer parks," I added.

"And have three names," my father said, winking at me. "Joe Bob Billy."

"Danny Lou Ray," I shouted.

"Bobby Will Paul."

"Tammy Sue Louise," Mom said. "They can be girls, too."

She leaned over to push my bangs off my forehead, staring at that part of me as if it contained the answer to world peace.

"What?" I asked.

"Nothing," she said, sighing. "You have such a wonderful forehead."

This was her habit. Forehead worshiping.

The petition didn't work and the poets kept coming.

Matthew Swan was still missing. The police at the Texas border were no longer searching for him, and the private detective told the Swans to give up. A completely stripped Dodge Dart that might have been the car they had taken was sitting in a garage outside of a Mexican town called La Ascensión. I took the atlas out and stared at the dot next to that name, but there was little to learn from knowing where it was. I had known Matthew since the first day of kindergarten, and we had been best friends for eleven years.

We were in love with each other every other year, but someone was always in love with someone else. Or not in love with anyone but obsessed with something like soccer (me) or the Ramones (Matthew), so we weren't into dating.

Still, we both knew that someday the timing would be right and we would end up running across a big field and then falling into each other's arms and kissing passionately. Actually, we'd done that once, but it was a joke. We knew we were going to be with each other forever because we'd already survived junior high. We'd survived recognizing the world wasn't the way our parents told us, that people frequently cheated and lied and hurt one another on purpose. We had learned about the big stuff like the Holocaust and the My Lai Massacre and Bosnia, and the smaller stuff like how petty some teachers were and how a girl being called a bust down could make her feel like she didn't have the right to live.

The year no one stayed with their original friends, we kept picking each other for cooperative group work and gym. People told us we should develop different criteria for our best friend but it didn't make a difference. When my mother took six girls to New York for dinner and a matinee of *Rent,* Matthew came, and I went on his annual rock-climbing expedition with his uncle and four other boys. When Camilla Crawford called Matthew "Granola Boy," I slapped her, and when Jeremy Pinkerton told Matthew he thought I was fat, Matthew let the air out of the tires of his new Mercedes SUV.

In cop shows when the police talked about "watching one another's back," we always knew what that meant. We were partners, and if I'd been in Mexico with him I think things would have turned out differently. I'm not saying I could have kept what happened from happening, but I think it would have been a different trip and no one would be searching for drugs or talking to bad people. We would have stayed in a youth hostel and called home, and no one would have disappeared. We would have been safe because my whole life had been about keeping Matthew safe so we could grow up and be in love and have children and all that other shit that's never going to happen.

Matt was really big for his age, for any age: at least six-three and still growing. Until ninth grade, we were the same height. My dad marked the wall every New Year's Day, and you could hardly tell the difference between us. Then Matthew grew seven inches one summer and left me behind. I still didn't have boobs or a butt, and it was awkward and weird. In all the books I read the girl was supposed to be the one to suddenly mature, but we were reversed. He still had a baby face, but he was so tall, no one noticed.

That was the summer Mr. Swan left. The Swan kids were hippies—three older sisters who were known as total bust downs and a younger brother who had too many learning disabilities to attend Millstone. He went to the public school, where they have these teams of special ed teachers who follow you around all day like an army. Ivan had always been sort of spacey, but he didn't seem dumb to me at all. He could read cereal boxes when he was four, and he understood the hardest video games when he was even younger than that.

They were all beautiful. Ivan's hair fell down his back in shiny yellow curls, and the girls were skinny, long-haired, and mean. They dressed in faded Indian print skirts and scarves they used as shirts. In the winter they wore layers of velvet and lace, ancient cashmere sweaters, and lamb's-wool coats. When it rained they smelled like patchouli, pot, and damp wool. The Swan sisters unnerved people. They tended to move as one, to whisper and giggle, and to say and do things that were bad. You couldn't go into stores with them because they stole stuff all the time. Stupid stuff like batteries and candy and hair dryers. They were banned from half the stores in Millstone.

So, I KNOW he's dead. That's all. I know it and so do his sisters. I've seen them standing in the parking lot of the 7-Eleven, smoking cigarettes or drinking from brown paper bags. Chloe, Samsara, and Nell. Their hair, no matter how dirty it is, shines like spun gold. Sometimes they wave at me, but mostly they pretend not to see me because I am too close to something that is lost. His mom acts like she doesn't know she's avoiding me. Maybe she thinks I let Matthew get killed. When we walked my dog, Pip, our parents always told us that we had to cross the street together holding hands, and if someone tried to talk to us we should yell and run. I let him go because I thought he would come back and then we could start our real lives. I let him go because people told me if our love was real it would survive his taking this trip even though he was with another girl. I didn't think someone in Mexico would kill two teenagers. So now she hates me or something. Who can blame her?

One day we ran into each other at the health food store. Mrs. Swan took off her dark glasses to sign a check, and when she looked up our eyes met and I saw how much she was suffering. Her eyes were dark inside, and there were these huge circles under them. She'd been in AA since Matt was eleven, but I was sure she was drinking again or taking drugs. Her eyes were terrible.

"Alice," she said, not even trying to smile. "How's school?"

"Great," I answered too fast.

I remembered how she'd started to go to twelve-step meetings and Matt went, too. I went once, and people didn't seem to notice or care. They were held in this big church basement, and Mrs. Swan got a year coin, and when she started to talk about how she stopped drinking, she kept pointing at Matthew and saying the word *love*, like that explained it all. I ate seven cookies and drank real coffee that was so strong, later I couldn't sleep.

That day at Heavenly Grains she stared at me and put her hand out like she was going to touch my face. I'd known her since I was six years old. She'd rocked me back to sleep when I had bad dreams during overnights. I wanted to move toward her, to go right into those arms so both of us could feel something. But I was frozen.

"Good," she said, putting her glasses back on like a mask. "Come see us," she added, although she knew I wasn't friends with any of her other children.

"I will," I said. "Sorry," I added and then stopped, but she didn't hear me.

As I passed the notice board I saw they still had the flyer up with Matt's photograph, a really bad one from the tenth-grade camping trip. MISSING it said in huge black letters. It was the same picture Mr. Jurgenson had put on his milk cartons, which was a really terrible thing because one morning we were eating breakfast and then we saw there was this picture of Matt on the milk with details about how he disappeared. My mother started to cry. We sat there with waffles in front of us and my mother crying and I felt like maybe it wasn't going to be possible to survive. It snowed on the tenth-grade camping trip, and we zipped our sleeping bags together and breathed each other's frozen breath and Matthew sang me a song about "Quinn the Eskimo," and then we slept and woke up to eat bacon and porridge, which tasted amazing.

I went to school the day after I saw Mrs. Swan with this tight feeling all through my body. And the prisoners were back.

Millstone Country Day is a private school and a public school. You can go there for free if you live in this teeny section right next to the school where houses cost at least a million dollars. Or you can be really, really poor and get a scholarship or you can be like me and be smart and middle class and your parents can pay a sliding scale to send you there. The Swans had lived in their house across the street from the school for a hundred years.

What can you say about New Jersey? It's called the Garden State, but it's famous for being the chosen home of the Mafia, Bruce Springsteen, and a bunch of people who couldn't afford to live in Manhattan. My dad likes to play a song called "I'm from New Jersey" by this singer-songwriter named John Gorka, which claims people from New Jersey don't expect much. He says it should be our state song, but I don't think the governor would agree to that.

Millstone Country Day is not like a normal school. There are fireplaces in the front hall that get lit on the first day of a frost and windows that make the hallways light and carpeting that an interior designer donated which is really beautiful and soft. The classrooms have cool tiled floors, and a painting company owned by a family that has ten children freshly paints the walls each summer. We don't sit at desks. There are tables, wooden tables with chairs, and then there are separate study "nooks," where you can curl up on cushions. There's this thing called the honor code, which is supposed to keep us from doing bad stuff. No one ever believed in it but Matt. He was always invoking various clauses and confessing to dorky crimes like cutting school so he could be absolved and set free by the clique that called itself the justice committee.

Our homeroom is one of two senior class homerooms. Ms. Hardwood is forty-four and gay. She and her partner adopted a Chinese baby girl and brought her home in a doll basket because she was so small. Her name's Grace, and if Ms. Hardwood hadn't adopted her she told us the hospital would have stopped taking care of her and she would have died. Before Matthew went to Mexico we used to walk Grace around the block in her stroller, stopping to let her get out and run, which she frequently wanted to do. Grace was four last year, and every time I see her now she runs up to me and says: "Where's Matt-Matt?"

The guy who runs the tire place told us we looked like a "happy little family." Me and Matt, Grace and Pip. Kind of a sick idea, since Matt and I would have had to have made Grace when we were thirteen, but in another way, kind of nice.

Ms. Hardwood's partner is a blacksmith. It's a rare thing to do in modern society, but it turns out a lot of people in Millstone have horses and they need to get new shoes. Also, she makes these very complicated metal thingies for the outsides of houses. My mother said rich people love metal sconces. Her name is Amy, and she used to play chess with Matthew. I think she loved him. I've known Ms. Hardwood since before I was born. She was in love with my uncle once, but he died, and sometimes I remember that and think I should ask her when it stops feeling like your throat is full of glass.

"The poets from Rahway Prison will be here today," Ms. Hardwood said after making several announcements about gym requirements and graduation.

We groaned.

"All right," she said, "let's try and remain open to the idea that Walt Whitman or Anne Sexton might be serving time for car jacking."

The poem that made me know that Matthew was never coming home wasn't about Mexico or dying or lost people. It was about pie and how hard it is to see one get eaten. And then you wonder if this could be the last piece of pie in the world. And you try to recall the way it had tasted, how the apples and the crust and the ice cream mixed together and melted in your mouth. You were screwed because you couldn't remember the flavor. There was this huge hole in your belly and no more pie.

I couldn't remember how Matthew's hand felt inside mine, the exact color of his eyes, or the way he smelled because, unlike most boys, he smelled wonderful. His sisters were always spraying him with perfume and giving him scented soaps. It wasn't easy anymore to find his voice in my head, the way he sang, "Go ask Alice, when she's ten feet tall . . ." His footsteps sounded a certain way, his cough, his sigh, his laugh, which kind of rumbled and then climbed until he could have been a girl giggling.

I used to be able to summon all those elements like a witch at a cauldron creating something from scattered pieces. But nothing came to me anymore. He was gone and I was left behind. The video-tapes and recordings didn't make any difference. It was watching a ghost, a shadow, an echo of a voice. It was worse than nothing.

The pie poem ended, and those of us still awake clapped. This friend of my mom's was writing an entire dissertation based on ado-lescent sleep patterns. He claimed we were sleep deprived because our circadian rhythms were based on nocturnal energy and school was totally wrong at 8:00 A.M. because we were still deep in REM. He interviewed a bunch of us and paid us to come into his sleep lab-oratory and take tests with electrodes attached to our heads. This was the reason we passed out like gassed bunnies during school assemblies.

I noticed Sigrid Anderson was leaning forward, her hands clutch-ing the seat in front of her so hard, the knuckles looked as white as chalk. Sigrid was pretty chalklike anyway, very blond, nearly albino, no natural color anywhere. I expected her to sit back, but she kept hunching forward and sounds like someone struggling to breathe were coming out of her mouth.

"Are you okay?" I whispered. Another poet was on a rant about Jell-O.

She said something I couldn't understand.

"What?" I asked. It was a hard situation. We weren't friends. I didn't know what to do.

She suddenly sat back and I could see she'd been crying. Her face was red and her eyes looked raw. I looked right and saw a long line of sleeping classmates.

"He killed my baby-sitter," Sigrid finally managed to say, her hand indicating the entire stage of prisoners.

"Which one?" I asked. This was a stupid question.

She pointed at a guy sitting at the end who hadn't read anything yet. Duncan Farley was right next to him, rocking on the balls of his feet, grinning his grin. The poet had a nearly shaved head, and his cheekbones stood out sharply. His biceps were enormous, and a tattoo of a phoenix rising from flames covered his upper arm. I had a moment of disappointment since he was so handsome in a prisoner sort of way. Why couldn't the person who killed Sigrid's baby-sitter have been the fat one? This one looked like a movie star.

I glanced back at Sigrid, who was now completely white except for two red splotches on each cheek. She wasn't breathing.

"When?" I asked, shaking her a little, surprised by the smallness of her arm.

"I was nine," she said in a hiss, like air leaving a tire. "Thor was four."

Eight years.

"Was he convicted of murder?"

Sigrid shook her head. "Involuntary manslaughter," she said as if the words were right there in her mouth.

"But you said he killed her."

Sigrid nodded.

"So he didn't do it on purpose?"

"Yes, he did." Her voice was low, but the tone was very sharp.

I waited.

"No one was home but us. He was behind the door and then he strangled her."

"In front of you?"

She didn't answer. I touched her arm. "You were there?"

She stared at me. Sigrid's eyes were too blue, like a crazy Siamese cat. I was getting a headache.

"I hid in the closet."

"Where was Thor?" I wanted to keep her talking. She looked so pale her skin seemed blue.

"Taking a nap."

This was the worst thing I'd ever heard in my life. The poet who killed Sigrid's baby-sitter was now reading a poem about the aurora borealis. Duncan Farley was staring at the ceiling as if he expected the sky to suddenly be revealed. To be left in the charge of such a moron filled me with a rage so sour I could taste it. Here my parents were paying for an education, and friends of mine disappeared while others were exposed to the bad poetry of murderers.

"Jesus, Sigrid," I said, putting my hand over her drawn knuckles, the skin as cold as ice. They were little-girl hands, nails bitten down to the nubs, fingers stained by ink.

"He called up while I was still in the closet, and when I finally picked up the phone he told me I'd better keep the secret or he'd kill my parents. He said he was going to turn himself in to the police but he would tell them it was an accident."

"What did you say?"

"I said, Don't kill my parents."

I looked around for a moment, wondering how anyone could manage to keep his or her sanity. Sigrid grabbed my hand. "Alice," she said, "don't tell anyone."

Why had she chosen me? Millstone's cliques probably seemed amorphous from the outsider's perspective, but we knew they were clearly delineated, enclosed worlds. My group was the hippie-environmentalist-rebel-art clique. We didn't do a thing together, but when times grew difficult we'd pull on black armbands, stage a guerrilla theater protest in the front hall, or simply leave school for the woods, where we sometimes dropped acid or smoked dope but mostly sat around talking about how much we pitied our parents and hated high school. The things I liked about us were our lack of a uniform, the general acceptance of extremely antisocial behavior, and a rejection of the importance of things like prom.

There were the preps—deck shoes, corduroy pants, Fair Isle sweaters for the girls with thin gold chains and stud gold earrings, oxford cotton shirts for the boys, no socks. The preps liked folky art rock and had parties at the country club. Their sports were field hockey, ice hockey, soccer, and lacrosse. They were intolerant of any deviation from what they considered "tradition," drank prodigiously, and acted middle-aged.

The socialites wore Lilly Pulitzer prints and carried baskets for purses. There were no boys in this group. I don't think they actually had any philosophy. It was mainly a fashion choice.

The kids who didn't live in the area were bused in from Trenton, and their clique was born from exclusion. They played ghetto games like basketball and listened to R&B and ignored all the social behavior of the rest of the school. Whenever there was any assembly on diversity, they ended up on stage dressed in FUBU looking bored. They used bad grammar, and they were usually cheerful and friendly. All the black kids were in this group, the kids from mixed marriages, and one boy from Ecuador, who was rich but ended up there by default. Peter Wong didn't belong in that group either, but being Chinese he was considered difficult to absorb, so they let him hang around even though he had no street cred and he was always winning awards for being a math genius.

The politicians ran the school, dressed like bankers in straight skirts, wool pants, ironed shirts, and sometimes jackets. They frequently participated in junior versions of adult institutions like the

United Nations and the Supreme Court. They were the ones who ran the justice committee and meted out the punishments earned by defying the honor code. All the members of the debating club came from this group, and they sat together at lunch having staged arguments. They followed Duncan Farley around like ducklings, and they made all the announcements in the morning over the P.A.

The politicians were sort of our enemies. The antisocial stance of our clique was an affront to their involved, get-with-the-program attitude. It's not like we were lazy, but we didn't think high school was the place to make a major impact. I considered it a staging area, a place where you gathered information.

Then there were kids like Sigrid who had no group, undocumented migrant worker kids who drifted the halls in search of sanctuary. They were dressed like children by their unobservant parents, they did their homework, and they never spoke in class or home room unless called upon. You'd see them walking home or waiting at the curb for their mothers to pick them up, their books clutched to their chests as protection, always alone.

Matthew didn't belong to any of these groups. He played basketball with the ghetto kids, he drank beer with the preps, he volunteered on committees run by the politicians, he sometimes even had tea with the socialites when one of their giggling ranks approached him with a muffin. He was friendly to the outcasts, and he was my best friend. Basically, he drew us together and encouraged us to forget how much we didn't like to be in high school. He helped us see that no one deserved to be treated badly. He did this without any effort. He was a boy who made people happy just by showing up.

And now I was stuck with Sigrid and her terrible secret.

Two

"WHEN DO PEOPLE GET PAROLE?"

My parents were in their after-dinner places, Mom on the couch finishing the morning crossword puzzle, Dad reading something hard and writing things in the margins with a black ballpoint. This was how it was every night. Usually it made me insane because they never did anything different, but after what Sigrid had told me I didn't mind how familiar it felt. Upstairs Alf was whispering secrets over the phone to his new best friend, Phil.

"What people?" my father asked.

"Who threw the winning pitch of the 1967 World Series?" my mother interjected.

Without skipping a beat, my father said someone's name and my mother wrote it down.

"Bingo," she murmured.

"People in jail," I said.

"Convicted criminals?"

"Uh-huh."

"And their crimes?" My dad was peering over his book, bifocals lowered.

"Has this anything to do with Matthew?" Mom had put her newspaper down and was staring at me.

I shook my head. The sound of his name brought a short, sharp pain.

"Maybe they sold drugs or they embezzled. Or maybe murder."

My father looked thoughtful. "I have no idea," he said. "I think people get paroled according to the circumstances around their crimes and depending on whether they behave themselves in jail."

"If they have good lawyers," my mom added, picking up the paper.

They didn't ask me any more questions. My parents had read a book called *Stop Asking Me Questions, I Hate You: Dialogues with Your Teen.* A doctor wrote it, and each chapter focused on a different problem. The chapter called "Death of a Peer" was bookmarked, and certain passages were highlighted.

I read the chapter, but it wasn't very helpful. The dead kids were killed in car crashes and gang fights. Nobody's best friend from kindergarten had just disappeared. There were some sample dialogues with parents starting conversations with statements like "I know you're in pain right now but it will get better." If my mother ever said anything that lame to me, I'd walk out of the house.

I got up and started to clear the table. My mother gave my father one of her looks. My father stood up and took the plates out of my hand.

"Relax," he said, and then he disappeared into the kitchen.

I moved toward the stairs.

"Alice . . ." my mother started.

"Yes?"

"Do you have any questions?"

I didn't want their attention, but I hated to be ignored.

"Do you ever think this is a dream?"

My father walked back in holding the same dirty plates he had just brought out.

"A good dream?" he asked me.

"No," I said. "A terrible dream. A nightmare. The feeling you get when you wake up and claw the sheets and you think you're being attacked by spiders."

My father stepped toward me. "We got rid of the spiders, honey!" He looked happy. "I bombed your whole room. Remember?"

"Jesus," I said. "You're just so literal, Daddy! It's pathetic!"

As I stomped up the stairs I heard him ask my mother, "What does she want, Julia? What does she want me to say?"

"Hush," my mother murmured, "she'll hear you."

I stomped back down and walked into the dining room.

"Okay," I said. "Why did I take so long to understand the meaning of life and what am I supposed to do now that it's been taken away from me?"

My father had put down the plates and was bent over my mom like he was trying to disappear into her body.

My mother drew her breath in so sharply I could feel how much it must have hurt.

"Good night," I said.

"Sweet dreams," she answered, her voice breaking a bit.

"You want some warm milk?" my father asked. "With honey?"

"No," I said, but I smiled at him sort of.

* * *

ON SUNDAY we were in our Sunday morning after too much breakfast positions. Dad was pretending to read *The New York Times Book Review*, but he'd nodded off. Mom was lying on the small couch we had on the sunporch trying to finish the magazine's puzzle.

"What band celebrated a famous girl in a child's story?" she asked me.

"Jefferson Airplane," I said, and then the pain hit again. I looked out the window to watch Alf where he was wrestling with Phil. They were like two puppies, falling down and rolling, hugging and kicking.

"God," I said, "life actually sucks."

My mother nodded. "What was that movie with Julia Roberts— the one that made her famous?"

"*Pretty Woman*," my father said.

"*Mystic Pizza*," I snapped.

"Define *sucks*," my father said.

"No," I said. "It's like being on a game show living here. You wake up and someone demands an answer."

My father loves to discuss things. He was the captain of the debate team in high school. Once he and Matthew spent an entire evening comparing the merits of mustard versus ketchup. Mainly, it's theoretical, which is much more irritating. The worst is when he tries to have an opinion about something he doesn't know anything about, like why rap isn't hip-hop.

"Define *life*," he said.

He also thinks he's funny. Sometimes he is, but he can't get past the fact that I no longer consider him the funniest man in the world. I'm nearly eighteen and I don't feel like laughing anymore.

"What happened to the Andersons' baby-sitter?" I asked.

My parents stopped what they were doing and looked at each other. Neither looked at me. They cleared their throats and smiled.

"You think I didn't know?"

"Know what?" my dad asked, slowly removing his glasses.

"That she was murdered."

"Alice—" My mother glanced at my father and stopped.

"It wasn't murder exactly—"

"Yes, it was," I said, forgetting my promise to Sigrid. I mean, this was worse than the secret about Midas whispered into the grass. This was a major thing.

"And how might you know this?"

"Sigrid Anderson told me."

"She told you her baby-sitter was murdered?"

"More or less." Then it struck me I should take it back.

"No," I said, trying to look confused.

My parents were staring at me. I decided I should stop talking.

I stood up. "I'm going to the library," I said. "We have a research paper due in a week."

"Sit down for a second," my father said. "Don't be in such a hurry."

"Didn't Sigrid change schools?" my mother asked. "Maggie Koning said she was attending that place where the kids rename themselves."

"Narnia," I said.

"Surely not?" my father asked, looking pained.

"Yup," I said. "It's a Waldorf school. The kids pretend to be elves and fairies. Then they go to normal school and deal drugs."

"Jim Anderson has liver cancer," my father said quietly.

"Oh no," my mother said. "Didn't Sigrid's mother die when they were in the other house?"

My father nodded. "Thus the full-time nanny."

This was very bad. A dead mother, a dying father, a murdered baby-sitter, and no friends. Life seemed really harsh.

"Look at those birds," my mother suddenly said, pointing at the cherry tree which stood right outside the window. It was full of birds for some reason, all of them chirping. "They think it's spring," she added, "instead of just a January thaw."

"He's never coming back," I said. "He's dead."

"Listen, Alice," my father said, "sometimes kids just take off—"

"Matthew didn't take off! He had permission to go to Mexico. His mom gave him her credit card, for God's sake! Anyway, he would never be completely out of touch!" I walked over to the sliding doors to look outside. "Hallie Swenson wanted to take this trip and he said yes because he was going to break up with her and he thought they could talk about it."

I turned back to stare at both of them. They looked frightened and small. They didn't contradict me.

"He loved me," I said.

"Alice—" my mother began.

"What? Look at the birdies? I'm not a baby anymore, Mom! You think I care about fucking birds when my best friend is dead and people's baby-sitters get strangled?"

"Who said she was strangled?" My father was staring at me.

"Oh, leave me alone," I screamed, stomping out onto the porch, scaring away the birds, which flew off in a swirling mass calling what sounded to me like "gone, gone, gone."

I contradicted my maturity rant by jumping on my pink three-speed Schwinn decorated with pink plastic streamers and riding away as fast as possible. In the little mirror attached to the handlebars I saw Alf standing alone in the driveway. He looked very small.

On the trip to Mexico, Matthew was going to tell Hallie Swenson that he couldn't be her boyfriend because we loved each other.

"Why can't you just call her up and tell her that?" I asked.

He had shaken his head. "She's a junkie, Alice," he said. "She'll overdose." He put his arms around me. "I don't want to go, but Hallie's really fragile."

Hallie Swenson was fragile like Courtney Love. She had graduated the year before us, but after three weeks she came back from Bard, where she apparently did nothing but walk around naked, crying.

I had said yes because I wanted to deserve him, I wanted to be his dream woman, his archetype for femininity, and the strong, faithful, heroic goddess, a combination of Emily Brontë, Joan Jett, and Joan of Arc. I had said yes because Matthew Swan had held my face in his hands and told me that he loved me with every part of himself, that he had loved me from the moment he saw me trip over my shoelaces, and while it had taken a while for us to grow up and get it right, we would get it so right that never, in the history of love affairs and marriages and big families with beautiful children and grandchildren, would anyone get it more right.

We had planned on a trip to Europe, cafés in Paris, and the beach in Greece. We were going to live in an apartment in either Seattle or Boston. We were going to be incredibly happy, and as I lay naked in our zipped together sleeping bags, my breasts and belly being kissed by him, I knew that when we finally made love, it would be better than anything I'd ever done. I felt safer, happier, stronger, and more hopeful than any time in my whole life. And my parents would understand because they loved him also.

Hallie Swenson hadn't been strong enough to destroy us until she got Matt to go with her to Mexico. He was sorry for her, which isn't love. He probably wanted to have sex with her too, but that isn't love either.

Things had happened that were bad. Mr. Swan ran away with a girl that he'd taught, an eighteen-year-old girl who was already pregnant. My parents went through a weird period my sophomore year when they kept fighting, and finally my dad moved for two months into a garden apartment where everything he ate had to be microwaved and you could hear if your neighbors breathed heavily.

Someone shot Darwin Mitchell in downtown Trenton because he was wearing gang colors by mistake. He was paralyzed from the waist down, and they named a basketball scholarship after him. Pets and grandparents and famous people we loved like Kurt Cobain had died. Terrorists blew up places in the Middle East and Oklahoma, and there was an incredible famine in Africa. But nothing so terrible as Matthew Swan. Nothing that twisted your insides so badly you thought you had cancer at least.

I rode as if I was racing against hundreds of people, my tires skidding along the road, and then I found myself outside his house, a place I'd avoided ever since he'd disappeared. I hammered on the door, sobbing like a child. After a moment, the door opened and Mrs. Swan stood there, and when she saw me her eyes filled with tears and she held her arms wide and I went to her. For this woman had given birth to him, and if I felt what I felt, her suffering was ten times worse.

Three

"YOU LIVE IN ART?"

Mrs. Swan said this is the first thing she heard me say when I was six and Matthew brought me into their house after one of our walks. I had asked him that because of the hallway where pictures lined the wall and a sculpture of Leda being raped by the swan was spotlighted at the far end, the bird's feathers ruffling slightly in the wake from a ceiling fan. I didn't know this was what the swan was doing. It took about ten years for my dad to finally let me read the Yeats poem and then to better understand how intense the whole thing was since *swan* wasn't just a bird but their family name.

Matthew's mother was no less exotic. Catherine Swan didn't dress like any of the other women I had seen in Millstone. She wore what I believed to be a costume but turned out to be a typical outfit—a velvet dress designed by a famous forties designer, shirred and ruffled in the front, slit up to the lower thigh, a satin shirt, which wrapped and tied around her waist, a silk scarf that covered her long, reddish gold hair. You wanted to touch and smell Catherine. She was all about sensory detail, smooth and fragrant and swirly with wild, exotic colors. Her bracelets jangled slightly, and sometimes her earrings tinkled. At first glance, she frightened me. It didn't seem appropriate for anyone's mother to be so beautiful and sexy. But soon I was following her around, sneaking into her bedroom to peek into jars of secret beauty potions, to lift the lids of boxes full of precious jewels. I thought she was Cleopatra. She hypnotized me.

My mother was beautiful but she didn't know it. I'd watched my father pull rubber bands out of her hair so it flowed nearly to her waist, dark and thick, brown with red highlights created by hours working in the garden. For a moment we would both stare at her, breathless and blinded by the transformation, her blue eyes suddenly bright as sapphires, her appearance like something from one of my fairy tales. But my mother was shy and didn't like to be looked at. She ducked her neck like a plain bird, a hen maybe. When we shopped together she would slip in and out of clothing, barely allowing herself to look at the mirror, frequently buying things without trying them on.

With me, she was different. I was more like her creation, her doll to dress and decorate. Until I rebelled at eight, my hair was kept long and braided or twisted into complicated arrangements around my head. I hated the whole Heidi thing. One Christmas my godmother sent me a dirndl, and somewhere my mother found a tiny pair of lederhosen for Alf, who looked completely ridiculous dressed like something on a beer stein.

Mrs. Swan allowed you to create yourself. Her three daughters swirled around her room in states of nakedness. Draping a feather boa around her neck, Samsara would shimmy into a lycra halter dress left over from the disco era, while Chloe was swathed in a severe Japanese tunic, and Nell was into a goth virgin thing with lots of white lace and leather. Matthew's sisters didn't appear ready to leave home. I think Samsara was the oldest at twenty-three, Nell was twenty-one, and Chloe, eighteen.

Nell was my favorite. She always asked me about school, and whenever I mentioned a teacher she didn't like, she'd roll her eyes and say, "Jesus, Alice! So-and-so is a total fuckhead!"

Samsara liked to take quaaludes, so it was hard to have a conversation with her, and Chloe, the youngest and most beautiful, was mean.

"She's jealous," Matthew told me once when we were fifteen and Chloe had told me my breath made her want to hurl.

"Why is she jealous of you?" I asked. I wanted to be pretty and to always smell like flowers.

"Not of me, doofus," Matt said, giving my head a rap. "Of you."

"Of me?"

"She doesn't like girls who are prettier than her."

I stared at him in dumb amazement. "She's gorgeous," I said.

"Everyone's gorgeous if they put on enough makeup," Matthew said, walking across his room to pick up a mirror. "It's being gorgeous when you've just been riding bikes and swimming and your hair's still wet."

I looked in the mirror, and then I ducked my head just like my mother.

Matthew looked down at me and gave me a noogie. "Forget it," he said. "This boy won't encourage female insecurity and objectification."

"Objectify me!" I wanted to scream. This was one of our disjunction times. I was totally in love with Matthew, and he was chasing some Zen Buddhist woman who was already a college freshman. I think they'd had sex. I lay awake at night and imagined them in the positions I'd studied in my parents' married-sex manual. It was pure torture. Who cared to ask what a college freshman would find fascinating in a fifteen-year-old boy?

The Swans' house had a variety of smells. The kitchen was the most overpowering, with its combination of yeast dough rising, spiced food cooking, and a scent that brought on hunger even if you had just finished a meal. Mrs. Swan was a natural and phenomenal cook. Her recipes were all memorized or invented. Cardamom and fennel seeds were crushed together in a mortar and pestle, heated until crackling in a cast-iron skillet, and then combined with olive oil and rice to begin the layering of flavors.

The Swans' house wasn't elegant at all. It was chaotic and dirty, and when Mr. Swan left and Catherine started to drink even more, it was dark and sad and scary. But I couldn't see those things. Or I saw them but I didn't care. If the red velvet couch was stained by years of kids spilling food, it was still much better than the Scotchgarded dark blue corduroy couch that graced my parents' living room.

Only once did I see the truth about Catherine's alcoholism. I came home from school with Matthew for lunch, and when we went into the kitchen, his mother was facedown at the table. I screamed.

"What do you want to eat?" he asked me, acting like there was no one at the table.

"Your mom . . ."

"Ignore her," he said. "She's fine. You want grilled cheese?"

I nodded. I was afraid to look at her. I had heard about grownups passing out, but I had never seen an actual example.

"Where's your dad?"

Matt's father taught poetry at Millstone. He frequently came home at lunchtime.

"Fucking his girlfriend."

At this, Catherine raised her head. It was pretty terrifying.

"Go upstairs, Mom."

I had never seen her like this. Her face was all puffy and white. Mascara streaked across her cheeks.

"Hello, Alice," she said, with the purr in her voice that I loved.

"Hi, Mrs. Swan."

"Call me Catherine."

"Get out of here, Mom."

"Excuse me," she said, standing up so suddenly the chair fell backwards. "Did you say something about your father?"

"I said he was fucking his girlfriend."

The mug flew past my face with so much force I felt its edge as a blow. But Matthew received the real impact. The thing hit him in the head so hard he staggered. I saw tears in his eyes, but he said nothing.

"Don't you ever speak to me like that again," his mother roared.

"Get out of here," Matt said, his shoulders shaking slightly.

And she did. Slowly, like an old woman.

"I hate her," Matt said as he put a grilled cheese sandwich down in front of me. "She made him do it."

It was impossible to understand what I'd just seen. My parents had fights, but there was no screaming and no throwing. I frequently screamed at and threw things at Alf, but he was forgiving and sunny in the face of my unfair and frequent bullying. Mrs. Swan had actually hurt Matthew. I could see a lump rising near his ear. The cheese sandwich stuck in my throat and I started to cry.

"Hey," he said, putting another plate down and looking at me with confusion. "Did that thing hit you?"

I shook my head. I was scared.

"Listen," Matt said, leaning over to hand me my sandwich like I was a little kid. "Don't mind her. She's really, really freaking out over my old man's leaving."

"He's leaving?"

Matt nodded. He stared out the window. "There's a baby," he said finally, "a baby and this chick who's the same age as Samsara."

"Are they getting married?"

He shrugged. "Marriage is a crock of shit," he said.

I didn't think that then. I thought it was a white dress encrusted in pearls, white satin slippers, and silk stockings and swirly dresses worn by beautiful bridesmaids. My cousin who lived in Baton Rouge married a very rich man, and they had a wedding that my father claimed cost more than our house. We were served caviar and oysters on ice and palate-cleansing sorbet and lobsters and steak and stuffed mushrooms and champagne, which I tasted and found too bubbly. Alf was dressed in a tiny tuxedo and held a puffy pillow with the ring sitting on it, and everyone said "ahh" when he came down the aisle. Later I danced with my father in my dress, a frilly, pink thing that my mother said made me look like something spun from sugar. This was marriage to me. Sugar and new clothes.

Mr. Swan taught senior English at Millstone. Some claimed he'd known Hemingway and fought a bull in Madrid. Others said he was a really famous writer who kept his identity secret. His classes were always shut on the first day of registration. He conducted them at a huge wooden table that filled a room in the coach house behind our school. Mr. Swan didn't believe in grades or parent conferences. When parents tried to visit him he'd lock the door of his office, and he never answered the telephone. Until he had the thing with this senior girl, no one expected him to lose his job. Duncan Farley was always referring to him as "our literary genius." But now he had gone too far.

The girl was a freshman at Harvard, expected to have a brilliant academic career, not to return to Millstone with a belly and a lawyer.

Mr. Swan liked me for some reason. He called me "that Alice creature" and told my parents I was a "deep, unconventional, and whimsical" child. He also told my mother she had a face like a Giotto Virgin, and my father said she immediately paid an unplanned visit to the Renaissance room in the Met to see what he meant.

My father found Gregory Swan ridiculous. "It's the Hemingway thing," I heard him telling my mother. "It's dated and dumb."

The thing was, he did remind you of Hemingway. Part of it was the wardrobe, which always included a worn suede shirt and corduroy pants tucked into hiking boots. His jackets had leather-patched elbows, and he smoked a pipe. Corny, but it worked. His hair was long and streaked with gray, and he was really, really handsome. You could see where the Swan kids got the majority of their looks. Mrs. Swan was very pretty, but Mr. Swan had this chiseled, high-cheekboned, piercing gray eyes thing that made most people, all people, a bit stupid.

Matthew hated him by the time we were both twelve.

"My father thinks he's being really deep when he tells me I should respect women and then he does it with one of his students."

There were girls at Millstone who had done stuff with boys by seventh grade. Not exactly sex but a lot of other stuff. I hadn't done anything. Being a tomboy kept me out of the circle of kids who had a social life. I never hung out at the shopping plaza, and my parents didn't belong to the country club. I had read the sex book my parents had under their bed. It was about six hundred Japanese women in strange sexual positions. I didn't quite understand how this information could possibly inspire my parents to anything but giggle.

Matthew's parents had other books—the Kama Sutra and Nancy Friday. We looked at these things, but really, it just wasn't us. Our passion for each other was very romantic. We wanted to make love someday, but in such a choreographed situation it would be less sex and more ballet.

The only person I discussed sex with was Amy, Ms. Hardwood's partner. I started riding my bike over to her smelting pit, and one day I asked her a question about why boys can't help getting hard-ons. Amy never stopped taking molten iron out of the fire or hitting things with her hammer. She didn't act like it was some big deal to be discussing penises, and she didn't ask me any dumb questions. She sort of mentioned her own experiences as a teenager, and she listened to me complain about how Larry Blake had tried to get me to touch his dick behind the field house. There was no sudden silence, nor did she seem all that shocked when I explained that half the girls in eighth grade had already had sex.

She mentioned AIDS, condoms, and emotional intimacy. She defined rape and said anything that was an imbalance of power was wrong. After a while, I forgot where I was.

"I'm in love with Matthew Swan," I whispered into the gathering darkness, Amy's anvil scattering sparks into the blue velvet. She raised her hammer and then stopped.

"How wonderful," she whispered back. "And he is truly worth loving."

I cried. Maybe because I hadn't told anyone, but mainly, I think, because saying what I felt about Matthew filled me with an equal amount of joy and sadness. Saying it made it so, and now I could drop it and smash it and stain it and ruin it.

One of Amy's horses walked up and nuzzled into my jacket, its soft nose a comfort against my skin. "Oh, Mockie," I whispered, "I'm in love with Matthew Swan." And Mockie, finding no apple, raised her head and whinnied, galloping away in search of a snack.

THE HOUSE WAS CLEAN. Not immaculate, but not filled by the clutter of five children. Samsara and Nell had rented an apartment closer to their bartending jobs; Chloe was never very messy; Ivan, obsessed by computers, lived in the basement; and Matthew, of course, was gone.

Without saying anything, we walked to the back of the house and into his room. One wall contained a huge poster of Che Guevera, another faced it featuring the guys from Rage Against the Machine. Matthew's last art project, a collage that included several photographs of me, was unfinished on his drafting board. Someone had dusted and preserved the very essence of him by allowing the room to simply wait. It was wonderful and terrible. I was afraid she would see what I had suddenly known about his being dead. But Catherine Swan wasn't looking at me. She was staring into space, her hands clenching at nothing.

"Why won't he come home?" she said finally.

"I don't know."

"For you." She didn't look at me but at one of the photographs.

"For everyone."

"Not his father." She spoke through clenched teeth, lips hard. "Not for him."

I nodded. Sitting down on his bed, my hand resting on the quilt his sisters had made the winter we spent in front of the fireplace playing endless games of euchre, I felt something, someone, somewhere.

"I had a psychic here," Catherine Swan said suddenly. "She did a reading of the room."

It was not good news.

"She said he was in another place and I should let him rest."

I looked at her and saw that tears were falling so rapidly down her cheeks, her eyes had nearly disappeared.

"He's tired," Catherine said, her voice soft and sweet. A mother's voice to a sick child.

"Then he needs to come back," I said, pettishly.

"I don't think he can, Alice."

I didn't say anything.

"She said he was sorry—"

I stood up suddenly. "He can come home if he wants to. He has to come home. I can't stay in high school, I can't live my life, I can't bear how this feels, I can't be anything without him. He was my Matt, my only Matt."

When Pip died, Matt sat with me in the kitchen and hugged me as I sobbed. Pip wasn't a particularly impressive dog, and no one had trained him to do anything but sit. We buried him in our secret space under a cherry tree and said a poem by a famous poet that Matt's father copied for us and placed a small, polished stone that just said PIP in beautifully shaped letters. Mrs. Swan had made that for me.

And now I was yelling at her as if it were her fault her favorite child had disappeared without a trace, like cars in the quarry, gone silently and deep. I was tired of praying and hoping and wishing and waiting and being patient. Nothing had come of any of it. I could remember the day he left and whispered in my ear, his breath sweet and warm. "Be my love," he said.

He wasn't a normal teenage boy. Normal teenage boys talk about sex like they talk about throwing up or playing soccer. They don't think about you as a person. They think about parts of your body, they separate you from yourself and then they rate those bits. Matthew cooked me dinner and lit candles and sat across from me asking how I'd written a poem that he read, or what did I think about the movie or how about we plan a rock-climbing trip, would I like that? He helped his mother stop drinking and he taught Ivan how to read and he arranged an intervention for Samsara, which didn't work but was still a pretty big thing for a kid to do.

I don't want to think about him anymore. If Adam and Eve needed one thing when they screwed up their situation, it was amnesia. You can live in original sin, guilt and misery, petty anger and self-ish greed as long as you have no basis for comparison.

Catherine was inhaling and puffing out her cheeks like a blowfish.

"What are you doing?" I asked.

"It's supposed to reduce wrinkles," she said.

Both of us started to laugh. I made a few fish faces.

"You don't have wrinkles," she said. "You have dimples."

"Do dimples segue into wrinkles?" I asked.

We were trying to leave his room without feeling like someone had ripped out our guts. Silliness helped

"You want something to eat?" Catherine put her hand on my shoulder. I was as tall as her now.

"No," I said.

Standing in the front hall, I inhaled deeply and tried to store that smell in my memory forever.

"I'm selling the house," Catherine said, as if she'd read my mind.

"What if he comes back?" I asked.

"They found some bones," she said slowly, "near where the car was last seen."

"Bones?" I asked, confused.

"Human bones, Alice, many, many, many human bones. They think there were drug people who did it."

I shook my head. "Matthew didn't do drugs," I said.

She nodded. "Hallie did," she said. "Her parents were about to put her back in rehab."

I hate Hallie Swenson. I'm sorry if she's dead, but I still hate her. It's because of her Matthew went on the trip, because she was a junkie and Matthew wanted to help her. Ever since Catherine Swan got sober he had this idea that he was some kind of sobriety tool, like a few words from him were going to get a druggie like Hallie to stop snorting and shooting junk. The thing was, Hallie looked innocent and much younger than eighteen. She wore baby doll nighties as dresses and glitter paint all over her cleavage, fishnet stockings and high heels. Boys didn't stand a chance.

"You knew about Hallie?"

"Of course not!" Mrs. Swan gave me an angry look. "You think I'd have let Matt go away with her if I knew that?"

"They weren't even friends," I muttered, looking to see how she reacted.

"Well, he did seem to have a crush on her . . ." Catherine paused. "I mean, a small one."

"A crush? On Hallie Swenson? No one gets crushes on evil people. They get stung and momentarily disoriented." I stopped. "He had a crush on her?"

Catherine shook her head. "I don't know, Alice. I think they spent the night together."

"Which night?"

"I had to go to New York to see a new doctor—" Catherine looked at me. "You can't be jealous. I mean, you have a boyfriend, don't you?"

I shook my head.

"Matt—" She stopped. "I don't understand teenage relationships," she said. "He didn't love Hallie. It was just a distraction."

"He was coming back," I said. "We were going to start our lives."

"Alice—"

"What?"

"He didn't think you'd want to go to college with a boyfriend." She said very fast.

I stared at her. "Boyfriend? I think we would have been married—"

Catherine sighed. "Which is very sweet but, Girl—" She shook her head. "He was worried about Samsara. He said he would take a year off to help her."

"He was coming to Madison with me."

"Eventually, but he wanted to help his sister first." She frowned. "We are so selfish," she muttered. "How could I have agreed to that?"

I imagined this line. This endless line of people waiting for Matthew to help them. Why did they think it was his job to make them better? Like he was a saint or something.

"Didn't he know I needed him?"

Catherine shook her head. "You didn't need him, Alice. You just loved him. You were the only person who offered him help in return. Hallie needed him, honey. That's very seductive."

Maybe he didn't love her but he'd slept with her. So this was what Mexico offered. A few more chances to be with Hallie Swenson while gaining credit for being an upstanding citizen.

We walked to the end of the hall. I looked back and thought that maybe I'd never see this place again. Catherine put her hand on my shoulder. "You were his favorite person in the whole world," she whispered. "His magical girlchick."

I nodded. "Keep me posted about the bones," I finally choked out, and then I ran out the door and grabbed my bike and rode away from town to where I could actually sit and scream and weep, keen, wail for Matthew and what was left for us to bury and forget.

Four

WHEN I WAS IN SECOND GRADE I won a perfect attendance
award. I had never missed a day of school since pre-k. Not even
when I broke my wrist or when the blizzard dropped nine inches
of snow on Millstone. School was like heaven. I hammered at its
gates.

That was then but this is now and now hates everything about
school. The thrill is gone. Seniors should be allowed to check in and
out. School is too small, too stupid, and too familiar. We've heard all
our teachers' jokes, we've seen every single assembly known to man,
we've checked out all the library books, we've broken most of the
rules, and it's still six months until commencement. We learn nothing. Ms. Hardwood said we reminded her of bitter old people in a
nursing home sitting around, waiting to die. Ms. Hardwood doesn't
have much time for anyone she considers a slacker. Last year she ran
a marathon for her sister who had breast cancer. We all raised

money, and Matthew and I made these huge banners we hung from trees that said: VALERIE ROCKS.

The trouble is, Ms. Hardwood and I are sort of in the same place as far as Matthew's concerned. Even though she's forty-four and a lesbian, I think she loved him as much as me and maybe part of her was in love with him. They were friends. He told her stuff I didn't know about: his mother's drunks and his father's lies and how Samsara was anorexic and Chloe was taking drugs. Ms. Hardwood has been distant with me since he disappeared. Amy said she's so upset about Matthew she's having trouble with people who remind her of him. I don't care all that much except it feels strange. We used to go over to their house to baby-sit Grace, and now I don't even know if Gracie's lost her front teeth or not.

One of my mother's brothers was killed in Vietnam right at the end of the war. On his last day of active duty, Uncle Adam stepped out of a jeep onto a land mine and died instantly, all of him broken so there was nothing left to bury.

Ms. Hardwood had been engaged to Uncle Adam. When my father told me I didn't understand.

"She's a lesbian," I said. "Isn't she?"

"Yes," my dad said. "But sometimes people are several things in their lives."

"You mean I could turn into a chipmunk or something?"

My father smiled. "No," he said. And then he looked upset. "Grown-ups don't stop wanting things," he said. "Just because we make certain choices that doesn't mean we're finished."

I had no idea in hell what he was talking about and I didn't want to know. Now I know, or I sort of know, and I still don't want to know. He's my father. He shouldn't want anything. He should just stop. I understand why the whole Birnam Wood thing is so radical. Macbeth went around cutting people's heads off but certain things needed to be dependable. Parents are like trees. They should stay in one place.

Looking at Ms. Hardwood, I could see a man loving her. The golf moms in our school were much more butch than she. They had these enormous, tanned, muscular forearms, while Ms. Hardwood was curvy and wore hip, pretty clothes. She was graceful and elegant. I couldn't help wondering if Uncle Adam would have been the only man who kept her from being gay or whether she turned gay because she was so sad or whether people have any idea of whether they actually like men or women but rather they're conditioned by social norms.

A bunch of kids at Millstone are openly out and they're sort of annoying. They always make a big deal of tongue kissing in the halls and feeling each other up in the lunchroom even though it's against the rules to do that stuff unless it's a dance and then you have to be a little bit subtle. Anyway, I almost asked Ms. Hardwood once but she isn't very approachable on a personal level. Matthew told her everything. I think he even told her about the time that the old soccer coach made a pass at him.

It was funny. When I heard about these things—dead fiancés, wars, deformed children, murders, divorces, and people never coming back—I thought, How could anyone possibly survive such horrible things? But while I could feel Matt's dying in every inch of me, skimming across the surface of my skin, soaking into my pores when I stood under the shower, I could still smile and sleep and do my homework.

Grief is fifty times harder than AP Calculus.

"EVERYBODY." Ms. Hardwood was standing at the end of the room, her hand raised like we were in grade school.

"Everybody," Isabelle Folonari whispered, perfectly imitating Ms. Hardwood's Brooklyn accent.

"Isabelle?"

"Yes?"

"Is there something you'd like to share with us all?"

"No."

"Then be quiet."

Isabelle arched a very thin eyebrow. "Dyke," she whispered under her breath.

"Cunt," whispered Wendy Henninger, head of the Gay/Lesbian Student Association.

"What did you call me?" Isabelle screamed.

"She called you a cat," Morgan Crawford said, barely looking up. "She called you a pussycat."

Then everyone looked at me, since I was sitting next to Isabelle.

"Did you hear anything, Alice?" Ms. Hardwood asked.

"No," I said.

"She's lying," Isabelle snarled.

"Fuck you," I said, forgetting where I was. "You called our teacher a dyke."

"I am a dyke," Ms. Hardwood said, calmly pulling out a pile of disciplinary slips. "And now you're all going to see our beloved headmaster."

NO ONE EVER sits on the comfy chair. The comfy chair swallows you whole and traps you while Farley paces back and forth, smiling of course, telling you all the reasons you have disappointed the "Millstone Country Day family" and why it's such a painful thing for him, Duncan Farley, to see you headed toward a meaningless life, which will start as soon as you fail to get into Yale, Harvard, or Princeton (Brown, Vassar, Stanford).

Isabelle Folonari started to cry as soon as we sat down and didn't stop until we left the room. She had been doing this trick since second grade, when an actress girlfriend of her movie producer father taught her how. Morgan Crawford was oblivious and asleep behind his tinted glasses that were prescription so Farley couldn't make him take them off.

Wendy sat with her arms crossed, glaring at the sobbing Isabelle. She had shaved her head over Christmas break, but now she had a light fuzz across her skull and so many ear piercings it was hard to see skin. I liked her but she scared me. I think her intention was to be strong but I found her mainly belligerent, although Matthew said she was angry because her father had walked out on their family after her mother was diagnosed with MS.

"Now," Farley said, bow tie bobbing, "I understand there is stress. Senior-year stress, after-Christmas stress, the stress of parental expectations—"

Isabelle raised her hand. "The death of someone I loved."

Farley paused. "Yes, Isabelle?" he asked tenderly.

"Our classmate," Isabelle looked right at me. "Matthew Swan."

"You bitch," Wendy muttered under her breath.

Morgan pushed his glasses up on his forehead. "Shut up," he said.

Farley was shaking his head slightly. "I've known Matt Swan since the day he was born. He used to come to our all-school meetings and sit on the floor smiling." He wiped his eyes quickly, and for the first time since I'd known him, I liked him.

"He was my boyfriend," Isabelle said.

"What?" I was already on my feet, already moving toward her, my hands outstretched as if to rip her head off.

Isabelle looked up at me. "Sorry, Alice," she said smoothly. "I know you guys were close. But we"—she paused—"were really close."

"He hated you," Wendy said. "You were the kind of girl he totally despised."

Isabelle tossed back her hair. "So? Boys always want women they hate."

Then we were all given warnings. Given warnings and offered shortbread from Farley's stash of imported cookies. Only Morgan took one.

Isabelle walked away without a word, Wendy gave me a brief hug and then followed her. I wanted to leave school but I couldn't move.

"You okay?" Morgan asked.

I shook my head.

"Come on," he said.

I followed him outside and across the main soccer field to the woods. There a rope course and survival jungle snaked for nearly a mile, donated by an alumnus who had climbed Everest. On one expedition he had sustained such severe frostbite, he had lost most of his nose. The air was still warm, almost sixty degrees, balmy for January. We walked along the path until we reached a tree that had been stepped and climbed up into the high branches. Morgan offered me a cigarette.

"This really sucks," he said.

"What?"

"His not coming back."

I didn't say anything.

"I think she was lying."

"Isabelle?"

"Yeah." He cleared his throat. "Or maybe not but you shouldn't give a shit. He loved you. Everybody knew that."

"They did?"

"Sure. You guys were always each other's favorites. Ever since kindergarten." Morgan drew a deep puff of smoke and then exhaled. "Remember when we were pilgrims in Mrs. Hannigan's class?"

"You were Proctor Adams."

"And you were Abigail Adams."

"Your daughter."

"I used to pretend you were really my wife," Morgan said.

"You did?" I tried to remember Morgan in fourth grade. He was very short and wore owlish glasses.

"Yeah." He laughed. I didn't remember ever hearing Morgan laugh before. "I had this thing for you in grade school."

"A thing?"

"I told my mother I thought you were the most evolved girl I had ever met." Morgan was blushing.

So we sat there and cut European history class, which was okay, since we were supposed to be working on our research paper in the library and Mrs. Kaplan never took attendance. You could tell her you were working in the audiovisual room and she'd believe you. The audiovisual room had become the specialized computer lab, but Mrs. Kaplan still talked about something called microfiche.

Sometimes I forgot about outside while I was in school. You're in this place that exists in a separate universe and everything that happens in there—bells ringing, teachers testing, kids being weird—is the only thing happening anywhere. But here there was an entirely different set of rules. Animals were eating, horses grazed, squirrels nibbled, birds pecked, and a fox darted past us with some small, furry, doomed thing in its mouth, the fox's fur like flame. If we hadn't come outside, I never would have noticed.

When we went back, it was lunchtime. I usually ate on the windowsill with the hippies, but I didn't feel like talking to anyone so I went into the cafeteria. Sigrid was sitting alone at a table, her sack lunch spread out, a sandwich, an apple, and a little bag of chips. It was the sort of lunch you ate in first grade. I sat down.

"Hi, Alice," she said.

I could tell by her face she was very glad to see me, and for some reason that was nice.

"Hey, Sigrid," I said.

"You want half my sandwich?"

I nodded.

Bologna on squishy white bread, not what my endive-eating, salsa-dipping, tabouli-consuming friends usually considered food. It tasted great.

"You okay?" Sigrid was looking at me with concern.

"Yeah."

"Did you get in trouble?"

I shook my head. "Farley gave us a cookie," I said.

"Really?"

"Uh-huh."

We sat in silence for a moment.

"Hey, Sigrid," I said, "can I ask you something?"

She nodded.

"Is your dad really sick?"

She looked away and then nodded.

"I'm sorry. I think my parents know him or something."

"He's got liver cancer." She looked back at me. "It's pretty bad."

"Who takes care of him?"

"There's a nurse."

I saw she was about to cry.

"I'm sorry," I said again.

"He's dying," she said.

"I'm sorry." I couldn't stop saying that.

"It's okay," Sigrid said. "He's been dying for a really long time." And then she started to laugh.

I started to laugh. The thing was, it was all there—Matthew's bones and Isabelle's lies and how Mrs. Swan's face looked when she stood in his room. Even the thought of Alf and how he still wanted me to wrestle with him made me feel like laughing.

Bologna was coming out of my mouth, I was giggling so hard. People stared at us, and some of the prep girls rolled their eyes. Probably I would be accused of being stoned. But I didn't care. There's a skull beneath the skin, I wanted to scream at them, and someday you'll know the truth and no one will have prepared you for that pain.

THAT NIGHT it rained. I slept and woke up and heard sounds outside. It was the kind of cold winter rain you imagine one of those unmarried girls in English folk songs carrying her baby through, carrying her baby until she fell over and died, and then, of course, the baby died too. This was the kind of music my mom played last year when she was mad at my dad. Alf and I called it dead baby music.

I thought about the wolves that chased the sleds in *My Antonia*. The story of how the Russian guy threw the bride to them had haunted me for weeks. "Everybody wants to live," Matthew had said, acting like it didn't bother him. I thought about the moors and how Heathclife and Eustacia Vye and Lear wandered around calling out for someone they couldn't have or something they had lost forever.

I tried to stop remembering books, but then I thought about hobos on boxcars and babies left in trash cans and cats tied up in sacks and thrown into water. I could not stop the way the pictures kept streaming into my head like some kind of speeded-up video. But I would not think about Matthew. If I did that I would get up and look through the window and see him standing outside, arms outstretched, calling for me. I could feel that he was there, everywhere, and I wanted to be there with him.

THE NEXT MORNING I stood outside on the verandah and felt the sun on my face. I was just in my pajamas, and it felt like spring. The droopy little white flowers were sticking their petals just above the dirt. My mother walked out with her coffee mug, a monstrous bowl my parents bought in Paris with a weird face painted on the side. "La Mère," it said. My dad swore it was a picture of Medusa, who ate her kids and turned people into stone.

"How's school?" she asked like I didn't know Farley's secretary had called already.

"Dandy." I stared down at the ground and dug my slipper into a mound of grass and earth. A bad thing to do.

"Alice."

"Yes?"

"Don't do that to the lawn."

I shrugged but continued to flex my toe, to exert downward pressure until a huge clod of mud was dislodged, landing at my mother's feet.

"Alice!"

"Sorry."

"Really—I mean—what's going on?"

She looked different in the morning. Younger but tired.

"Nothing. Just the usual shit."

"Alice."

"Oh, Mother, stop saying my name, okay? Just stop saying it over and over again. It makes me want to kill myself."

I didn't look at her. I shouldn't have said that. I heard her sigh. I waited. Go away, I thought, go away.

Here we were. At the mother-daughter moment everyone had described in health class. They gave us these case studies about the situation, how our mothers felt when we walked away from them, making it clear they were passé, pathetic, no longer fashion forward enough to care about. And the daughters? Suddenly alone, empowered, sexualized, full of fear and mixed emotions, teetering on the brink of womanhood. They got that part wrong. We had plunged. I think the only virgin in my class was Sigrid. I had had terrible sex with a Princeton boy who invited me to his dorm room to watch a movie. When he made it clear we were supposed to sleep together, I didn't know how to tell him I didn't want to. It wasn't like he was hideous or anything, but I didn't know him. I didn't tell anyone. When I thought about it, I got this cold feeling in my chest.

My mother still picked me up when I was eleven, twelve, and almost thirteen. She was strong and I was skinny until eighth grade, and she picked me up when I was scared, hurt, and sometimes after we had terrible fights. We had a sort of dance. She would get closer and closer and then sort of jump at me and grab me, all of me, into her arms and whisper, "Hush, stop now, Alice," and I'd feel all the rage and pain and fear start to leave. But where did it go? Did she absorb it like a sponge? Was it her job to take the dark stuff and let it seep into her own tissue? What if it proved toxic, like those drugs they gave women to cure morning sickness?

My grandfather built a rocking chair for his wife, Dad's mother, who had nine children. It was very sturdy. We'd sit in the chair, and my mom would sing the song from *Jesus Christ Superstar* that Mary

Magdalene sang to Jesus just before they crucified him. She tells him not to worry and that everything's fine. And it was. Just fine. Even though my legs dangled down to her ankles and I could barely fit inside her arms, I did fit. I made myself small, she grew, and we wrapped ourselves back into one another for a little while. I would give up anything to fit there again.

My friends spoke of their mothers like enemies, describing fights, which ended up with them stealing money, or clothes, or breaking something their moms loved. These arguments seemed senseless to me, but I didn't have a mother who had my body fat measured or read my journal or tried to kiss my boyfriends. These mothers were critical and mean. They told lies, and they didn't like it when their daughters were pretty. They were exactly like the stepmothers in "Cinderella," "Snow White," and "Hansel and Gretel," but they were real.

My mother wasn't mean. She was just sad. Some of it was in her own mind, and some of it was because of winter. But most of it was her family. Her family was screwed up. Her parents both died when she was fourteen in a weird accident. They were drunk, but they didn't die in a car crash. I think they fell off someone's roof or something. I never got the whole story.

Dad said she had to be a mother to the whole family, which was two younger brothers and a sister who was retarded. When Mom's parents died, her aunt moved in, but she wasn't very responsible. She didn't drink, but she played the numbers and bet on horses and she basically spent all the money her mom had left in insurance and lost the house.

Finally, Mom got old enough to not have anyone take care of her and she got a full-time job and went to night school and her sister was accepted into a good group home for retarded people. But then her brothers were drafted and went to Vietnam and one of them, her favorite one, was killed in the war. Adam had been like her own kid, I think because he was eight years younger than she was. He had a twin brother, Eddie, who wasn't so sweet. He didn't die like Adam, but when he got back from Vietnam, he was addicted to heroin. Aunt Barbara died when she was forty. I didn't ever meet her.

Uncle Eddie had all these jobs and he kept getting arrested, but finally he moved to Montana, where he joined a cult that believed in Armageddon. He spent one Christmas with us, and he taught me and Alf how to be sure the feds aren't listening when you talk on the phone. My dad says Uncle Eddie specializes in advanced paranoia.

When my mother gets sad, I feel sick. I want it to stop immediately, because once she was sad for a month and didn't get up in the morning to make us breakfast.

Matthew used to say my mother was the sweetest person he knew. But he didn't realize that sometimes it's better to have someone like his mother who you can tell the truth to. My mother couldn't talk about Matt disappearing. I could see in her face that she was remembering her brother dying and her sister and maybe her parents. And besides all the memories, there was the reality of missing Matthew. He had flirted with her and read her poetry and acted like her opinion was important to him. When he first disappeared, she helped to put up flyers and she answered the hot line after work. But gradually she stopped doing anything, and then she stopped talking about him.

That's when my father started to go over to the Swans' to stuff envelopes and help answer the phones when Catherine Swan was getting all these calls, mostly from psychics and people who didn't know anything but wanted to talk. Sometimes I went with him, but mostly he went by himself. I asked my mom to go over there with me one night about six months after Matthew had disappeared. "You go," she said, but I could tell she didn't want me to leave her alone. So I stayed home with her, and when my father got back late that night I heard them arguing late into the night. He didn't go back to the Swans' after that.

I FOLLOWED my mother into the kitchen after I stuck the lump of lawn back in the hole. "I don't want to kill myself," I said, hugging her from behind, burying my face into the space between her backbones. Her hair smelled like roses.

"Go to school," she said. "Go to school, you terrible child."

MS. HARDWOOD CAME IN the lunchroom. I could tell she was looking for me. She looked businesslike, which meant she was stressed. "Alice," she said, "come and talk to me."

I nodded and stood up.

"Thanks for sitting with me," Sigrid said.

I smiled at her. The fact was I liked outsiders. No one had prepared me for the hierarchy of coolness in school. My parents weren't socially competitive; when I came home demanding to be enrolled in whatever dance class or activity would guarantee my acceptance into the rich kids' club at Millstone, they suggested I ride my bike or take a class at the Y or wrestle with Alf, who was always ready for combat.

"Are you and Sigrid friends?" Ms. Hardwood asked as she opened the door to her office.

I shrugged.

"She could use some friends," Ms. Hardwood said, her fingers rubbing her temples, exhaling a small breath before she began to tell me how this recent incident affected my academic career.

"So what's new?" she asked.

I stared at the poster just above her head. It was an Atget photograph, a misty, black-and-white print of a secret garden, a beckoning, misty, peaceful landscape. For a moment I saw two children, a boy and a girl, hand in hand, walking through the gate of the picture. I had let in the memory, and there was nothing to stop what came next. Bones. Blood. Blackness. Death. His hands outstretched toward me, pleading, entreating, good-bye, good-bye, good-bye.

"Alice?"

My body was convulsing without any warning. The temperature in the room dropped to the point where I was sure I would freeze to death. At the same time, I felt the inside of my throat parch, a deep, choking, terrible pain swept across my chest and I fell down on my hands and knees, curled up into a ball, and screamed. Minutes later the nurse was standing over me. I was under a blanket, and through the window I saw my mother running across the parking lot.

Bones.

Catherine Swan had called my mother to tell her about the bones and to apologize for what was probably a bad thing to tell me. My mother had called Ms. Hardwood to give her the heads-up in case anything weird happened at school, and now all their fears were made manifest in the spectacle of a screaming, hysterical, tearstained, and almost suspended adolescent girl.

"Alice?"

"What?"

"Darling."

"What?"

"Alice?"

"Yes?"

"What happened?"

"Nothing."

"Nothing?" Ms. Hardwood was white and holding my mother as if to keep herself from being blown over. "Don't you remember?"

"Of course I remember. I was upset—"

"Alice!" Ms. Hardwood looked furious. "I think you had some kind of a fit."

"I'm fine." I looked at my mother. "Why are you here?"

"Catherine Swan called me." My mother looked really, really sad.

"Ms. Hardwood told you I said 'fuck' in homeroom?"

"Alice!" My mother looked pained. As if she and Ms. Hardwood couldn't imagine anyone using such a word.

"What?"

"It's about Matt."

I frowned. "Don't start," I said. "Don't try and explain anything to me!"

She stared at my hands. They were trembling so violently I could barely hold the blanket around me.

"Honey." My mother had started to cry. Ms. Hardwood put her arm around her.

"Do you want to go back to class, Alice?"

I nodded.

Ms. Hardwood wrote me a pass. My mother was sitting on the couch looking confused. It was weird to have her in school.

"I'm okay," I said, leaning down to kiss her.

"No," she said fiercely, "you are not okay. Your darling boy is dead."

I stared down at her, wondering how she dared to put such a fact into words.

"Go," she whispered. "I'll see you later."

I understand some things. During Holocaust Week we watched documentaries narrated by survivors, and they kept talking about the human instinct to stay alive. That was how I felt now, walking into my chemistry class; even Mr. Larabee, unattractive at best, appeared somehow beautiful and full of grace. I slid myself into the desk, and right away Amanda Stevens turned around and smiled at me. In all the time I had known Amanda Stevens, she had never, ever smiled at me. Twelve years of school together and not a single friendly word had passed between us. I don't know why.

"We're on page two hundred," she whispered.

"Thanks," I said in a sweet voice I had never used in my life.

I proceeded to flunk a snap quiz and not care. I looked out the window and watched a second-grade class launch weather balloons, most of them blowing straight into the elm trees that shaded the front of our school and staying there while the kids shouted and stamped their feet. Life seemed very fragile. I felt my own breath on my arm and watched as a fly attempted to land on Kyle Flutter's Mohawk.

"Alice?"

Mr. Larabee was staring at me.

"Yes, Mr. Larabee?"

"Are you all right?"

I nodded and smiled at him. He looked slightly startled. He glanced at my quiz and frowned. How sad, I thought, how incredibly sad it was to believe a quiz held any importance when nothing in the world mattered except survival and common decency.

This was my mood when I arrived at my house to discover both my parents and my mother's friend Laura Youngblood, a Sioux Indian and a shrink, sitting in the living room, talking in hushed voices. I went straight into the kitchen and began to assemble smoothie ingredients. As I peeled and chopped, the grown-ups gradually filed into the kitchen.

"Smoothie?" I asked politely.

They shook their heads as if afraid to interrupt the ceremony.

A banana, a peach, frozen strawberries, cranberry juice, plain yogurt.

"Hi, Alice," Laura said.

"Hi, Laura," I responded over the din of the blender.

"How are you feeling?" my father asked.

"I'm fine," I said. "Did Mom tell you what happened?"

They all nodded. It was a little weird.

"Well, she called Ms. Hardwood a dyke."

"Who did?"

"Isabelle Folonari."

"Is that why you got so upset?"

"No. I said 'fuck you,' and we all had to go see Mr. Farley."

"Did he smile?" My father winked at me and I laughed.

"He gave us a Scottish shortbread."

I looked around for a smoothie glass, and my mother quickly handed me one.

"We heard the news about Matthew," Laura said quietly after I drank out of my glass. "It's very hard to accept."

Laura Youngblood is beautiful. She has hair so black it reflects light, an oval face, high cheekbones, and very dark blue eyes. Her back is so straight; she always seems like the tallest person in the room. And she's graceful; her feet don't seem to make any noise when they touch the ground. I had known her all my life, but I didn't feel relaxed around her. She was too aware of all the things you do to cover your feelings.

"I accept it," I said slowly. "Something already told me he was dead. Now we can bury something."

I heard my mother sob. My father put his arm around her.

"You're very brave, Alice," he said.

"I think when you love someone as much as I love Matthew you can't allow the loss of them to take away your life." Who was talking,

I wondered? Someone very wise. "Or you'll end up psycho like Heathcliff and ruin everything you touch."

Laura nodded. "Can we ask you a favor?"

"Sure."

"If you feel psycho, if you feel like not eating or running away or anything different that might hurt you, will you tell someone, one of us or someone?"

"Of course," I said graciously. I walked over to my mother and hugged her.

"I love you," I said.

"Oh, Alice," my mother said, sobbing, "my precious darling."

I gently let her go and walked upstairs, drinking my smoothie, contemplating the future as a bleak and terrible wasteland, my prince a pile of bones, my dreams dashed to dust.

Five

MAYBE THIS IS WHY I decided to go to the prison. The darkness of the human condition was revealed to me and I was illuminated by this truth. Tyger! Tyger! burning bright.

Spring term of senior year meant one thing: independent projects. Accepting that most of us were already mentally AWOL, the administration of Millstone Country Day had developed a program that fostered independence and encouraged creative expression. At least they said it did. Mainly kids got jobs and hung out in cool places or volunteered to build huts in third-world countries or sat in Tuscany drinking wine and pretending to be influenced by the pottery of Tuscany peasants.

This was the time to intern, to apprentice, to suck up to your parents' friends who had desirable vocations so they'd allow you to name them in your proposal. There were also outside contractors who came to school hoping to attract senior-year volunteers, and the Literacy Behind Bars project was one of those.

Rahway Prison was medium security and about thirty years old. The literacy program had existed from the beginning, and Rahway Community College considered it an important part of their class on penal reform. Two teachers from the Rahway Community College English faculty worked there full-time, and two graduate students assisted. They would accept one high school senior as part of their program, and when I walked over to the table I was quite sure I would be the one. This certainty came with the enthusiasm with which I was greeted and the fact that there was not a single other student clustered around their presentation as there were around Habitat for Humanity, Save the Rainforest, Musicians Against Violence, and Global Warning.

Prison literacy was too local and didn't sound much different from tutoring inner-city gang members, a program most Millstone seniors had been exposed to.

After I filled out the one-page application, the woman behind the table smiled up at me. "Hi, Alice," she said. "I'm Sonia Goldberg. Why do you want to work with prisoners?"

"I think writing can change people's lives and they need their lives to change."

This was impromptu. I wasn't sure if writing could change anything, and I had no idea what a prisoner needed.

Sonia nodded. She was about forty-five with thick, wavy blond hair and very pretty brown eyes.

"Okay," she said. "Can you start a week from Monday?"

I nodded.

"You need to get your parents' permission and to have them sign a waiver for entering Rahway Prison. Also, Duncan Farley needs to sign off on all the paperwork and you'll be given a drug test. Have you ever been convicted of a felony?"

I shook my head.

"Fabulous. Are you good at English, grammar, poetry, all that sort of stuff?"

I nodded. It wasn't something I felt comfortable saying, but it seemed to me that the prisoners needed to try something different, like haikus or short stories.

She looked at me for a minute.

"One other thing, Alice. I'd recommend you put your hair back and not wear any makeup. Dress as if you were auditioning for an Amish play. These men don't see women very often, and they almost never see exquisitely beautiful teenage girls."

"I'm not exquisitely beautiful," I said. It felt like she was making fun of me.

Sonia shrugged. "Trust me," she said. "In their eyes, I'm a Playboy centerfold."

I spent the weekend being very sisterly and making my mother feel better about the fit she'd witnessed. Alf was interested in seeing a terrible movie about skateboarding, and I actually took him to the multiplex, driving my dad's horrible station wagon, not pretending I didn't know who Alf was, buying him a jumbo popcorn instead of keeping the change the way I usually did.

I attended a lecture with my mother on global warming and found the sight of penguins fighting over the shrinking area of an ice floe oddly comforting. We walked through town afterward, looked at furniture and bought a hideous top at my mother's favorite store, a place that sold handmade clothing designed by inner-city children. Stopping to get cafe au lait, my mother turned and hugged me.

"I'll never have children," I said as we sat eating biscotti at a table by the window. There was snow falling, and the statues already had white hats.

"Why not?" my mother asked.

I stared out at the town square. People were trying to start a snowman. A very small boy in a red sweater had his head tipped back, tongue outstretched. I thought of Alf and then of Catherine Swan.

"Too much," I said. "Too dangerous."

My mother smiled a little. "Isn't love dangerous?" she asked.

"Love sucks," I said.

"Sometimes." My mother glanced outside. "Oh," she whispered, "but it's so worth it, Alice!"

"How can you say that? After Uncle Adam and Aunt Barbara and the other stuff?"

The mother was holding the red sweater boy high in her arms so he could catch all the snowflakes before they hit the ground and melted. This was the lie your parents told you. Life is sweet, they said, taste and nothing bad will happen.

"It's the truth," she said.

"What if I can't manage?" I asked, feeling the weight of my question against the wall of my chest.

INRI, it said on the crucifix. Iron nails ran in. Jesus had yelled at God—what did he yell? "My Lord, why have you forsaken me?" I imagined for a moment what Matthew might have asked. Or did he yell? Did he beg for his life? Did he try and run away, or did he protect Hallie until the bitter end? The bitter end. What was God thinking when he let his only son die like that?

My mother looked startled. I had allowed my coffee to spill, and I was muttering.

"I'm sorry." I didn't want to frighten her again. "I was trying to remember a famous question."

She smiled. This was a common thing for a person who did crossword puzzles. We walked home while the snow fell in huge flakes.

"Look at this," my mother said, sliding down our street. "Lovely snow to cover it up."

Yes, I thought, cover it up. Hide the dirt and the dead leaves and the old things that will never be new again. Bury the bones, bury the dead, ashes to ashes.

As we came in the front door, I saw that my father and Alf had started a fire. My heart lurched to feel the joy of it as my father held his arms out to us both, crying, "Look at the angels, Alfred, snow angels come to life!"

SCHOOL WAS NORMAL except for Thursday, when Ms Hardwood stopped me during homeroom. "Are you serious about helping at the prison?" she asked.

I nodded.

"It's not going to be much fun. What about that thing with Amy—" She stopped. "I guess it isn't really the thing anymore, is it?"

I shook my head.

"We could come up with something better than the prison poets, couldn't we?"

"I want to do it," I said, trying to look excited. "Anyway, they need people."

Her eyes were full of tears as she squeezed my shoulder and walked away.

MATTHEW AND I HAD DECIDED to spend our senior project learning how to properly shoe horses. Then we were going to trek all the way from New Jersey to Canada, traveling on small country roads. He was going to videotape people, and I was going to write a daily journal. We had the use of a video production house in New York, where we had a vague plan for a documentary. Mostly it was going to be our first chance to be alone together. I had imagined mornings in the cold, clean air, drinking coffee out of tin cups, my hair all tangled, and wild sex on rocks.

No more. Now I would dress like the Amish and listen to the clichéd sonnets of convicted felons.

On Monday, I put on my chosen outfit, gray corduroy pants, a white oxford shirt, a black cardigan buttoned to my neck. I brushed my hair and pulled it back so nothing but unmade-up face was visible. I looked hideous, but my parents acted like a movie star had just arrived.

"Hey," said my dad, "very *jeune fille*. You look like a young Natalie Wood."

By the time I reached the high walls of Rahway Prison, I had pulled out the ponytail. To hell with these horny old men, I thought. Let 'em leer!

The guard at the gate checked my ID and waved me forward. It didn't seem all that scary in terms of the outside, except when I looked up, men with guns stood in sentry towers, and when the gate closed behind me I felt trapped.

"Hi, I'm Hal Ransom. We'll be teaming up for the whole project."

Hal Ransom was wearing a suit like a stockbroker.

"Are you a writer?" I asked as we were buzzed through a series of metal doors.

"Not exactly. I'm doing my dissertation on prison reform—"

"Princeton?"

"Rutgers. Political science."

It helped to talk, because walking through the halls of the prison was extremely disconcerting. Doors opened and swung shut, and fluorescent lights glared into your eyes at every corner. It felt like the worst high school in the world. It felt like you'd never, ever graduate.

We were separated and searched; not exactly a strip search, but the woman guard did put her hands down my shirt and inside my underwear. She patted me all over and checked my notebook and pencil case.

"I'm Officer Costa," she said. "You need anything, you let me know." She pointed at the badge on her chest. "Officer Costa," she said very slowly, like I was a little kid.

"Thanks," I said.

"You going to college?"

"High school. This is my final project."

She handed me my pencil case. "Pretty depressing, isn't it?"

I shook my head. "Not really."

"You don't think prison's depressing?"

I shrugged.

She looked at me for a minute. "Did something bad happen to you?" she asked.

"To my friend."

She nodded. "So is this like penance or something?"

I nodded.

We walked out the door, but Officer Costa stayed back when I headed toward the lockup.

"Get felt up?" Hal asked me as we were reunited in front of a gunmetal door with barred windows.

I stood on tiptoes and peeped inside. A small circle of chairs was in the middle of the room. Nothing else. In each chair sat a man with a yellow legal pad and pen. There were eight chairs, five men. I felt like I was going to throw up.

Hal looked down at me. He was very tall. Dark and a bit funny-looking but also handsome. "You feel okay?" he asked.

I nodded, but I thought I was going to faint.

"We get to leave," he murmured, leaning over me. "Breathe."

I nodded. The guard on the other side opened the door. Officer Costa reappeared behind Hal. "I'll be in here all the time and take you to the bathroom," she said.

Hal made a scared face. "Who takes me to the bathroom?" he asked.

"The guard at the door will switch off with me," she said. "Is it Alice?"

I nodded.

"Don't forget that you're dealing with the scum of society. Every guy in here will tell you they didn't do what it says on their rap sheet. They did that and fifty other things they didn't get caught doing. If they ask for anything outside of a dictionary, you tell me. The only way they get to take this class is through personal recommendation, and that's a violation."

Officer Costa walked over to a side table and sat down. She picked up a book that was lying there. *Love in the Time of Cholera*.

"She's reading," Hal hissed. "That is so radical."

She lowered her book and glared at Hal. "Don't assume anything," she said. "This place is full of surprises."

THEY ALL HAD TATTOOS. They all wore the same clothes and sort of had the same haircut. Other than that, they were totally different.

Kenny was a Puerto Rican, about twenty-nine, a gang leader who had been shot in both kneecaps and had a major limp.

Howard was in his late forties, had been an accountant for a famous law firm and embezzled so much of their money the place had gone broke. He had also gone to Harvard, which he liked to mention at least once every session.

Curtis was black, from South Carolina, had killed two people while drunk, and wrote about his hometown almost exclusively.

Roger was from Macedonia and had an accent sort of like Dracula. The guys called him Count. He wrote ballad poetry about Macedonia history. I think he did something terrible, but I wasn't sure what it was.

Lincoln was also black, had a huge Afro, and hated white people but said he would work with us because he needed to find his "authenticate voice." His writing was based on the teaching of Malcolm X, and poetry didn't ever enter his mind.

The first thing we did was go around the room and introduce ourselves. The guys all knew each other, so they didn't say much.

First up was Curtis. "My name is Curtis," he said. "Curtis Leonard Whiting III. I'm from North Carolina and my great-great-grandparents were slaves. I killed two people and I wish I didn't. One out of self-defense and the other outta sheer spite." He looked at me. "Sorry, young lady," he said.

"That's okay," I replied, startled by his apology.

"You think?" Curtis smiled at me almost like he was flirting but not in a gross way.

I shrugged.

"Well," said Hal, "maybe we should say who we are. I'm Hal Ransom—"

Roger raised his hand.

"Yes," Hal said. "And you can just ask a question, by the way."

"Okay," Roger said. "Are you a Jew?"

"Methodist," Hal said.

"What's that?"

"Uh, it's sort of like Protestant—"

Roger waved his hand like he was shooing away a bug. "I thought you were Jewish."

"Now that we've established my religious preference . . . I am getting my Ph.D. at Rutgers in political science and hope we can establish a dialogue about as many things as possible. The food here, for example. Maybe you can tell me how the food is."

I couldn't believe Hal had said anything about food. It was like mentioning Harry Potter to Alf.

"Food stinks," Roger said. "Let's hear about her."

He pointed at me as if I was deaf or something. All the men sat a little bit forward on their seats. If I ever craved attention, this was it. I thought about that Madonna video when she's a dancer and men or women put money in a coin slot to watch her perform.

"I'm Alice," I said. I saw them all mouth the word *Alice.* "I go to Millstone Country Day, and I'm doing this for my senior project."

Curtis raised his hand. "What's a senior project?"

"It's—uh—it's like this thing you do instead of regular classes. You try a job or you help with other stuff . . . like a project or community service."

Lincoln glared at me. "You mean," he said slowly, "we're like your project?"

"No." If there was a prison riot, I really hoped Lincoln didn't end up near me. "It's more like I want to be a writer and so I'm here to help."

Howard smiled at me. "Which is a very nice gesture," he said.

All the men except Lincoln nodded. Lincoln muttered something that sounded like "Fuckin cracker-ass, motherfuckin, goddamn whitey."

"Well," Hal said. "Shall we get started?"

The guys picked up their yellow legal pads and stared at me. For some reason they thought I was the one to listen to. I glanced at Hal, who smiled encouragingly.

"Okay," I said. "Let's start with a one-page autobiography. Just one page in which you tell the story of your life."

Kenny raised his hand. "Can I write in Spanish?" he asked softly.

"Of course," I said.

"Can I write about you?" Curtis asked. The other men glared at him.

"It's the story of *your* life," Hal said.

"Maybe my life's just starting," Curtis said, looking at me like I was something amazing. "Maybe she's what's the thing that gave me life."

OFFICER COSTA WALKED US to the front door. "How'd it go?" she asked.

"Great," Hal said. "I can't wait to hear their stories."

She fitted a key into the door. "Don't they all end exactly the same?"

"Do you believe in redemption, Officer Costa?" Hal was giving her this earnest stare.

She squinted at both of us. "You mean like with coupons?"

I laughed.

"What is it they give that returns their souls to them? Those lives they ended? I don't think they have anything to trade in, so I don't believe redemption's much of an issue." Officer Costa turned around and went back inside.

Hal dropped me off at my house. We sat in the car for a second before I got out.

"So," he said, "you did a great job."

I nodded. It didn't seem like I'd done anything but let a bunch of prisoners stare at me.

"They'll calm down," he said. "You just shook them up a bit."

I nodded.

My dad was in the kitchen chopping things. I could hear NPR; the obscure-movie guy was talking about a French movie director who had just died. My father was standing at the counter, a pile of chopped onions in front of him, tears rolling down his face.

"Hey," I said, "you want bread?"

If you held a piece of bread in your mouth it made the onions less potent.

"No," he said, wiping his eyes on his sleeve. "Most of these are real." He pushed the onions aside and started to tear apart a yellow pepper. "I can't believe he's dead," he said.

"Was he old?"

"No. Sort of. What's old to you, anyway?"

"Sixty." I saw his expression. "Ninety."

"He had a stroke." He threw a piece of pepper at me.

We didn't have anything to eat at the jail. The cafeteria wasn't where we wanted to be during the break. Instead, we went outside and gulped down air. Two short pieces about parents torturing their little kids had nearly destroyed me. The prisoners wrote as if they were recording their crimes. But these were crimes done to them by people who were meant to cherish them. Mothers, fathers, uncles and aunts. Neither of my parents had ever hit me. Once my father called me an "ungrateful brat," and then we made up and he apologized. I didn't even get punished for bad things I did. They loved me no matter what. It seemed really unfair. No wonder the prisoners grew up and killed people.

"What movies did he make?"

"Oh, probably nothing you would have heard of." My dad paused. "What movies do you like?"

"Ones with people trying to change their lives. Or trying to love someone . . ." I stopped.

"Give me an example."

"*Drugstore Cowboy,*" I said. "This guy's a junkie but he's trying to stop and then someone dies and he realizes he'll die too if he keeps shooting heroin."

He nodded. "One of the movies this guy made was almost about nothing—just the moment you feel that you truly love someone." He smiled at me. "That's twice for me," he said. "Your mother coming down a street in Manhattan when her umbrella blew inside out, and you."

"Me?"

"Two seconds after you were born. Eyes like sapphires and no crying." He wiped away a tear. "And Alf, of course."

I remembered Alf as a newborn. He didn't cry at all unless he was absolutely starving. "Alf was a good baby," I said.

My father nodded. "But no one ever put me in my place like you did, Alice," he said, opening the refrigerator. "I stared into your eyes, and you told me you were as old as the pyramids. Your mom and I didn't know what to say to you. Baby talk seemed beneath such an infant."

He was teasing me.

"How were the prisoners?"

"Sort of normal. I mean, what you'd expect. They were all abused and neglected or left, and then they grew up and killed people or stole money."

My father looked uncomfortable. He unwrapped the sausage he had bought at the Trenton Farmers' Market. "Your mom and I were thinking," he began, tossing the sausage into a huge black skillet that was older than me. The room smelled of sage, garlic, and meat.

"Maybe you want to go away to a nice place or try something a bit less grim."

I shook my head.

"No?"

"Anyway, it's too late to change."

"Well"—he pushed the sausage around with a wooden spoon— "Ms. Hardwood could get a waiver from Farley on this one."

"I want to teach in the prison," I said, feeling my face getting red. "Why can't I just do that?"

"You can but—" My father looked at me. "Wouldn't it be easier to go away?"

"The prisoners need me," I said, trying not to cry. "And Sigrid's dad is dying."

He looked surprised. "Sigrid?"

"She's my friend." This wasn't true. I barely knew her. "If you had fatal liver cancer I wouldn't want all my friends to leave me."

"Jesus, Alice. What are you thinking? You're going to spend the last spring of high school listening to criminals talk about their terrible childhoods and comforting Sigrid?" He looked angry. "And what about this Mexico thing?" He stopped.

"You mean Matt? You mean those bones?"

He winced.

"If the dental records match, I guess he won't come back."

My father pushed the meat around so it wouldn't burn. "Couldn't you do something mindless, Alice? Learn how to windsurf or something?"

"You always complain about how selfish my friends are—that kids used to do things for world hunger and now they just save their money to buy cell phones."

"You want a cell phone?"

"No," I said. "I just want to be of use."

"That's unnatural," he snapped. "Why are you talking like this? Where's my horrid little greedy girl who takes the credit card and buys twenty-dollar thongs?"

I couldn't believe he would say something so gross.

"Alice," he spoke very quietly, "what do you want?"

"I want to be with Matthew Swan," I said, not looking at him.

"I know."

"I don't want to survive this."

He started to move toward me with his arms out.

"Don't touch me, Daddy," I whispered. "I love you but don't touch me."

He stopped. "If I could make him come back," he said, "if I could make him ring the bell and say, 'Good evening, sir, can your daughter Alice come out to play?' I would give my right hand. I swear to God, Alice, I would give my right hand to let him come back to you."

"I know." He wasn't crying about the stupid dead French director at all.

As I walked upstairs I saw him sit down at the kitchen table and bury his face in his hands.

We used to play Lancelot and Guinevere from the myths of King Arthur. Matthew wanted me to be the Lady of Shalott so we could fix up his raft with flowers and candles and float me down the river behind the Forest Preserve and pretend I had died of love.

"Nobody does that," I told him. "Queen Guinevere cheats on Arthur and feels really bad and becomes a nun. I can do that, but I can't just die of love."

It was a disaster. The raft started to sink and I got sucked underneath. I stayed down for so long, Matt thought I was unconscious and came in the water and we both got in lots of trouble.

Now I think you can die. I think you can feel so terrible and so alone, so choked up and so angry, so frightened and so sad, so disappointed and so tired, that you lie down and you don't ever get up again. You can't sleep or eat or talk or laugh or get excited or be amazed by anything ever again. And you die for love, after all. You die for its absence.

LUCINDA BAKER WAS the person who had volunteered to coordinate graduation, and she was waging a campaign against dresses that weren't dead white, snow, or vanilla. Any girl who showed up in cream, mauve, eggshell, or bisque wasn't going to be allowed in the processional. When Wesley Turner said he didn't know white came in a spectrum, Lucinda got snippy.

"Well, it does," she snapped. "Anything other than pure white looks muddy, yellow, or gray."

So our graduation would be totally white. White roses, boys in Gatsby suits, white-draped chairs, white doves that someone's dad could get on discount.

"It's racist," Kenny Lee said, putting up his hand. "Seems to me we're sending a very Ku Klux Klan–type message."

Ms. Hardwood nodded. "Are hoods optional?" she asked Lucinda, who looked confused, probably because she didn't possess a single strand of irony in her liposuctioned soul.

This was the moment Isabelle Folonari chose to make her announcement. "On behalf of the yearbook staff, we'd like to present our photo tribute to a fallen classmate."

And then she unrolled this huge poster of Matthew. I had been standing next to him in the original picture, but someone had cropped me out of the frame. Matthew was up to his knees in seafoam, a wave breaking behind him. It was our class trip to the New Jersey shore the previous spring, taken one month before he disappeared. The water was freezing but the day was gorgeous. He had kissed me in the water, our faces nearly frozen with cold. He told me of his plans to break up with Hallie. We dried our hair with our underwear and he told me he loved me. I believed we would be together for life.

"Isabelle," Ms. Hardwood said. "This is inappropriate."

Then the whole room turned and stared at me instead of Isabelle. Like I was his wife or something. And I stared back. I didn't look down, I didn't cry. I didn't do anything but stare.

"The yearbook committee would like to border this picture with black and have it be the first page of the yearbook."

I jumped up. "He hasn't been found yet," I said. "They don't know if those bones are even human."

Isabelle smiled. "I'm so sorry, Alice," she said. "My mother heard from her friend at the district attorney's office. They made a positive identification with Matthew's dental records. Those are his bones."

It was like everyone sucked in their breath at the same moment.

Ms. Hardwood tried to stop her, but it was too late.

"They think it happened months ago."

She shouldn't have said that. Even though I knew if Matthew had been alive he would have been in touch, I had this idea of him safe and maybe with amnesia or maybe just not able to call. Each night before I went to sleep I imagined exactly how his hand felt inside mine, the calluses at the base of each finger, the ring he inherited from his grandfather, heavy inside my palm. And I told him how much I loved him, and also what was happening with Gracie and Alf and Amy and my parents and his mom and his sisters. Whispering in the dark like when we were little and slept over at each other's house, sleeping in his bunk bed, telling secrets until one of us dropped off the edge of the night.

"I'm sorry," Isabelle said, not talking to me but facing the homeroom. "It's a tragedy, the tragedy of our entire class, but Matthew Swan needs to be remembered and not given nothing just because certain people seem to think he's their personal property—"

"Sit down, Isabelle!" Ms. Hardwood's voice could freeze you sometimes.

Isabelle's mouth opened.

"Not another word, young lady!"

Six

"ALICE?"

I was sitting behind the planetarium that the Sobol family had donated to the school. Mr. Sobol won a Nobel Prize for finding a black hole in the universe and then his oldest son died of childhood leukemia. It was a good place to hide when you were cutting class.

It was Ms. Hardwood. She sat down next to me and pulled her knees up, hugging them like a child. She didn't say anything.

"I don't have a class," I said finally.

She didn't speak.

"He's dead," I said.

"I'd like Isabelle Folonari's scalp," Ms. Hardwood said into her knees so her voice sounded strange. "Amy could weld some kind of trophy cabinet."

"Maybe she's right."

Ms. Hardwood scowled at me. "No, she's wrong. Except the brat was right about his being your personal property." She looked at the ground. "Alice, if you only knew how much that boy loved you."

"I knew," I said, looking at the mural on the side of the planetarium globe, Daedalus and Icarus flying with their wax wings. He would have done it. He would have jumped off a cliff if he thought it would take a long time to land, even if it meant he might die. Matthew was reckless with things that mattered. For a moment, I really hated him.

Ms. Hardwood stood up and brushed off her skirt. "Come on," she said, holding out her hand. "It's lunchtime. Amy made some soup."

I hadn't had breakfast and I don't think there was dinner. I felt the empty space in my stomach. It reminded me of what had happened. I started to shake, and for a moment the idea of tumbling over quietly, being unconscious, letting go, getting hooked to an IV, staying in the hospital, seemed really, really attractive.

"Breathe," Ms. Hardwood said, holding my arm tightly. "Start taking deep, even breaths."

They lived in a stone carriage house on the very edge of the original property that now belonged to the school. Amy's great-grandmother had donated it because the only girls' school in town taught mindless stuff like baking and tea preparation. All the women in Amy's family were feminists. One of them had been a suffragette who went on a hunger strike and was force-fed until she died.

No one minded a lesbian couple with an adopted Asian baby, which was one of the things you had to say was good about Millstone. It was pretty tolerant of things other communities might not have liked. Also, Amy's family was loaded. More than loaded, filthy rich. Her great-great-grandfather had invented a part that made rifles repeat, and during World War I it was the thing they put on millions of rifles. Another relative had struck gold in California.

If anyone had tried to evict Amy and Ms. Hardwood, she could have bought the whole town and turned it into a lesbian health spa. She was an only child and both her parents were dead. Even though she could have done anything, she chose to be a blacksmith and live beside a school. She could have bought a skyscraper in Manhattan and dressed in haute couture, but instead she spent her days smelting and being someone's mom. There were several buildings at the community college with her name on them, and she had endowed a scholarship at Millstone for female scholars attending Smith.

I used to be very jealous of Amy. She's six feet tall and has blond thick hair and dark blue eyes. Her blond thing isn't like Sigrid's at all. She's very warm and tinted and slightly tan all the time. She seems not to know how incredibly gorgeous she is, that she could be on the cover of *Vogue* and no one would say, "Who put her on the cover of *Vogue?*"

The other thing is her body. From being a swimmer in high school and then the blacksmith stuff, her arms are total muscle and her shoulders are just incredible. You know they are a woman's shoulders but still, they could hold up a building.

I used to watch Matt looking at her and think, Thank God she's a lesbian, which is really pathetic. She never would have made a move on him because Amy is the most moral human being I've ever known in my life. Sometimes I imagined those two having a child, and I couldn't help thinking their baby would be like something from a myth. A baby like Paul Bunyan. I wouldn't mind if everyone was happy and not dead. I'd even baby-sit their wonder child.

It was delicious soup. Carrot soup with pesto and homemade bread. Gracie came out of her room from her nap and wordlessly climbed into my arms, holding her blue bunny and a piece of a quilt she called her softie. She smelled like peaches. Ms. Hardwood went into the kitchen with Amy for a moment, and I heard Amy groan.

We said a prayer before lunch. Nothing much, just a prayer for the dead and the lonely. I ate my soup holding Grace. It's weird how little kids seem to know when you need them. I missed my brother suddenly.

After lunch I stayed and played with Grace for a little while. When I left, I looked back, and the three of them were waving from the doorway. I could see that Amy had started to cry. Ms. Hardwood was stroking her hair and Grace was hugging her legs.

EVERY DAY we headed out to the Jersey Turnpike toward Rahway Prison. Hal brought his lunch, enough lunch for three people, and he insisted I eat some. He said he was allergic to a lot of stuff, dairy and wheat. People who eat healthily always seem to have allergies to things like eggs. I don't get it. If you're so healthy, why aren't you allergic to Big Macs or something? Maybe they are but they never test the allergy. Anyway, he made bread from an alternative grain, and once you got past the texture, which was very strange, sort of like Play-Doh and particleboard combined, it was good.

Hal like to make his own CD mixes. My favorite was an Irish music mix which was sort of dangerous because these women's voices were so beautiful and full of longing I'd start to cry just listening, not even thinking about Matt or anything, just because the sound pierced your heart in a way that made you remember everything you had forgotten or lost.

We didn't talk much. I was trying to get ready for the watching, the observing of me, which was so intense I felt like I was in a vampire movie and my soul was being fought over by five men who had done something seriously bad.

Officer Costa was nice. She stopped searching me after the

second week, but we usually talked about movies or politics or something that had happened in Millstone. She ran a group for screwed-up teenage girls in Hackensack and told me some terrible things that had happened to them. They all had at least one baby and were dependent on drugs or alcohol, usually both. She thought teenage mothers were the worst thing in the world.

"You gotta understand, Alice. We find these dead babies, little people just lying cold in their cribs. These girls spent all the money in BabyGap and they let them get sick and die. People are stupider than anything. Much stupider than dogs."

Officer Costa loved dogs.

It was two weeks after the first day that Frank joined us. The extra chair should have been a warning, but when he walked in, the fire-bird glistening on his biceps, I was completely freaked. I knew he was a prisoner, I knew he was in the literacy program, I knew he'd killed Sigrid's baby-sitter, but somehow, I never thought he'd turn up. I felt danger where previously I had felt none. The others had told us about their crimes—Curtis had killed two men—but they didn't seem real. Real was Sigrid's baby-sitter. Real was a child watching from the closet. Real was what someone remembered after someone she loved was taken away.

The class was in a bad mood. The radio show they listened to that broadcast out of Houston had contained a message from Lincoln's wife. She was leaving him, it had said. She wasn't going to spend her life waiting tables in Newark when she could go live in California with her ex-boyfriend who sold used Lexuses.

"Pray for her," Roger said. "She is a child of God."

"I'll pray for that fat-ass bitch," Lincoln said. "I pray that my man takes the box cutter like I told him—" Lincoln saw the guard starting to enter the room, and he gave him a big, fake smile.

"At least she ain't dead," Frank muttered, staring at the floor.

"You okay, man?" Lincoln asked in a tone so tender, I was shocked.

Frank nodded.

We handed out the assignment. They had to describe an emotion in as many ways as possible without making any direct reference to it. The exercise was supposed to get you out of abstractions.

Frank read first. "Mom forgot you. Kids went home. No birthday. Nothing under the tree. The guy at work you talked to disappeared. You laugh at something dumb and the dog stares. The baby turns her face away."

"Good," Hal said, "really, really good work."

Howard put his hand up. "Bone in throat. Something at the tip of your fingers, electricity ache. No breath, scrape against the windpipe."

"Right there," Kenny said. "Hit in the belly like that time Freddy sucker-punched you behind the 7-Eleven."

"Powerful stuff," Hal said. "Now, anyone write anything positive?"

We all stared at him. My words on the page: fuck no, over and over again.

"Alice?"

"Broken-winged bird frozen on the street outside of Saks Fifth Avenue. Ice in belly, guts feel twisted."

I stopped. All the men in the room were staring at me. They looked horrified.

"Well," Hal said. "At least I wrote something light."

"Baby's neck, warm sun cat back. Lilac smell on first day of spring. Thick red hair sun glint, arch of white back and neck."

There was a long silence. I think Frank was crying. We all sat there without doing anything until the guard hit the door with his club.

"Jesus loves you," Howard said to me as they filed out.

"Shut the fuck up," Lincoln muttered. "She could be Jewish."

WE DROVE without speaking until we'd passed the line between Rahway and East Millstone.

"So," Hal said, clearing his throat. "Ready for this?"

"What?"

"The source of Frank's pain?"

"Did his mother die?"

"Nope. Ever hear of the term *punk*?"

"You mean the music?"

Hal shook his head. "It's what they call their wives in prison. The men who've agreed to be wives—"

"Wives?"

"Guys inside take wives. A jailhouse lover who will also iron your uniform—"

"You're kidding—"

"Old-timers choose newbies to be their bitches, and the rest of the prisoners have to leave them alone. Otherwise it's a free-for-all." Hal paused and looked at me. "I probably shouldn't tell you about this," he said. "What are you, sixteen?"

"Almost eighteen," I said. "Anyway, it's not like I don't know about gang rape." But I was shocked.

"Frank's lover died. The guard said he'd nursed him for the past two weeks, slept by his bed and everything. AIDS." Hal shook his head. "I wouldn't last a minute in that place."

I didn't say anything. Outside I watched a lady pull a wagon full of groceries across the highway. Sigrid's baby-sitter had been strangled by this man and now he was spending his life in jail. Why should he feel close to anyone?

"You okay with this?" Hal patted my knee.

I nodded, but all of a sudden tears were just there, like when you are going to throw up, no warning, nothing. I tried to keep them inside, so I screamed. Then the sobs started.

"Hey," Hal said, looking completely scared, "Alice? Jesus, Alice—" He put on his right-turn signal and got into the exit lane. "Hold on," he yelled, like I was having a baby in a cheesy made-for-TV movie, "just hold on!"

We exited off the ramp and drove into an industrial park. He parked next to a factory called Wayne Electronics. He turned toward me, and I sort of fell on him, still crying but sort of pushing it now. He started to kiss me, my mouth, the side of my nose, across my eyelids. It felt wonderful. He pulled me toward him, and then he put my seat down like he was a dentist and unbuttoned my shirt. My nipples glistened, and I arched up to meet his tongue. He sucked and nibbled, muttering, "Oh, baby, sweet baby, you beautiful girl."

I didn't do anything. Hal covered my breasts and belly with kisses and licked his way down until he unzipped my pants, lifted me so he could pull them to my ankles, and then he put his face between my legs, cold tongue, a shock, each finger another pressure. It happened fast and then slow. I was without any thought of where we were or who was inside me. It just kept happening over and over again, the tongue on me, the fingers pressing in and up, his words against my skin, screaming and pushing and coming.

"Yes," he said. "Yes, yes, yes, yes, yes."

When I got home I found a note from my parents that said they'd gone to a neighborhood association meeting which was also a potluck and would I make sure Alf got fed. Like he was a dog or something.

Alf's room was pretty awesome. He'd painted the ceiling so it looked like the planetarium, with the entire solar system in silver fluorescent paint. He wasn't messy like most boys. He was really organized and into having everything stored in these cool boxes. Matt had made a lot of those boxes with him. They had a box construction project every holiday—dad boxes for tools and cuff links; mom boxes for sewing, jewelry, and whatever; even a girlie box for me, which was the ugliest thing I'd ever seen in my life, covered with shells and glitter.

"You want spaghetti?" I asked him.

He was sitting on his bed, and I couldn't believe how tall he was. He was as tall as my father. Taller maybe.

"Okay," he said and his voice cracked.

"Okay," I said, mimicking him.

But then I saw his eyes. He'd been crying long and hard.

"What's wrong, Alf?"

"Nothing." He picked up the electronic calendar thing and started pushing buttons.

"Are you in trouble?"

He shook his head.

"Did somebody hurt you?"

A tear landed on the bed. It had been a long time since my little brother cried in front of me.

"Honey—"

"I found out," he said. "I found out about the bones."

I sat down and stared at a clear Lucite box containing all the stuff Matthew had given, loaned, or persuaded Alf to buy. Rollerblades, pastels for drawing, CDs by obscure, screaming groups of men, books no one would read unless they were trying to impress someone. The thing was, Alf didn't do or read or listen to anything I ever recommended to him. It wasn't fair, I thought darkly, it wasn't appropriate.

"What should I do with this stuff?" he asked.

"Burn it," I muttered.

He pulled away to look at me. "What?" he asked, his lower lip trembling.

"Nothing," I said. "Give it to his sisters."

"The three witches?"

After we read *Macbeth* in junior year, Matt never failed to mutter "Fair is foul, and foul is fair," when Samsara, Chloe, or Nell appeared.

"They don't have any taste," he said.

"Look," I snapped, "just because Matthew was willing to talk to you doesn't mean he was right about everything."

His sisters' lack of discipline and the way they dismissed all his obsessions as boring drove Matt crazy. He couldn't get them to pay attention to any of the things he cared about: nuclear disarmament, voters' rights, acid rain, or the proliferation of chemical warfare. They liked clothes, boys, stupid music, and drugs. None of them had any respect for any rule that had ever been used to keep them from walking out of school, kissing a boy, or saying what they felt in whatever language they deemed appropriate. They adored Matthew but they would not listen to him. They liked to work easy, dumb jobs, collect their money, and spend it on things that got them high or made them pretty.

Once when he was trying to lecture Samsara about respecting her body, she raised one eyebrow and said, "Hey, we aren't the Brontë sisters and this isn't three hundred years ago and you aren't the only thing that makes us live and breathe. Get over yourself, little boy!"

I was shocked that she made such a literary reference, but Mrs. Swan told me all the girls had IQs in the genius range and their SATs were the highest in the school. Samsara had been eligible for several full scholarships but she refused to apply. After their father left they decided to be dumb and beautiful, Matt told me.

"Why should they have things they won't appreciate?" Alf asked me, tears still in his eyes.

I shrugged. "To remember him by."

"That's not how to remember people," Alf muttered.

"Like you know," I snapped.

"Just because I never had anyone die doesn't mean I don't miss people."

"Who do you miss?"

"Jonathan."

Jonathan Friedman, Alf's best friend since he was practically born, had moved away during the summer. Everyone had tried to make it seem like it would be easy for them to keep in touch, but it was hard to watch the two boys saying good-bye. They had been babies together and went to the Sunshine Nursery School and kissed and hugged one another without a thought until first grade, when they started to shake hands, which was stupid but, I guess, necessary. Neither of them was very athletic, but they were odd and they liked each other and one friend can save you from total misery. The day Jonathan's family moved away, Alf cried on my mother's lap for an hour. We took him out and bought him an enormous magic kit, but it didn't do much to make him less sad.

"How do you remember Jonathan?"

Alf showed me his laptop. There was a file on the desktop labeled Personal. When he clicked on it, a floating box in 3-D appeared. Alf clicked, and things began to come out of the box: a photograph of their kindergarten play, a map of the Millstone river system, a Slinky, a homemade airplane, and a hologram of several of the rapidly aging female stars of some lame teen sitcom.

"Did he think those babes were hot or something?"

Alf nodded.

"What will you do for Matt?"

His question took me by surprise. I never was that sort of a kid. After memorable events, I purged. My father called me the Shredder from my habit of disposing of old papers from school immediately. I couldn't stand to have little things at the bottom of my book bag or my purse. I needed to know what I carried.

There was a bundle of notes and cards that Matthew had sent or given me over the years. Most of them were unromantic and self-absorbed, defending his behavior or attacking mine. I had a file in my computer of saved e-mails that were sort of like love letters. There was a dead rose and a ticket stub from an Ani DiFranco concert we attended on our first official date, where he had kissed me so deeply I felt my skin start to radiate heat and the people sitting behind us applauded when we finished.

And I had a T-shirt of his I would never wash. Never. I would be buried in that T-shirt, which contained all that was left of his essence. If I let his mother smell it she would cry, but I knew she had enough dirty laundry to keep her happy. Once I had thought to call the FBI and ask them if they could use the T-shirt to track him with those special dogs.

There were other things, too. Maybe I thought we would grow apart when we were older so I had started to archive the past. I kept stuff I pretended to have lost and stuff he had given me that I always meant to throw away but never did. Sometimes I think we are born knowing certain parts of our lives are too precious to survive.

"Nothing," I said. "I can't keep him in a box."

"I'll give his stuff to his sisters," he said.

"Keep something, Alf," I said, patting his head. "You want some dinner?"

"Okay."

I started to leave.

"Where are you going?"

"To the kitchen."

"Can I come?"

Visions of my little brother trying to follow me appeared, and I pulled him up to his huge feet and hugged him hard. For the ten years we had walked Pip, I had refused to let him tag along. Matthew tried to persuade me to let him but I was without mercy. We left him with his small nose pressed against the screen door, the wires ticktacktoeing across his skin or, when it was cold, standing on the living-room couch watching us walk away. Why? What was the matter with me? My heart was a box of rocks. "I love you," I whispered into his neck.

And he melted there for a moment, his cheeks still slightly wet from crying.

We went downstairs and made garbage macaroni and cheese. It's really good, but the idea is sort of gross. You put much more than macaroni in the homemade cheese sauce. We grilled portobello mushrooms and found some chicken and steamed a big chunk of cauliflower. All of this went into the pot, and then we ate it in big bowls my parents had bought on a trip to Japan. We kept the TV on the whole time, but we talked, too. Alf told me about a kid in his class who'd been stealing things over the Internet, things that were very expensive. The kid had a whole warehouse full of state-of-the-art video equipment and laptop computers and really expensive sneakers. This kid had access to a credit card number through one of his father's clients, and the person was so rich, he didn't notice how huge his bills were. Or at least this is what the kid told Alf.

"He has a CD burner I want to give to Dad, but I know it's stolen." Alf shook his head. "You know his father is the CEO of Gray Technologies. He doesn't need to do this."

I didn't give him any advice except I told him a little about the Rahway setup and how bad it felt to walk into that prison. We watched MTV, and Alf showed me a juking step which started with a swing and then you went under and over your partner in some very complicated way. He's a great dancer. I heard something, and there were my parents standing at the front door, watching us with that look parents get on their faces when you're actually doing something nice or positive. I remember loving that look, wanting to see it on their faces, wishing and hoping I'd make them feel good. It's hard not to hate everything that reminds you of childhood.

Seven

THERE WAS SCHOOL THE NEXT DAY for the losers who
didn't manage to leave the country. Isabelle, thank God, was in Tuscany or Milan, someplace she could find her inner diva bitch. Ten of
us turned up in Ms. Hardwood's homeroom, including Morgan
Crawford, Wendy Henninger, and Sigrid. Wendy's hair was an amazing shade of purple, and she seemed to have pierced several new
parts of her face. Morgan looked exactly the same, and Sigrid had
on jeans which I had never seen her wearing.

"Cool jeans," Ms. Hardwood said, sitting down next to her,
putting her hand lightly on her arm. "How's Dad?" she asked quietly.

Sigrid had blushed when her jeans were mentioned, but now she
looked pale. "His blood count is bad," she said. "But they don't want
him in the hospital."

Ms. Hardwood nodded. "Morgan?"

"Ms. Hardwood."

It was sort of cool being left by all the hoi polloi, as my mother would call my globe-trotting classmates. Ms. Hardwood was like a parent with too many children. She never had time to focus on us.

"What are you doing at that recording studio?"

Morgan cleared his throat and tried to look cool. "Actually . . ." His voice was high and squeaky, and several of us began to laugh.

Ms. Hardwood sighed. "Don't make me hate you," she said, turning to face the gigglers. "Morgan?" she asked, turning back to face him.

"I have an internship at Slick-G Sound Studio."

"Met any of my rock-and-roll heroes?"

"Elvis is dead, Ms. Hardwood. Dion retired."

She made a face. "I'm not that old, Morgan. What about Springsteen?"

"Nope."

"Tom Petty?"

"Nope."

"Bonnie Raitt?"

"Who?"

"The Ramones?"

Morgan looked disgusted. "Jesus," he said, "that's like ancient history. Mary J. Blige came by."

"I've heard of her," Ms. Hardwood said. "Are you learning anything?"

"How to remember twelve different coffee orders and not to put ketchup on Smoke Papa's burgers."

"Who's Smoke Papa?" Ms. Hardwood asked.

"He used to be Terence the Stud," I said, trying to be helpful.

"He was engaged to Dellabella," Wendy added.

Ms. Hardwood raised her eyebrows. "And Dellabelle is who, again?"

We laughed politely, but it was also annoying. We're supposed to pay attention to what matters to them but they don't listen to our music properly. My father makes fun of the fact that I like Jakob Dylan more than his dad, and my mother groans when I talk about movies that were based on earlier movies. "You should see the real thing," she says. "The original."

But this *is* the real thing for us. This is all we have and all we will ever have. They don't like what we like and they don't like us imitating them. Grown-ups don't know when to move over. They still block out the light and suck up the oxygen and just when you're ready to actually say something, they don't listen or they change the subject.

"Dellabella had a gangsta girl ska group, but now she's on her own," Morgan said.

Ms. Hardwood nodded. "What are you learning, Morgan?" she asked.

"How to deal with diverse, strange, and talented yet stupid people," Morgan answered gravely.

"It sounds like teaching," Ms. Hardwood said, smiling. "Sigrid, did you bring the tape?"

Sigrid nodded and pulled a cassette out of her book bag. Ms. Hardwood took it and put it in the boom box.

"Do you want to tell the others what you're working on?"

She shook her head.

"Can I tell them the story at least?"

Sigrid nodded.

"It's a modern opera based on 'Hansel and Gretel' told from Gretel's point of view. Sigrid submitted this to Juilliard in November, and she was accepted early admission with a full scholarship."

We were stunned. No one kept news like this quiet around Millstone Country Day. When Tamara Thorpe was given a partial scholarship to Harvard, Mr. Farley announced it over the loudspeaker. When Hecky Douglas won some lame award for being the best hockey player in the Northeast, he was given a standing ovation in the morning assembly. Parents sent out engraved announcements when their kids got into Brown. It wasn't considered boasting. It was like you won the lottery and everybody should know.

The opera stuff was hard to appreciate at first. It was dark and weird and no one sang like the women in those Broadway musicals. The sound wasn't melodic and the lyrics weren't full of pretty images. But after a minute or two, you recognized greatness. It made you want to do something—to cry or laugh or talk or say something to Sigrid—but you had to listen.

Sigrid had been studying the violin since she was three with all the other Suzuki midgets. She could play anything stringed—cello, guitar, mandolin—and she wrote beautiful music. The song that Gretel sings to Hansel to help him keep going when they're lost in the woods was so sad but also beautiful. She basically tells him that if they die they will always be together, that they will sprout roots and become part of the forest and their branches will entwine and no one will ever separate them. It took a minute for me to realize I was crying. That was how good it was.

I wasn't thinking about me or Alf or even Matthew. I was thinking about how it must be for Sigrid without her mother, trying to take care of Thor. Toward the end of the piece the music got really light and happy, but Gretel was telling Hansel to lie down and go to sleep because she's accepted they are dying. I think it's called the rapture of the deep when drowning people decide to let themselves sink. It's supposed to be the sweetest feeling in the world.

I wonder if it's just easier sometimes to stop struggling. I remember when we went to this production of *Othello* in New York where Desdemona looked totally blissed-out when she was finally strangled. Our teacher said it was all about sex. How can it be about sex if someone's dead?

When the music stopped, there was a minute of total silence, and then the ten of us applauded. Sigrid had walked out of the room, so we were applauding the tape recorder. But we had to do something. We didn't act all bitter and stingy like we usually did when somebody did something amazing. Listening to Sigrid's music made us better human beings. It was that good. I opened the door and she was standing in the hall.

"You wrote that?" I asked.

Sigrid nodded.

"Are you coming back in?"

"Do I have to?"

"Come on. We're all totally self-absorbed. No one even noticed you left."

She followed me back in, and Ms. Hardwood hugged her. There were tears streaming down her face. "Listen," she said, "when you win the Nobel Prize you can tell the world I'm a lesbian. As long as you mention my name."

"Hey!" Morgan Crawford was standing right next to me throwing his car keys in the air and catching them. When I looked up, he fumbled and they fell on my foot.

"Sorry." He bent down to pick them up and turned really red, totally glowing, his ears like brake lights. "You want to get some lunch?"

I looked over to where Sigrid was now sitting, pretending to be absorbed in putting her cassette away.

"Sure," I said. "But let's see if Sigrid can come."

Morgan didn't roll his eyes or indicate he didn't want her included. "Someone will have to take the boot."

He had an amazing car that was made in England and was so small you could barely fit three people into it. I think it was called a Triumph Spider. It was bright yellow and went about a hundred miles per hour if you put your foot down just a little.

I took the boot. Sigrid had to be threatened before she agreed to sit up front, but it was worth it to see how much she blushed when I pointed out that she had much longer legs than me.

"Right, Morgan?" I said.

He blushed and didn't look. "Yeah, I guess," he mumbled.

The countryside around Millstone was still undeveloped. Rich people realized their views were going to be blocked by minimalls, and they got together and bought up the fields that surrounded their farms and estates. Some of them were rented to local farmers, but others were returned to being woodland. We took the back roads, and Morgan accelerated so when we sped over the edges of the hills, the tires came away from the road and for a moment we actually flew. Other than screaming, no one spoke. I was the apex of the triangle, and if I didn't start a conversation there would be nothing said until we reached town.

"So, Morgan," I shouted above the engine noise. "How did you get into that studio?"

He blushed. Then Sigrid blushed. I swear to God, they were made for each other.

"My mom's partner represents him on all his drug and firearm stuff," Morgan said. "They wanted a slave."

"Is it fun?" Sigrid asked, blushing.

"Yeah." Malcolm turned onto Main Street, his tires screeching. "I get to help with the sound edit if there's not a rush to get the thing done."

"You mix?"

"Uh-huh."

A woman in a Hummer was signaling to pull out of a parking space. Her car was so huge; she had actually used two meters. She looked to be about twenty-two, and there was no evidence of a family the size of the Israeli Army to justify her driving such a tank. God, people are horrible sometimes. Morgan pulled into the space and turned off the engine.

"Are you using the board?" Sigrid asked, not blushing at all.

I felt my legs turn to stone, but I didn't want to move. It seemed to me I had found the perfect couple and someone had to push them together. So what if sitting on my own feet permanently crippled me?

They started to talk about sound editing, and I stared out the window. I'm not musical. In fact, I'm musically learning disabled. I was forced to take piano, then guitar, violin, and flute. I sucked at them all. I sucked at recorder and triangle. I sucked at drums and singing. No one could stay in the room with me when I practiced. My father said I had a tin ear. But some jerk at *The New York Times* wrote an article insisting all children had musical talent, and if it wasn't nurtured, they would lack a certain brain development that could cripple their creativity for life.

I spent three years being yelled at and criticized by music teachers. One said listening to me made him want to cut his throat with a rusty piece of metal. I figured this was too much and I told my father, who nodded and said, "Amen." After that I went on a hunger strike that lasted an entire day. My parents capitulated, and my musical training came to an end.

So I didn't enjoy listening to musical geniuses talk about chords and sampling. It made me feel stupid and left out. I stared out the window, and then I saw Hal. He was walking down the street holding a bag from the health food store, looking sort of smug. I ducked down as much as I could in a space too small for a largish dog.

"Hey," Morgan said, "you must feel like your feet have turned to stone by now."

He and Sigrid were looking back at me where I was scrunched down, trying not to be noticed by Hal.

"I'm fine," I said.

They didn't turn back around.

"Stop staring at me!" I snapped. "I like it in here."

Morgan glanced at Sigrid, and she blushed.

"Go in without me. I'm sort of thinking about something I want to do with the prisoners."

They finally got out, and I rolled into the front seat, my legs totally cramped. What had I done? I was going to be alone with this person for another month. Not alone, in a small room with six other men who seemed to have nothing better to do with their time than stare at me. Now Hal would probably act weird and try and get me alone to kiss me or talk to me.

I'd been groped before by baby-sitting clients and one friend of my parents who always stuck his tongue in my mouth when he kissed me. It was never that bad except one time with Mr. Blackstock. He had been drinking with some friends and came home and drank more while I was checking on his son, and he followed me upstairs and sort of lunged. Thank God for all the wrestling practice I'd had with Alf. I flipped him over and locked myself in the bathroom. Before this, I'd felt bad for him. His wife was young and beautiful and mean and had left him for her tennis instructor, left him with their four-year-old son, Joe, who was a very sweet little boy.

The Blackstocks were so rich they had several garages for all their cars and Harley-Davidsons, and they had phones in every room including the bathroom. After I called Matthew from the phone next to the bidet, I went through the medicine cabinet and stole Mrs. Blackstock's lipstick, which was this amazing brand that you could only buy in Paris. Also, I slipped a prescription bottle of Dexedrine into my pocket and several bars of really expensive Italian soap.

Mr. Blackstock was outside the door whispering about how sorry he was and that he wouldn't touch me if I'd just come out. Samsara's VW bus didn't have a muffler so you could hear it as it came up the long driveway. Matthew knocked on the door, and after a moment I came out and he was standing there, taller than Mr. Blackstock, holding my coat and bag. Mr. Blackstock was holding Joe, who reached his arms out for me.

I never saw his mother pay attention to him except to unpeel his hands when he tried to hug her. She was a terrible person, but she always had her picture taken at charity events, usually cuddling some sick kid. The Blackstocks owned the other half of Millstone that Amy didn't own. Mrs. Blackstock didn't act like anyone's mother. When they went out, it was always Mr. Blackstock who hugged and kissed Joe good night while she looked bored and checked her nails for chips. Maybe he'd gotten too big to be an effective fashion accessory.

Matt just nodded at Mr. Blackstock. He put his arm around me, and we walked downstairs. At the door, Mr. Blackstock pushed all this money into my hand and said he was sorry. Joe kissed me. I felt terrible. We drove to the Donut Palace and Matthew acted angry. I thought about Joe and felt guilty about leaving. We sat in the car for about a minute without talking. Matt scowled like I had somehow made Mr. Blackstock attack me.

"Sorry you had to leave your precious whatever," I said. "Next time I'll just suck his dick!"

I opened the car door and started to walk toward the Donut Palace. I heard Matthew slam his door and then his feet behind me.

Matt grabbed my hand and squeezed so hard I thought my bones would crack. "Don't ever talk like that," he said.

"Ouch," I said. "Why not?"

"Because you know better." He sounded like a teacher. "You aren't like that."

"Like what?" I asked. "You hurt my fingers," I whined.

"Never mind," he said, taking my hand and kissing it, kissing each knuckle.

"Do you hate me?" I asked as we entered the diner. The smell of coffee and hot doughnuts hit you in the face, bitter followed by sweet.

He stopped and leaned over, tipped my chin back, and said, "You're my perfect Alice. No one else can ever be that." And then he kissed me but really sweetly, like my dad, lips closed and no tongue. He had tears in his eyes but they weren't because of me.

It turned out Catherine Swan had been taking Xanax or Valium or something and she'd taken too many and fallen. Before she fell, she had a fight with Ivan about his going to bed and hit him, not hard, just a spank on the bottom. Then she fell and cut her head; it wasn't serious but she needed stitches to make it stop bleeding.

Matthew had taken her to the emergency room, where Ivan told someone they had to come there because his mother hit him. That person had called the police. The police had wanted to put Ivan and Matt in protective custody. Catherine Swan wasn't a perfect mother or anything, but she loved her kids. Until Matthew got a chance to explain everything, it had been very bad.

Then he got a message on his beeper that I was in trouble, so after he dropped his mom and brother off at home, he came over to the Blackstock's to rescue me.

Sometimes I wonder when Matt's childhood really ended. I think people believed he could do anything and not get worn out or worried. He was amazing at taking care of people. But he wouldn't let you do things in return. I had this dream that someday I would be there when he needed backup and I'd be able to shoot all the bad guys, or get my sled dogs to pull him out of the avalanche, or just be this earth goddess that could soothe his aching psyche.

When we were married I was going to be very helpful and supportive, and I was going to help build things and make bread. We'd be partners. I was trying to learn how to knit so I could make him a sweater. My job on the horse trek project was going to be shoeing the horses because Amy thought it was a good role reversal if Matt cooked and I was the real hard labor gal. When I started, the whole thing had freaked me out. I was sure the horse was going to crush me and never put his leg up to be shoed. But I had learned how to do it. I wasn't afraid or timid anymore.

None of those things will ever happen. I spent ninety dollars on heather cashmere wool yarn, and my mom's going to take it back to the Knitter's Niche and see if we can get store credit. I never helped him with anything that was hard. I read this article that talked about how couples evolve and the way we fit the profile was selfish/giver. I was in my selfish period, but then it would be Matt's turn. You couldn't both be selfish together. But now he's dead and I can't ever take care of him. I will just stay selfish and find some loser who's willing to put up with me.

During Vietnam they brought home all these boys in coffins and they gave their mothers or their wives American flags. What's that about? You love someone, you give birth to someone, or you have a baby with someone and they get killed and the government gives you a piece of cloth? I wanted the boy. The man-boy with the strong hands, the sweet-smelling skin, and the thick hair. I wanted his life inside me, not the hollow, flat memory part. I wanted him to have fucked me until I was full of him, to have made a child from our two selves; two children that grew up and found a perfect fit.

Maybe it would have been terrible. Maybe he would have been a bad father. His father was a liar and his mother was a drunk. His sisters are sluts and his brother can't read at grade level. According to the latest statistics, your chances of staying married after one year are like one in fifty. Who can deal with odds like that? Matthew used to tell me, "Swans mate for life," but that was the bird, not the person.

Mrs. Albright, the health teacher, said passion wasn't a healthy foundation for a relationship. "The fire that's built with paper and starter fluid won't burn through the night."

"Then let it flame," Nick Sanders said. "I'd rather die a beautiful corpse than be someone's hot water bottle."

Mrs. Albright's husband had recently died. I think she was offended by the idea of someone just being with you to warm your feet.

I'M GOING INSANE.

After my parents came home we made hot chocolate with marshmallows, and the four of us sat in the kitchen like a family on a commercial. But I couldn't stay in my place like the cool older sister. I felt sick.

"Kids," my father said. "Maybe Matthew came to earth to do exactly what he did."

"Like his mission was over or something?" Alf asked, his voice squeaking.

I glared at my dad. "He didn't have a mission. We were going to get married."

"Alice," my dad said. "Things would have changed. Nothing stays the same."

"You don't know," I muttered, "you don't know what we would have been like."

"No." My father sighed, reaching for me. "One can only imagine."

I stood an inch beyond his hands. "We would have lasted forever," I said. "We would have been together until we died."

"Don't get bitter," my mother said. "Someday you'll be able to tell everyone about him."

I started up the stairs and then stopped. "I'll never say anything," I said, not looking at my mother. "But it doesn't matter because it never really happened."

AND THEN THERE WAS Hal. When he picked me up the next morning there was an old paperback book lying on the passenger seat. A book that had once sold for $1.25. I turned it over after I fastened my seat belt and saw it was *Catch-22*. Matthew had a reading list and this was number five. Although I'd hated *Zen and the Art of Motorcycle Maintenance,* which was number four, I thought Heller was a great writer. Most of Matthew's favorite books were about people getting killed by nature or men trying to figure out why they were assholes. We didn't have the same idea of what made a book great.

"An awesome novel," Hal said, putting his hand on my leg.

This was a mistake. I stared at his hand with this look I'd perfected in second grade that actually sent heat toward its focus. He took his hand away. I stared out the window.

"Have you read it?" he asked after a few minutes of silence.

"Uh-huh."

"Did you understand it?"

I couldn't believe he asked me this. What would I say? No, I'm just a teenage slut with a great pussy, or Yes, fuck you. I stayed quiet.

"Alice?"

"Yes?"

"Can we have a decent conversation?"

"Sure." I smiled at him like Snow White's stepmother smiling at the dwarfs. "Tell me why you like it so much," I suggested.

It turned out Hal had been an American lit major in college and had actually met Heller on several occasions. "He's really a smokin' guy," Hal said.

I nodded. The tendency to attempt the teenage vernacular struck me as pathetic.

Then he started to talk about Mark Twain and Sylvia Plath and EE Cummings and Zora Neale Hurston like maybe I'd never heard of any of these people. The thing is, Millstone has the most AP classes of any school in America, and most smart kids that graduate from there end up skipping two years of English and history when they go to college.

Hal started to list every single book I should read at the endless red light by the soft ice cream stand. For some reason that light had never been fixed. My dad used to ask Matthew to run out and get us cones while we sat waiting, and there was nearly always enough time before the cars behind began to beep.

The books reflected the same taste as Matthew's, a taste instilled in him by Mr. Swan, the Hemingway wanna-be.

By the time we reached Rahway Prison, Hal was deep into the Raymond Carver spiel. How Carver had been this unrepentant drunk and then got sober and then met this woman poet and then wrote hopeful stuff and then got cancer and died. Like I cared.

Matt would have loved Hal, I suddenly thought. They both considered themselves brilliant.

"Alice?"

I was opening my side of the car, having kicked his special edition of *Catch-22* deep under the seat. "Yes?"

"Are you freaked out about what happened?"

"No," I said slowly. "Are you?"

Hal looked thoughtful. I waited. He looked pensive. I slammed the car door and started to walk toward the gate. I was looking forward to seeing the men. At least they were honestly fucked up.

"Alice?" He put his hand on my shoulder but I shook it off.

"Look," I said, "my boyfriend's bones were just found buried in a field in southern Mexico." He looked stunned, which was really enjoyable. "The thing is"—I stared into his eyes—"nothing happened the other day. I might as well have been lying there dead, my veins filled with embalming fluid." I smiled at him sweetly, "But I hope it was good for you," I said, entering the prison on the third shrill sound, the iron doors slamming shut as I walked toward the metal detector.

Eight

THE TROUBLE WITH BOYS IS they aren't girls. They can't help how they are. Alf is a fine person. He just isn't a girl.

When I saw Samsara Swan in Glittertrash, I turned so she could avoid me if she wanted to. But she acted like I was her best friend, screaming my name and running over to where I was standing looking at this rack of really ugly vintage swimsuits. Her arms were full of velvet dresses.

"Alice," she said. "I knew that was you because your hair is exquisite."

My hair was pulled up in one of those clips you use to keep potato chip bags sealed.

"Sweet Alice." She dropped the dresses into a pile of clogs and hugged me. I couldn't believe how thin she felt. Like a very underfed child. She was so small and her heart was close, so close to the surface. I could feel it against my body.

She pulled away and stared into my eyes. "Alice?"

"Yes?"

"He's dead. Did you know? He's dead. My perfect baby brother, my little man, my puppy. Someone killed him, someone shot my Matthew, my prince, light, and sunshine."

I kept nodding. What could I say? Her eyes were very weird. I tried to remember what they said in health about drugs and pupil size. Her pupils seemed enormous, but maybe it was just her eyes were full of tears and things looked bigger.

"Did you know how much I loved him?" Before I could answer, she continued. "It probably seemed like I didn't but I did, so much, so much he made me crazy. I mean, you shouldn't love your brother so much you want to marry him, should you?"

I didn't say anything.

"He wanted to send me into treatment. He said I was much more than a beautiful, smart woman. He said I had a perfect soul and that I would get my core revealed and then it would be like nuclear fission."

This was the sort of shit Matthew could talk.

"I was so stoned, I just laughed at him. He cried. He said I had to get better so he could have the most beautiful sister in the world. And now he's dead, Alice, fucking dead. Someone shot him in the head like a dog, like you'd kill a bad dog." She stared at me. "No one will ever love me like that again."

No, I thought, they won't.

"Samsara," I started, "I'm so sorry—"

She put her hand against my mouth. "No," she said, "that's inappropriate. You are as broken as we are. We watched *West Side Story* last night and Chloe said, 'It's like Matt and Alice.'" Samsara saw my face and smiled. "She never hated you, Alice. It's just Matt chose you over her and that hurt."

I started to pick up the fallen dresses. Samsara pulled me up and shook me hard. For a skinny girl, she was strong.

"You were going to marry him, weren't you? In my mother's wedding dress, all beads and white lace. He told us right before he left for Mexico with that dumb bitch. He told us you had finally found each other and that when he came home, he was going to make you marry him."

I didn't believe her.

"He's so old-fashioned." She gently stroked my hair. "Will you always love him?" she asked.

"Yes," I said.

"I'm too thin," she said. "I need to start to eat again. Nothing tastes like food. It's just stuff and I don't want it in my mouth." She started to turn away, but then she stopped. "I can still remember the first day I met you," she said. "You were six and I was twelve. Do you remember what you asked me?"

I shook my head.

"You said: 'My name is Alice and I'm six years old. Are you a movie star?'"

Samsara had answered the door wearing a pair of Cathcrine's high-heeled, fur-trimmed mules, a feather boa, a silk kimono, sunglasses, and dark red lipstick.

"I thought you were the most glamorous woman I'd ever seen," I said.

Samsara shook her head. "I was a little girl," she whispered. "I loved my mother, my father, my sisters, my little brother. I thought everyone was going to be happy, so happy." She kneeled down on the floor and started to gather up the fallen dresses.

"I'll do that," I said.

She smiled up at me. "You have always been really kind, Alice."

She stood and brushed off the dust. "We're having a thing for Matthew tomorrow—at the house. My mother is going to call you, but just come." She reached out and touched my face; her skin was soft and sweet-smelling, sandalwood. She was using his soap. "My mother needs you to be there. She wants all the pieces of Matthew to be in one place so we can let him go together." A shiver passed through her body. I could almost see the ripple in her skin. "We have to let him go," she whispered.

I nodded.

"He loved you for eleven years," she said. "Almost all his life. His short fucking life."

As she left, I heard an odd whisper, the sound of something, like the wind but also a murmur, distant music or wind chimes. But there was nothing to make that noise. It was like a sigh. The world had sighed.

CLOTHES DON'T INTEREST ME. Alf is the clotheshorse in our house. He worked for nothing at Abercrombie & Fitch so he could learn folding techniques. I swear to God, that boy folds like Michelangelo. Sometimes he sneaks into my room and folds all this stuff I have rolled up at the bottom of my closet. He has a reverence and affection for things like thread count, the weight of silk, the drape of a dress. He and my mom visit fabric stores together like they were making a pilgrimage to a shrine.

He's designing my graduation dress. It's made from this cloth with a name I can't pronounce, but I just see white.

I've been engaged to Matthew Swan since second grade. We turned in our Chuck E. Cheese tickets and picked out matching rings. I still have mine, and I'll bet his is someplace in his room. When I read *Wuthering Heights* I got worried. The way Cathy defines herself as Heathcliff and tells him, "You are me." It's beautiful but it's also sick. Laura Youngblood said we have this thing called a shadow self that is the part of our brain that's unregulated, which is a weird idea. But I guess maturity tells you whether certain things are acceptable.

Last year there was this girl who transferred into Millstone from someplace in south Jersey, and she was definitely deregulated. She bit three teachers and climbed on Mr. Rosenwald's piano during the annual choral concert and farted right into his face. I think she was expelled.

Anyway, I think Heathcliff was supposed to be Cathy's shadow self, and so they couldn't separate themselves but they also couldn't be together. Cathy needed Heathcliff to be a whole person, but he also was a destructive force because she needed to be regulated, especially back then, when women were not supposed to do things like sleep with anyone other than their husbands or get jobs or run marathons. Or teach prisoners how to write.

I wrote my junior honors research paper about *Wuthering Heights* and all the psychological stuff. Ms. Hardwood loved it. She read the opening and most of the conclusion to the whole class. Isabelle Folonari did all this eye rolling, and then she raised her hand and asked why I'd quoted this "Jung guy" when we were supposed to be using our own opinion and anyway, what did it matter whether he was young or not?

It took Morgan a second, but he turned around and smiled at Isabelle. "Listen," he said, "we know you aren't as stupid as you act. We know it's all a ruse because you want to be an international supermodel and no one would hire a supermodel who didn't have marshmallow fluff for a brain."

She didn't get it. I wondered then why Morgan had been so quick to defend me. Matthew had taken one of the hyphenated courses,

Jamaican-feminist literature, I think. They kept taking field trips to Jamaican restaurants in Newark. I gave him the paper to read, but he didn't ever say anything about it.

My prom dress was burnt rose, sheer over a satin slip. Alf designed it. I think this is a real thing for him, but he's sort of embarrassed about liking to sew. The thing is, Alf has all kinds of gifts. He's really good at math and writing. I don't think he even has a shadow self. The dress is in the back of my closet full of pins. I only tried it on once, and it looked amazing. I think he had this idea of me as a Greek goddess, and the dress makes me seem perfect. Thin but strong and beautiful but not cute and not slutty like most dresses for teenage girls.

He started sewing it when Matthew was still expected to come back from Mexico. So it's nearly finished, but it doesn't have anywhere to go. The back of my closet is my shrine to Matthew Swan. All the things he gave me or lent me are in there. If I grow up and get married, I won't ever tell my husband or my children about him because they will never understand how anyone could go on living when she loved someone so much it felt like having most of her destroyed, burned away, when he died. He's dead and I can't believe I'll never see him again.

Heathcliff can't live without Cathy, so he just lets himself die. He says he doesn't exist without her alive on earth even if he can't be with her. But I'm not quite that shadowed. He was an orphan and no one really loved him. I have all these people attached to me by fine gold wire you can't always see, but it's there and they won't let go. It starts with my mother and father and Alf, but there are other people, Ms. Hardwood and Amy and Mrs. Swan and Morgan and even Sigrid. You aren't free to put yourself onto the pyre like those Indian widows. You have to accept the responsibility of being loved.

*　　*　　*

SIGRID DIDN'T KNOW I was teaching Frank. It wouldn't be so bad, but he was actually turning out to be a good writer and I sort of liked him, too. His stories were powerful and not always ending with everyone down on their knees thanking "the Lord Jesus Christ" for a second chance or in some stupidly ironic twist of fate that makes you want to barf. My dad gave me a book of exercises that he used in college, and the prisoners started to do their homework and actually revised some of their poetry. But they wanted only me to read their work.

The thing was, nobody liked Hal. He was too judgmental, and when he criticized their writing he started by saying stuff like "Man, I know where you're coming from," which sounded really dumb considering Roger had come from Macedonia, where he had seen an entire village shot, the bodies piled up and burned afterward.

Lincoln grew up in this insane family where everyone except him took drugs and then he got old enough and started to work for "the man" as he called the dealer.

Kenny was left on the steps of a Puerto Rican orphanage when he was two hours old and then found out that the lady who was the town whore was actually his mother. He started running numbers for the gang when he was eight, killing at twelve.

If Hal was like anyone it was Howard, the Harvard graduate, and Howard was really annoying. When he wasn't complaining about a lack of "literary integrity," he was forcing us to listen to an endless adaptation of *Remembrance of Things Past*. Howard and Hal could go on about Proust until you wanted to start a prison riot. Everyone there was obsessed with time, so maybe it wasn't such a stretch to study the minutiae of daily existence and also to try and re-create the exact moments in the past that were lovely. Certainly I did that when I allowed myself to think about Matthew.

But the prison routine was exactly the same 365 days a year, unless you were lucky enough to be allowed to do something like study art or writing.

"We come in here to think about something different," Frank said one day in response to Howard's latest chapter, a ten-minute description of him washing a plate and contemplating his hands in soap. "You write this horseshit about boredom and endless repetition and it makes me want to cut my throat!"

Hal coughed. "What about 'write what you know'?" he asked.

Frank shook his head. "This isn't what we know, Junior! This place is just this passage, this long, dark, scary corridor which leads us someplace else."

"I know where you're coming from," Hal said. Nodding.

Frank stared at Hal. "You ever do anything wrong?" he asked.

Maybe it was just a coincidence, but Frank looked at me after he asked the question.

"Of course."

"Ever get caught?"

"Uh, my mom found my stash of pot when I was in ninth grade." Hal laughed but no one else did.

"You end up in juvie?"

"No."

"Did anything bad happen?"

"I got grounded."

Lincoln leaned forward, arms coiled muscles on his knees. "I got caught with stuff when I was twelve, got beat, sent up to Stonington for three years."

Kenny nodded. "My cousin shoplifted a fucking bag of potatoes and ended up at Rikers."

Frank nodded. "The difference between you and us is we got caught." He looked at me. "And they made sure we paid our big debt to society. Most people are bad inside 'cause they want something they can't have. Macbeth kills everybody to be king. And then he's upset because no one likes him. You gotta do your time, Hal. Be a man."

Frank smiled at me. "Then you look at Alice, there, and realize that other people are pure inside and just good."

All the other men smiled, too.

Hal looked pissed off. "Because she's a woman?" he asked suddenly.

Curtis looked horrified. "You don't have respect," he said. "Look at her. She's not just a woman she's like an angel. She sits here and she listens to us and never makes us feel stupid for what we trying to say."

"She's kind," Kenny said. "She believes we got something to say."

Roger put his hand up. "You see," he said in his Count Dracula accent, "we are like you, Hal. You don't accept that so you treat us differently and we are smart enough"—he tapped his temple—"to understand. You think we deserve to be here." Roger looked at me. "She doesn't judge that. She came here to help with a pure heart. Because she's suffering and she wants to understand life better."

"She got our respect because she can see we can teach her, too. She's here with us, not far away like you, slick," Lincoln added, nodding at me like I should know he'd watch my back if it came to some kind of bad time.

Hal looked hurt, but I felt wonderful. The prisoners liked me. They thought I was an angel. I wondered how they knew I was in pain, but it didn't matter. Even Lincoln didn't hate me or think I was a stupid "cracker-ass."

*   *   *

WE DIDN'T TALK until we were on the New Jersey Turnpike, when I realized Hal was crying. I didn't know what to say so I just patted his shoulder.

"I'm an asshole," he said, finally.

"No, you're not," I murmured.

"You agree with them, don't you?"

I thought for a moment. "Not entirely," I said. "You're the real teacher and I'm the student teacher. I can have fun with them, but you're actually teaching so they get mad."

This was a major stretch. Hal wasn't really teaching them more than I was and he was an arrogant twerp, but I felt bad.

"They're all in love with you," he said suddenly.

I shook my head. "It's not love," I said. "It's what Frank was saying about wanting something you can't have. It's not me. It's a memory or a dream of a girl."

Hal sighed. "How can you be so wise at seventeen?" he asked.

"I'll be eighteen soon," I answered, staring out the window at where the gasoline fires were burning west of Newark.

I HAD BEEN over to Sigrid's several times since our friendship started. Her father's wing was in the back on the second floor, so it didn't seem like someone was sick in the house. The place was amazing, a Mies van der Rohe–designed spaceship filled with gorgeous Scandinavian furniture and expensive electronics.

The house was divided into three spaces and a common area. Thor's wing was gothic. He was a major fan of Marilyn Manson and all things punk and black-tinged. While his father was undergoing chemo, Thor had shaved his own head and had a grim reaper tattooed on his lower back. There was a tattoo artist in Asbury Park who would probably tattoo a baby if offered enough cash. While Thor was only twelve, he had enough piercings and body decorations to last the rest of his life.

Sigrid's wing was exactly what you'd expect. The colors were very pale and slightly jarring, mauve-tinged walls combined with pale yellow ceilings. It was sparsely furnished and incredibly neat and clean. The overall effect was gorgeous. I was jealous of her house but not of her life.

I have never known anyone who was so alone. While I was there, no one called or knocked on her door; the house was silent except for a distant echo of Thor's gothic rock filtering down the hallway. It reminded me of the movie of *Beauty and the Beast,* the French one, where the invisible servants take care of Beauty while the Beast sleeps away the day.

"You want to come to a thing?" I had asked Sigrid when I called the day of the Swans' party.

"A thing?"

"Matthew's family's doing this sort of . . . celebration. Well, a wake or something."

There was a pause. It occurred to me that Sigrid had known too many dead people.

"I wasn't invited."

"I'm inviting you."

The fact was, I didn't want to go there alone. The Swan girls intimidated me.

"Well—"

"Come on, Sigrid. It will be weird, but you liked Matt."

I didn't know much about her and Matt. One day when we were

making grilled cheese sandwiches on the huge Vulcan range in the Andersons' kitchen, Sigrid slammed the door of the refrigerator and said: "Matthew Swan used to come over here." I knew they were biology partners, which requires a fair amount of time spent collecting things from various local ecosystems. My partner did all the work for us, and I wrote her English essays.

"Did you guys have fun?" I sounded like someone's mother.

"He's very smart," she said, slicing the cheese in perfect pieces. "I told him about my baby-sitter."

I was shocked. Not that she told him but that he didn't tell me. I had always told him everything, even when people made me swear to God that I wouldn't tell anyone else. Matthew wasn't anyone else.

"Really?"

"Yeah." She looked at me with her icy blue eyes. "Sorry."

"It's okay," I said. "I don't own him or anything."

No one owned him. The calcium from his bones was seeping into the mud in Mexico.

"He talked about you a lot."

"He did?" Then I felt afraid. Like I would hear something bad about myself.

"All the time. He told me we should be friends."

The Andersons had all these Scandinavian gadgets for weird things like pitting olives or making lumpfish. The cheese slicer produced paper-thin, uniform slices of cheese. Sigrid had a very tall pile of these in front of her, but she was still cutting.

"Matthew liked deciding things for people," I said, a little nastily.

"Is that bad?"

I shrugged. To tell the truth, it irritated me that Sigrid hadn't chosen me as a confidante without prompting. What would happen now that he was dead? Would I be passed over for the rest of my life?

"Did he talk about Hallie?"

Sigrid put the sandwich into this amazing cheese sandwich grill she said all Norwegians own because they are obsessed with cheese sandwiches.

"Sometimes. It was a total pity thing."

Yeah, and her looking like Fiona Apple on a good day.

"He was really into damaged people," I said, ripping the top off a bag of imported potato chips. All the food at the Andersons' reminded me of the stuff you get in fancy Christmas baskets.

"Like me." Sigrid spoke so quietly I could hardly hear her.

I looked over to where Sigrid was now making the second sandwich. A tear was sliding down her nose.

"That's not true."

"You didn't even know we were friends."

"So?"

"He wasn't proud of me like he was of you."

There wasn't anything I could say to contradict this. I didn't have any idea Matthew had ever even talked to Sigrid. He collected broken people, stray animals, and stories that people told him without knowing who he was or whether they'd ever see him again. He was the sort of guy old ladies sat down next to on long bus rides and explained exactly how they'd lost their families, their houses, their husbands, sometimes their minds.

He'd be called into counseling to discuss his SAT scores and the secretary would tell him that her mother had Alzheimer's and the counselor would tell him about how bad her dating life was after her divorce. He could have started a cult of people who wanted to tell him things.

We ate our cheese sandwiches, and then we went to try on stuff to wear to Matthew's thing. It wasn't a wake or a funeral or sitting shivah. It didn't seem appropriate to label it a celebration since the event marked the discovery of his bones. I decided to view it as a

weird party and a way to say good-bye to the Swans. No matter what
we promised one another, he was what held us together, and his
absence meant I had no place in their lives. I had spent more than
half of my childhood in their house, but like school, I would leave
and not look back except to remember small things in a false and
dreamy way.

We were putting on makeup in Sigrid's bathroom. It was huge,
like a bathroom in a nightclub with a mirror that went from floor to
ceiling. You didn't have to stand on the tub to see your lower half
like you had to in the tiny one that connected my room with Alf's.

"Do you still think about your baby-sitter?"

There was always a long pause before Sigrid answered questions.
I think this was why some people didn't like her very much.

"Yes," she said. "I think about her every day."

"Really? But— Why? I mean—how can you remember anything?"

"I remember exactly what she looked like, how she smelled, the
sound of her voice, the feel of her hands brushing my hair, sleeping
in her bed, walking down to the mailbox . . ." Sigrid paused. "Love is
a permanent thing, Alice. Like hate."

Her face was very serious.

"Do you actually hate anyone? I mean, I don't even hate Isabelle
Folonari."

Sigrid nodded. "Of course not. She's just a stupid girl. You only
hate people who do something evil and permanent. Like Hitler or
Mark David Chapman or him."

I knew she meant Frank.

Sigrid didn't have any eye makeup, so I loaned her some mascara
even though you're not supposed to share it. The mascara made her
lashes appear, and they were incredibly long. She put on a little red
lipstick, and I almost felt jealous of how pretty she was.

I had found this vintage seventies dress in the back of my closet that Matt had loved. It was hippie-peasant with huge bell sleeves, a tie around the waist, and an uneven hem cut on the bias. Underneath I wore my Doc Martens lace-up mountain boots and a pair of his socks I'd never returned. Sigrid put on a gray turtleneck and ironed jeans. She looked normal, if a little young and nerdy. Like someone going to the public library.

When I came out of the bathroom, Sigrid had a box open on her bed that was full of photographs. She pulled out a picture of a beautiful woman holding a little girl in her lap. Both of them were wearing birthday party hats and laughing.

"Is this your mom?"

"That's Antoinette."

"The baby-sitter?"

"Yes."

They looked alike, and then I remembered Frank and how he had killed this person, this laughing person who had loved Sigrid, and I thought I was going to throw up. There were many more pictures.

"Can I look at these?"

"Sure."

Sigrid went into her bathroom, and without a real idea of why, I took one of the photographs, Antoinette in shorts, standing at the edge of what appeared to be a huge lake. I slipped it into my pocket and continued to look at the other pictures, Thor as a tiny baby in the arms of a woman who must have been Sigrid's mother. She had a sweet, thin face, but she looked tired and sick. There were also pictures of Sigrid's dad, who was very tall and Scandinavian-looking.

"How's your father?"

She smiled. Now she was really, really pretty, and I was happy that she was.

"God, Alice," she said, "he's getting better! He can eat and he's talking about going back to work and maybe we'll do something dumb like go to Disneyland or Club Med—" She stopped. Her eyes were full of tears.

I put my hand on her arm. "That's not dumb, Sigrid. Normal people need to do silly things."

She laughed. "We're not normal."

"Why not?"

"People who have such horrible things happen to them aren't normal, Alice. There was a kid who wasn't allowed to play with Thor because his mother said our family was depressing."

"That's disgusting."

But I knew what she meant. Ever since Matthew Swan had been identified as dead, I felt strange. Things like that separate you; so when you watch TV and everyone else is laughing you think nothing will ever be funny again. Famous people can act dramatic and talk about their loss. Normal people are supposed to behave like nothing happened and not upset everyone else's state of denial.

It's horrible to talk about it because you can't express the essence of the thing. There are no words, just pictures, and you can't go around screaming: "Boy who loved me! Hair smelled like lemons. Hands made me whole."

It's the ache I had when my parents left me with my grandma for a week to go to Italy. Lying alone in the room, holding my stuffed cat, tears rolling into my ears and saying over and over again, "I want my mommy, I want my daddy." But I knew they'd come back and hug me and kiss me and it would be better than it ever was because for a short while I'd suffered. But he won't ever come back. He's a book you close and will never read again. He's gone.

*   *   *

THE SWANS' THING was huge. Cars lined their driveway and went down the block. Neighbors had given permission for people to block their driveways, and there were still people walking up the path. A person greeted guests at the door and, taking our coats, asked us to sign a guest book like it was a wedding or a museum opening or something.

Catherine Swan was standing outside the entrance to the huge family room, which seemed empty. In fact, the whole house was nearly unfurnished. The move must have started. Each room felt completely different without the old clutter of books, kids' toys, sports equipment, music stuff, art supplies.

"Alice." Catherine Swan held her arms out, and I walked over to hug her. She was very thin, not quite as bony as Samsara but without any softness or give.

"You're so skinny," I said, trying to smile at her.

"Yes," she said, pushing my hair away from my forehead, just like my mother. "And it doesn't give me any pleasure at all." She paused. "Life is so short, Alice. How can it be easy to waste?"

I didn't know how to answer her. We were never going to be together again. Matthew had died and left us without an excuse to love each other.

"Is Samsara here?" I asked, trying to say something.

Catherine Swan nodded. "Of course. Everyone's here," she said, her eyes focusing across the room, "everyone in the whole fucking world." And then she gave my shoulder a small squeeze and drifted toward another group of people.

"She looks so sad," Sigrid said, watching Catherine disappear into the crowd.

I walked over to where people were standing around a mural of photographs, Matthew's pictures from babyhood to last year. I was in many of them, and it was not possible to look without starting to cry. People were wiping their eyes and glancing away. It was terrible and I thought about leaving but I knew Catherine had wanted me to be there.

I saw Sigrid standing near a life-size plaster sculpture of a man trying to pick another man's pocket. Catherine had liked George Segal enough to convince all of us that we owed her a session of body casting. Over a single weekend, Matt and I had submitted to being stripped to our underwear, wrapped in gauze, and covered in papier-mâché glue that smelled really bad. It took me a week to get the stuff out of my hair, and my mom was furious until Catherine gave her a beautiful bronze mask she had made of my face.

There was a boy standing next to Sigrid who appeared as geeky and out of place as she did. When he waved, I realized it was Morgan. He, too, looked like an ad for a well-dressed preppie— deck shoes, corduroy pants, a button-down oxford shirt. Most of the crowd was in costumes of some sort, ranging from ghetto FUBU to Dolce & Gabbana off-the-runway designer rags. Clothes were nothing but a historical record in Matthew's opinion. He claimed they didn't reflect individual choice but were merely signs of our enslavement to cultural reductionism. I remember this because he took a course at NYU in fashion anthropology for no credit on Saturday mornings and I ended up typing his final term paper because Hallie Swenson had some sort of bad reaction to her meds.

"Alice! Little smart girl Alice!" I had forgotten how tall Mr. Swan looked when you stood next to him. He was drunk.

"Hi, Mr. Swan."

He stared down at me, put a finger under my chin, and tipped up my face. "The girl of his dreams," he said. "The girl who would make everything possible."

He looked terrible. I think the worst thing about people drinking too much is how their faces lose structure and get puffy. Mr. Swan's perfect cheekbones had begun to disappear in the flesh of his face. His eyes were circled by extra, sagging skin.

"I'm an ugly, old man, aren't I?" he asked me softly, holding my face.

"No," I said. "I'm sorry," I added.

"Why are you sorry?"

"About Matthew."

Mr. Swan sighed. "Did you break his heart? Were you his Helen of Troy?"

I shook my head.

"Did that girl? What is her name again—Helen?"

"Hallie."

He shook his head. "Never mind. Listen, Alice. Did you love my boy?"

"Yes."

"Truly, madly, deeply?" Now he was smiling like the old Mr. Swan when he wasn't yelling at someone for a comma splice or a dull metaphor.

"Yes."

"You were such a funny little thing. One day you came into my study, and you just stood there staring at me. I looked up and asked you what you wanted. 'Well,' you said, 'someday I'll be married to Matthew and he'll be really old like you and I'll need to know what he looks like.'"

We both laughed. I saw through the arch three shimmering girls dancing under a strobe light. Samsara, Nell, and Chloe.

"The three graces, eh?" he muttered. He looked at me. "My sirens who lure sailors into the coral deep." He let my chin go. "What about Ivan?"

"Ivan?"

"Would you marry him? We'd keep you in the family at least."

"I'm sorry, Mr. Swan."

He nodded. "What about you, Alice?"

"I'm fine."

He looked annoyed. "I think not," he said. "You assumed your life was going to be perfect and now you don't have a single idea about the next moment. My son was going to marry you, baby Alice. I had given him my mother's diamond ring, her pearl necklace, all these things that some terrorist drug-peddling murdering Mexican stole from their corpses!"

He was yelling so loudly that people had stopped dancing and stared.

"Daddy—Daddy, stop." And then color, silk scarves, velvet dresses, soft skin, and the scent of roses surrounded me. Matthew's sisters were shimmering in front of me, Samsara pulled me away, Nell and Chloe wrapped their arms around their father, their long blond hair swirling across his sad face.

"Come dance," Samsara murmured.

"No," I said.

"Come on." She held her hand out, putting a pill into the palm of my hand. "Take it," she said. "It's just E."

I didn't do drugs anymore. I mean, sometimes I still smoked reefer but nothing else. In fact, I never did much of anything. The one time I tried a half hit of acid it gave me a really bad headache and my jaw hurt and I felt too much about stupid things. My parents were away and we had a baby-sitter named Mrs. Dunbart and I ended up watching *The X-Files* with her and getting so freaked out I had to sleep on Alf's bottom bunk.

But I took the E because I felt weird explaining this to Samsara. Actually, I stuck it in the pocket of my dress.

Nell came up to me and put her arm around my shoulder. "How's your dad?" she asked, which I thought was strange.

"Fine," I said.

"He's really cool," she said.

I nodded. But I wondered how she even knew who he was.

"My mother misses him," she said. Then she put her hand over her mouth. There was sparkly stuff all over her face and something silver woven into her hair.

"Oh dear," she said, putting her mouth against my ear. "I promised Matthew I'd never say that."

"What?"

The music had this weird beat. Like someone having a heart attack.

"About my mother and your father." She shrugged. "Oh well," she said, "he's dead anyway."

I didn't understand still.

"So you knew?"

I nodded.

"From the beginning?"

And then I remembered how two years earlier it seemed that my parents were going to get divorced and my dad moved into the efficiency at Walnut Acres and my mother wouldn't tell Alf or me anything. Matthew kept making excuses as to why he couldn't come over to my house, and then one day I saw my father having a weirdly intense conversation with Mrs. Swan at the sushi place and I thought to myself, How did that happen?

"Yeah," I said, putting some space between Nell and me. "Of course I knew."

"Are they still married?"

"Uh-huh."

"That's good." She pushed the hair out of her eyes and smiled at me like we were best friends.

"My brother's dead," she said, after a moment, tears filling her eyes.

"I'm sorry, Nell," I said, even though I pretty much hated her.

"My brother's dead," she whispered again, and then she danced away with a boy wearing a Liberate Paraguay T-shirt.

I looked over to where Morgan and Sigrid were standing, almost huddling together like Hansel and Gretel. I knew Morgan had this major crush on me, but I also thought Sigrid had hoped that Morgan might end up as her boyfriend. I swallowed the E and decided I wasn't a nice person. The prisoners were wrong about my true nature. I was a greedy, cruel human being. I was as bad as Lady Macbeth when she told Macbeth she would bash the brains out of her own child if she had promised to do so.

This is what I was thinking. I had never completely made love with Matthew, but my dad had done it with his mother. It felt like someone had put a knife between my ribs. I walked over to where Morgan and Sigrid were standing and gave Morgan a big kiss right on the lips.

"Hey," he said, looking dazed, pushing his glasses back up.

"What are you doing here?" I asked him, ignoring Sigrid.

"I don't know," he said. "I just wanted to do something."

"You knew I'd be here, didn't you?" I whispered this in his ear. I was acting disgusting, but the E made it seem very cool, very sensual, very fine and sort of cosmically correct.

"Yes," he squeaked.

"Come on." I led him out to the dance floor, not looking back to see Sigrid, now alone. The music had a pulsating beat, a beat that anyone could use on any level. I saw older people, even really older people in their seventies, getting down, and some toddlers, diapers and all, shaking their big butts.

Morgan was a good dancer. I don't know why that was such a surprise but it was. Maybe because he was so smart and ironic. He seemed too ironic to boogie. We danced apart, and then I came up close to him and rubbed up and down his body. I wanted sex. Maybe it was the drug or Matthew or finding out what really happened to my parents. Maybe it was normal.

"Is your mom out of town?"

He nodded. Morgan's mother was famous for leaving him alone in their house. She had let him not have a baby-sitter since eighth grade. He was also known for never, ever letting anyone party there.

"Can we go to your house?"

This time, he kissed me. His tongue went into my mouth and moved slowly, softly but with perfect pressure. He knew what he was doing. I wondered if Sigrid had kissed him or whether he'd practiced on an exchange student or something. His lips moved down my neck, and I shivered. I don't know how long we were kissing. Long enough for Sigrid to leave and for the lights to get low. My whole body felt totally relaxed but also very alive. Like I was getting a massage and electrical shocks at the same time.

I unbuttoned my dress in the car, and while Morgan drove, he touched me. I felt like my skin was nothing but nerves. I put my hand between my legs and started to rub. I had never done anything like that in front of anyone, but he seemed completely fine with it. And he drove really well considering I was rubbing his crotch at the same time I had three fingers inside myself.

We started in the car. Morgan pushed the seats down and sort of swarmed on top of me. He licked down my front, pushed his face inside my underwear, and stayed there, licking, sucking, and eating me. I was becoming the sort of person who had sex in cars. The swimming pool steamed under a glass dome, hidden by trees but glowing like a planet. We slipped into the water, swam into each other, and kissed until I couldn't take it anymore and dragged Morgan out, muttering "condom" into his ear. Someone knew something because he had one, and lying back on one of his mother's expensive chaise longues, Morgan pulled me into him so I was facing backwards, went up inside, put his hand between my legs, and fucked me so long I turned around and asked if he were okay.

"Jesus," he muttered through clenched teeth, "you are unbelievably gorgeous."

This was nice, so I leaned back and had nothing but feelings, mostly about how high I was and how good the sex felt and how much I wanted to be dead but at the same time I still just wanted to be seventeen and fucking this boy. The bad feelings would come later. I knew this and I didn't care. I was in my own movie, the main character was headed toward the edge of the cliff, but for now, it was good.

Morgan must have saved up for this night. He pulled out of me, pushed me to my feet, took me inside, backed me up against the wall of the living room, and did it for another twenty minutes or so. We ended up on the rug of his room; my legs wrapped around his shoulders, the whole thing improbably wild and sort of insane.

"I love you" was what he said to me when we were finally quiet, our bodies covered with sweat and saliva and God knows what.

"Thanks," I said.

"I love you, Alice," he said again, staring into my eyes.

I saw he meant it and realized the bad part of what I had done was going to be worse then I'd expected. The whole time I felt like I was in a music video, maybe that old Fiona Apple one where she keeps taking off her underwear. It was sexy and sleazy and didn't matter. But it mattered to him. And it mattered to Sigrid.

"I shouldn't have done this," I said, putting my face into the coverlet. Morgan seemed ready to go to sleep, but I was wide awake and needed to do some more damage.

"Why not?"

"Because . . . I'm not ready." I stopped. Matthew Swan had been gone for almost a year. Most people didn't know he was planning on marrying me.

"Ready for what?" Morgan sat up. "You seemed pretty ready to me."

I glared at him. The drug was fading fast. "That was the E."

"What E?"

"Samsara gave it to me."

He looked a little hurt.

"It's not like it made me insane or anything," I said, trying to be nice. "It was really cool what we did."

"Cool?" Now he looked insulted.

"I never fucked anyone on a chaise longue before." I sounded like a total whore.

I got up and started to get dressed.

"Where are you going?"

"I'm supposed to be at Sigrid's."

"I'll drive you."

As we walked through the empty house I thought about how so many of my friends are alone much of the time.

"Do you ever see your father?" I asked Morgan as he turned on the security system and opened the garage door with the remote control.

"He's a prick," Morgan said, stopping. "The last time I saw him he told me he didn't think fatherhood fit him properly. Like it was a suit or something. You don't know how lucky you are."

"Yes I do," I said, opening the passenger side of his car. "But people aren't always as perfect as they seem," I added, remembering what I now knew about my father.

Morgan started the car and then turned off the engine.

"I'm sorry," he said.

"What for?"

"Matthew was it, wasn't he?"

"Yes."

Morgan leaned back in his seat. "If this was a while ago you could become a nun or something."

I found this annoying. "I don't want to be a nun," I said. "Anyway, we aren't Catholic."

He nodded. "So how will you know when you're finished?"

"Finished what?"

"This grief thing, sitting shivah, whatever you call it."

"Shivah? Jesus, Morgan, we're not Jewish, either." I stared out the window. The sky was getting slightly pink. "I don't know what will happen," I said. "No one I know was ever murdered before."

"What if you meet someone and it would be the right thing and you were just totally depressed and that person might be the only one to make you happy?"

I sighed. "Take me to Sigrid's," I said. "Before someone finds out I never slept there."

As I was getting out of Morgan's car, I put my hand on his arm. "Look," I said. "If I feel better before we all go away to college, I'll come over and we can do it again on your mother's chaise longue."

Morgan nodded.

Sigrid's brother, Thor, answered the door. I don't think he had been asleep. His hair was dyed Marilyn Manson black, and he was wearing a T-shirt that said DEATH ROCKS. He should have creeped me out, but he didn't. Basically, he was just a little kid like Ivan and Alf. Boys weren't scary when you knew them close up.

"Hey," Thor said, "did you go to that thing at the Swans'?"

I nodded. I walked toward Sigrid's wing with Thor behind me.

"Were you there when the police came?"

I shook my head.

"His sisters were dancing naked or something. Some kind of pagan grief thing." Thor looked sad. "I always miss the great stuff," he said.

"Hey." Sigrid didn't look angry. She looked glad to see me.

"I'm sorry."

"It's okay."

"Did my mom call?"

"No."

"Did your dad ask where I was?"

"I said you were still asleep."

I sat down on the side of Sigrid's bed, which was already made, perfectly unwrinkled, a bed that would make my mother weep with joy.

"I took E last night."

She looked up from the music she was writing or correcting or whatever musical people do with sheet music. "Really?"

"Samsara gave it to me."

"Was it fun?"

"I guess so." I looked at Sigrid's part. She had a perfect line down the center of her head. For early morning she set an impossible standard. "Sigrid?"

"Uh-huh?"

"Do you like Morgan?"

She continued to work on her music.

"I mean, do you want him to be your boyfriend?"

"I'm going to college, Alice. I'm not taking Morgan to college with me."

The image was actually pretty funny. Morgan was the sort of person you could imagine packing into a trunk. More so than having sex with him on a chaise longue.

She looked up at me. "Why? Did you sleep with him?"

I nodded. Sigrid's eyes were very, very blue.

"Was it nice?"

"I don't know." Suddenly I was starving. "Can we eat breakfast?"

"Sure." She put down her sheet music and stood up. "My dad made blueberry muffins."

I wanted to cry. The night before had been bad and weird, and it wasn't clear how many things were true. Nell said my father had been her mother's lover. Or she implied it. Or maybe it was an inference. There had been too many standardized tests in my life. I felt dizzy with all the literary terms that were swirling around my brain.

"I'm sorry, Sigrid," I said.

"That's okay." She turned toward me. "Morgan always had a thing for you. Every time you left us alone in the car he talked about how much he liked you."

And I thought they were flirting.

The Andersons' house was pretty hard to navigate. The kitchen was downstairs but also through another hallway, so you could easily take a wrong turn and end up back where you started. Mr. Anderson was sitting at the table reading *The New York Times*. He was wearing a light blue, totally pressed oxford shirt and pressed khaki pants and nice shoes. For a Sunday morning, he looked like a Ralph Lauren ad.

"This must be the infamous Alice."

Sigrid frowned.

"Hi, Mr. Anderson."

"It's nice to finally meet you." He stood up and put out his hand, which I shook. He didn't seem sick at all. "Muffin?"

I nodded.

"Are you doing a senior project, Alice?"

I nodded. Sigrid put a muffin in front of me on a white plate and I took a big bite. I was starving and couldn't remember the last time I'd eaten anything.

"At the prison," I mumbled through a mouthful of the best muffin I'd tasted in my life.

"Which prison?" Mr. Anderson asked.

"Rahway." I swallowed and took a big sip of the milk Sigrid placed on a coaster at my elbow. These people were very different from my family on a Sunday, Daddy in his ripped, bleached Megadeth T-shirt and my mother in her completely worn-out Laura Ashley pajamas until noon at least. "I'm teaching in the literacy program."

Mr. Anderson nodded. "Is it hard to go there?"

I nodded. "Yeah, but they aren't insane or anything. Actually, they probably are, but I think they might be like normal people—" I suddenly remembered Frank and how he had murdered the Andersons' baby-sitter. I took another bite of muffin.

"So they're just like us?"

I shook my head. "No, but they all had so many bad things happen to them I can't help thinking it makes sense that they did terrible things."

He frowned. "But we've all had bad things happen to us." He gestured toward Sigrid. "Should she start killing people because her mother died?"

"Daddy!" Sigrid looked pained.

"No," I said. "But at least it's not totally arbitrary, like those Columbine kids." This was a weak argument. If evil was evil, a rose was a rose. I was still a little high.

"Nothing's arbitrary, Alice."

"What about the people that killed Matthew and Hallie?" Sigrid's face flushed a little.

Mr. Anderson flinched. Most parents did that. They felt it someplace deep inside their bodies and it hurt.

"I don't know, Sigrid," he said, reaching out his hand to touch her shoulder. He looked at me. "You were Matthew's best friend, Sigrid told me."

I nodded.

"This must be very hard for you."

I nodded again.

There wasn't much to say about it. The three of us looked out the window to watch Thor hit a stick against a tree. His dyed black hair hung down his back.

"That boy would cry his eyes out if he stepped on a mouse, but he looks like someone's idea of a teenage killer." Mr. Anderson sighed and knocked on the window.

Thor turned around and smiled at us. His piercings shone in the sunshine. He waved. We waved back.

Nine

SOMETIMES I WONDER HOW MUCH Amy tells Ms. Hardwood about the stuff she knows about us. If Ms. Hardwood knew certain things, like what I did with Hal in his car, she would have to tell someone.

The Monday after I had sex with Morgan on his mother's chaise longue I went to see Amy at the farm. Ms. Hardwood had postponed our senior meeting until Tuesday because she was attending a seminar on whether kids should be required to read *Huckleberry Finn* when they are in high school.

The prison session was canceled because there was a problem with two guys who tried to escape when their wives told them they were pregnant by other men. There was a food fight, and they briefly took a guard hostage with a smuggled pair of tweezers. Hal said none of our guys was involved, which I was glad to hear because if they had been they wouldn't be allowed back to the writing class. The whole place was in lockdown.

"Why did they tell them they were pregnant?" I asked Hal. "If I were pregnant and my old man was in the slammer, I'd wait until I had to tell him."

Hal laughed. "Let's hope you don't end up with an old man in the slammer," he said. "But if you do, I'd keep the dating to a minimum."

Mockie was galloping across the field when I got there, running so fast you could see all four feet lift off the ground. She whinnied and flung herself on the grass and stomped so hard, dust rose in clouds.

"She's got spring up her nose," Amy said. "She's feeling wiggly." Amy looked at me and frowned. "What's with the purple circles, waif girl?" she asked, coiling a rope in her hands.

I walked over to watch Grace, who was wearing an old pair of snow pants with a sweatshirt over them, sitting in the center of an enormous puddle of mud. She was making mud pies and singing "Have you seen the muffin man?"

"Hey, piggy," Amy called. "Look who came to see us."

Grace looked up, looked around, and looked over my shoulder. "Matt Matt?"

"No."

Grace threw a mud pie at the fence. "Go 'way," she said, not looking up again.

I sat down on a big spool that had once held splicing wire.

"The bones are his," I said.

Amy finished winding the rope. It kept slipping toward the end. Finally she hooked it over the fence. "I heard," she said. She stared at something far away. "I'll never believe he won't just show up. My boy Matt."

"There was a wake last night."

"Yeah." Amy sat down on the edge of the fence. "We were invited but—" I could see her throat working to swallow. "Were people keening and drinking whiskey?"

"Dancing and taking E."

"You did E?"

I nodded.

"You probably shouldn't tell me some things." Amy put her foot on the fence. "I like your parents, remember?"

"And I had sex with Morgan Crawford on his mother's chaise longue."

Amy looked amazed. "Lord," she said. "What's up with your bad self, Alice?"

I shook my head.

"Don't take drugs," she said. "Not unless you're prepared to lose everything."

"I've already lost everything."

"No you haven't, honey." Amy sighed. "Doesn't Morgan have that incredible car—the yellow Triumph Spider?"

I nodded. I put my hand on my chest. "I think I have breast cancer," I said.

Amy shook her head. "Of course you do. Valerie thinks she has a brain tumor. It's bad, but we'll probably survive." She stood up. "Was that the first time you had sex?"

I shook my head.

"Truthfully?"

"It's the first time I saw the point."

Amy smiled. "So Morgan's some kind of stud-muffin?"

I frowned. "Don't be disgusting," I said. "Aren't you supposed to yell at me or something?"

"Hey, mud girl," she called out to Grace. "Wallow out of there."

She turned to me. "You need to tell your parents," she said. "You need to talk to someone."

I made a face. "Mom, Dad, I fucked a boy on lawn furniture?"

Amy was carefully wiping down each tool to make sure it was clean and dry before she put them away. I had nothing to take care of. Adrift like a space shuttle.

"Why do we exist?"

Amy looked annoyed. "Listen," she said. "One reason we let you teens hang around was that you didn't ask those stupid questions."

"Matt always did."

"Yeah, well, he cleaned out the sump pump, Alice. People will tolerate certain things from someone who does gross jobs."

"There's no God," I said.

"Probably not."

"If God existed he wouldn't have let six million Jews die."

"I would have been executed also," Amy said. "For being a lesbian." She clicked the padlock on the toolbox. "You don't have to go back so far," she said. "Last year the Serbs marched hundreds of men into the woods and shot them all. Then the Bosnians took all these Serbs and ground them up in a factory that was supposed to make paper." Amy shrugged. "Don't ever worry that anything bad won't happen again."

"Life totally sucks," I said, picking up Grace and smelling her head. She smelled of baby shampoo and dirt.

"There's God in our little girl," Amy said, smiling at me. "And in you despite all the original sins you recently committed."

I pressed my face into Grace's neck.

"Where's Matt?" she asked. It had been nearly a year since she had seen him.

"Bye-bye," I whispered.

She pulled my face down next to hers. She was strong for such a small thing. "Matt go bye-bye?" she asked.

"Yes," I said.

She looked at her mother. "Bye-bye?"

Amy nodded. I think she was crying.

"Okay," Grace said. And then she kissed me.

T HE SENIOR MEETING WAS boring. People were running out of the initial energy they felt about their projects and didn't want to give what Ms. Hardwood called quickie updates. We sulked and drank the cappuccinos we'd bought at Café Java and yawned. Morgan stared at me the entire time with this look on his face, like I'd killed his cat. Sigrid was absent. Before the time was up, I went to the bathroom. I looked like someone who was staying up too late and not getting fresh air.

When I walked outside, my father was standing at the curb. For a minute I was glad to see him because Morgan was right on my heels, trying to express his deep feelings about my body. But then I saw my dad's eyes and I knew he knew something about what had gone on at the party.

"Bye, Morgan," I said.

We drove for about five minutes without talking. Finally he sneezed.

"Bless you," I said.

"Thanks," he said. "Can we discuss this?"

I didn't know what he meant. Which this was this this? It could be anything ranging from Hal's calling the house to my taking drugs.

"No." I stared out the window. "I can go see Laura."

"Laura?"

"She said she can deal with trauma."

"What has traumatized you besides the obvious?"

It didn't seem like I had a choice. "Finding out you slept with Catherine Swan," I muttered.

He went through a stop sign. In all the years I had driven with my father, I had never seen him break a single law.

"Whoa," I said as cars honked at us.

He sneezed again.

"God bless you," I said.

"Thanks," he said. And then he sneezed twice. Maybe it was some kind of allergic reaction to guilt.

"We aren't getting divorced," he said finally.

"I don't care," I answered. But I did care. I cared so much, I thought my heart was going to burst.

"Fine. But we aren't."

"I don't care," I said again. This reminded me of that kid in the story, Pierre, who said "I don't care" until a lion ate him. I smiled a bit, and my father looked relieved.

"I'm dropping out of high school," I said.

"We love each other," he said.

"I don't care," I said again. I cared more than anything else on earth. Just love each other, I thought. Just stay.

"And we love you and Alf, totally," my father said, his voice breaking.

I didn't say anything. My father had lived in Montana once and branded cattle for a whole year. He was a cowboy and lived on the trail with a bunch of other cowboys. He said it cured him forever of wanting to work with his hands and convinced him to go to graduate school.

"I'm not going to college," I said.

He nodded. "Do you want to ask me any questions?"

I looked out the window again and watched as a lady with a shopping cart full of cans crossed the intersection. Her hair was so tangled and dirty it stuck out like a piece of solid material. Someone had given birth to that lady, held her and nursed her and rocked her to sleep. Maybe they had smiled at her whenever she looked at them. Or maybe not. Maybe they had wrapped her in a piece of sheet and left her to die.

Life seemed overwhelmingly bad to me at that moment. I felt this terrible pain just beneath my collarbone. I opened my window but I still couldn't breathe. I was having another fit thing. The car was going slowly through a school zone, and without thinking, I opened the door to get fresh air. My seat belt was off and I fell out. Slowly, like a package, in a ball. I could feel the asphalt scraping my skin and my bones hitting the road. Tires squealed and people were honking and I heard my father screaming my name. I was still trying to inhale.

Nobody believed it was an accident. The people in the emergency room kept asking over and over again, "You just fell out of the car?" Like it was something incredible, as if the effort to understand the event was beyond anything they had ever encountered. And there was nothing to make them leave me alone, no natural disaster or school shooting. I had at least three doctors and several nurses leaning over me, examining me and asking their stupid question. The nurses gently removed the gravel while the doctors shone penlights into my eyes to look for concussion.

"She fell out of the car?" It was my mother, her voice very high and thin.

"Jesus Christ," I muttered.

The nurse stopped swabbing.

"What?" I asked since she was giving me this intense look.

"Are you suicidal, Alice?" she asked, her tone casual, but I could tell she really wanted to be the one to save the fucked-up teen.

"No," I said. "Are you?" I asked politely.

She gave me this sort of sisterly smile. "I didn't jump out of a moving car," she said softly.

"Nor did I," I said. "The seat belt wasn't fastened," I added.

"Because you wanted to die?"

"No," I said. "Because I'm a moron."

They released me to my parents, who walked on either side of me, shoulder to shoulder, as if I were a criminal. Nothing serious had happened. I was scraped and bruised, my knees were covered with gauze.

We got in the car, but my father didn't put the key in the ignition. After a minute, my mother spoke. "Are we leaving?"

"Yes." But my father didn't move. "Alice knows about Catherine Swan."

"How?" She didn't sound very upset.

"Nell told me."

"Sweet girl," my mother said sarcastically. "We should get her a nice fruit basket." She twisted around to look at me. "Is that why you jumped out of the car?"

"No," I said. "I didn't jump. I was having another fit, and I needed air."

I could see she believed me. She seemed very calm.

"Okay," my mom said.

"Okay?" my father asked.

"No," she said. "But I hate hospitals as you know, and we aren't discussing this thing right now in front of Alice in the car in the hospital parking lot." She turned back to look at me again. "Honey," she said. "It was nothing, nothing real."

"But he slept with her!"

My mother nodded. "People have sex, honey. Didn't you have sex with Matthew?"

I couldn't believe she asked me that. I didn't say anything. My muscles were beginning to hurt already. Waking up was going to be terrible.

It was.

AFTER TWO SECONDS at the breakfast table, Alf felt excluded.

"What's going on?"

"Your sister fell out of the car," my mother said very clearly, as if Alf was slightly learning disabled.

"By mistake," my father added

"By accident," I amended.

"No seat belt," my mother contributed.

"Not buckled," my father interjected as if to clarify the presence of the seat belt but my decision not to use it.

"I know," Alf said. "I was here when you got back, remember?"

We nodded in unison.

"Hey," Alf said, his voice cracking a little. "When did the alien spaceship abduct my real family?"

Instead of being mean, I smiled at his feeble attempt at humor. "It's late," I said, standing up. "Gotta go teach those worthy social misfits," I said to Alf, patting his shoulder.

"Duh," Alf said.

"Well, shut up." I decided meanness would make him feel better.

"Alice." My mother sighed.

"You shut up," Alf snarled.

"Don't talk to your sister like that," my father said.

"She started," Alf whined.

"I fell out of a car," I mumbled, trying to look fragile.

Alf laughed. "You're a moron," he screamed as I went out the door. "No one falls out of cars unless they're pushed!"

Ten

HAL DIDN'T SAY ANYTHING BUT "HOWDY" when I got
in the car. Things were a little weird between us since the men had
made it clear they didn't like him. The only one who allowed him to
edit his writing was Howard, the Harvard graduate. Howard's memoir, *Harvard Made Me a Con,* was dense, repetitive, and full of clichés.
Each time Hal tried to cross something out, Howard would put it
back in and, when possible, add more.

The other guys had an opposite problem. They could barely write
a sentence without deciding it was stupid and ripping out the page
before I had a chance to read it. Their poetry was mostly literal.
They wrote things like "You are hot, mama."

"Define *hot,*" I'd say.

"Black stockings, garter belt."

"Fat butt."

"Sweaty but clean."

"Little fat roll at the hip."

"Tattoo on lower back."

I'd write these down, and then I'd suggest they get into sounds and rhythms. My dad lent me a collection of poetry that came with original recordings on CDs, and I played Sylvia Plath reading "Daddy" to them.

The prisoners thought she had a very bad attitude. They argued that people need to respect their parents unless they did something so incredibly terrible it was impossible.

Hal explained that Sylvia had been really depressed and blamed her father for her misery.

"You have to reach inside yourself," Roger said suddenly. "You can't point fingers."

"Maybe she just wanted to write a poem which made her father sound like a bastard," Lincoln said, glaring at all of us. "I say that is one sweet poem."

"She killed herself," Frank said, not looking at any of us. "She stuck her head in an oven with two kids in the house."

The prisoners marked stuff they wanted me to read. So far, nothing had been very shocking. They weren't trying to scare me with their crimes or be too explicit in the way they described their wives or girlfriends or the lack of them. They were much cornier than the kids I knew at school. My friends weren't romantic at all. The prisoners seemed to think love was the only thing that really mattered.

FRANK HANDED ME his journal with a section paper-clipped. "Read that," he said. I sat down and started to read, trying not to think about what I already knew of his history. He watched me over a copy of Raymond Carver's short stories. He looked like someone waiting to know the outcome of a serious operation.

WHAT I DID

by Frank Perone

Othello was a stupid bastard. He had this thing in him already. Who knows why? Maybe because he was black but probably not. I went to school with this kid named Sammy Didonato and he was mean. Short and mean. I thought he must have a mean mother to be such a little shit but he didn't. Mrs. Didonato was one of those moms you can talk to like she was your best friend. But Sammy was always trying to hurt stuff, kittens and puppies and other kids.

The counselor told me to focus on what I did. I can't do that because if I do that I will curl up and die. I should have never gone near someone so far away from where I came from but I couldn't help myself. You always want what isn't yours, what's different, what's better.

I closed the journal. It felt wrong to be sitting there, to be reading Frank's writing—like cheating on an exam or taking money from my mother's wallet. I knew what happened from another perspective, from the eyes of the child who watched him kill her baby-sitter. If I was Sigrid's friend, what was I doing? Frank's life was sad and I felt sorry for him. I didn't know Sigrid's baby-sitter, so I could only imagine her and that was hard. Frank was right there, skin and bones and hair and eyes. Just like me.

"You lost interest already?" He was at my shoulder.

"No," I said. "It's hard to read."

"Why? Is it overwritten? Are the transitions confusing?"

"No!" I shook my head. "You killed somebody."

"It's the truth," Frank said, sitting down. "Finally, it's the truth."

"The truth is good," I said, not looking at him.

"Did you finish it?"

"Not yet." I looked at him. "Maybe Hal should read it."

Frank looked angry. "Okay," he said. "You don't have to read it. But that full-of-shit bastard isn't reading my story."

I held on to the journal. "Look," I said. "I'm from this town."

"So?"

"I've heard my parents talk about this murder."

"Don't call it murder, Alice," he said. "It was involuntary manslaughter. I didn't even mean to hurt her. We just got into this thing and I tried to hold her down. Murder's something you plan." He shuddered. "That's why I said that stuff about Othello. He never meant to kill Desdemona." He looked at me. "We must seem like space aliens or something."

"Why?"

"You come from a nice family."

"My mother's parents were sort of crazy," I said.

Frank looked unimpressed.

"My boyfriend was murdered," I whispered.

"Come again?"

"My boyfriend was murdered. They just found his bones in Mexico. He was missing since last year."

"Your boyfriend's bones?" Frank looked shocked.

"They found these bones and matched them with missing people's dental records."

"Your boyfriend?"

"We were in kindergarten together."

Frank shook his head.

"He asked me out when we were six."

"That's pretty cute." Frank smiled. He looked around the room. No one was paying any attention to us. Hal and Howard were working on his manuscript. Lincoln was listening to something on his Walkman and writing. Officer Costa was reading *Catch-22,* which I'd taken from Hal's car.

Frank put his hand over mine. "I swear on her grave, Alice," he said. "I've never been so sorry to hear anything in my life. We all want so much for you."

"Who does?"

"Me and the guys. Even Howard, that stupid putz. We want you to go someplace kick-ass for college, and then we think you'll write some kind of novel or movie after you spend a year or two going all over Europe. See all those things in the books. After that, we figured you might hook up with a doctor or a lawyer or somethin', a guy who's got major earning potential but also realizes he's got himself the finest woman in the world. You'll have babies and send us pictures."

I couldn't believe that six convicted murderers had spun this fairy-tale life for me. It was weird but also really sweet. I had my own private fan club.

"Lincoln, too?"

Frank nodded. His eyes looked shiny. "They know who killed him?"

"Drug dealers, maybe. There was a girl with him—not his girlfriend anymore." I stopped. "She was a junkie."

"Who was?"

"Hallie. She graduated from my school."

"You got junkies at Millstone?" Frank looked outraged. "High school graduates?"

I nodded.

"What kind of scummy private school got drug addicts?"

"Lots of rich kids do heroin," I said, trying to look jaded.

Frank glared at me. "Listen, Alice," he said. "Don't talk any shit." He stared at the scrape on the side of my face, and a muscle twitched in his cheek. "Fall off your skateboard?"

"No."

"Dirt bike?"

"No."

"Rollerblades?"

"No."

"Go bodysurfing on concrete?"

"Something like that."

Frank shook his head.

"You know what Kenny said?"

I shook my head.

"He said seeing you makes it possible for him to remember love. You're smart and kind and you believe in us for some fucked-up reason. You tell us what we write has meaning and you listen, so we think you're gonna have an excellent life."

"What if I don't want an excellent life?" I snapped, pulling my hand away. "Hallie Swenson was pretty—"

"She was a loser."

I glared at him. "That's mean."

"So? The girl decides boohoo, life sucks I'm gonna stick a needle in my arm?" Frank made a gesture of dismissal. He leaned forward to stare into my eyes. His eyes were these amazing cat eyes, green-gray, yellow flames. "Listen to me, Alice. There are six men betting that you'll make us proud. None of us are ever gonna leave this place. Every time we get a parole hearing more people show up to tell those people how badly we destroyed their lives. We're society's scum and they've given up on us. Nobody takes what you got and throws it away. That boy who loved you—what was his name?"

"Matthew Swan."

"This Matthew Swan—he wanted you to have a wonderful life, the moon and the stars and everything sweet and good, didn't he?"

I had started crying, but no one seemed to notice. I nodded.

"You keep yourself clean and keep learning things and help us a bit more, and then you get the hell out and let us read about you."

"What if I can't do anything that makes me famous?"

Frank smiled. "You just be happy, Alice. A girl like you happy makes the world a better place."

"Can I interrupt?" Hal was standing behind Frank looking concerned.

"Sure," I said, still holding Frank's journal.

"The warning bell rang," Hal said.

I stood and started to hand back Frank's notebook.

"Take it home and read it," he said. "Write down what I should do next."

I nodded. In the car I stared out the window without talking. I could feel Hal watching me.

"What happened to your face?" he finally asked.

"I fell out of my father's car," I said.

"No shit," Hal said. "I did that once."

He really was an idiot.

"What were you and Frankie talking about? It looked pretty intense."

"Metaphors," I answered. "Why they shouldn't get mixed."

"Yeah." Hal sighed deeply. "Howard's really got a problem with that. Last week he compared a woman to a coyote and a hailstorm in the same sentence."

BEFORE I WENT to sleep, I read more of Frank's journal.

I was born to a kid who'd been raised by wolves. Mean wolves. My mother's mother was a loan shark, took things that people didn't want to pawn, never gave them back, just paid too little and passed them on. She would have been a grave robber back in the day.

My mother was fourteen when she was knocked up. She didn't have a chance. My dad was something else. He wasn't rich but his mother was a schoolteacher who raised him alone and wanted him to go to college.

But my dad was only fifteen when he made that baby. He asked the loan shark grandmother for a job so he could be a big man for his infant son. She wanted to get rid of him so she sent him to these two lower capos in the jersey Mafia and they took him outside and shot him—just like that—they didn't even know his name. His mother was devastated. She packed up and left. Never saw me or nothin'.

So my mom had a two-week-old baby, a dead lover, and a witch who only thought about how to use people. Nothing could feel darker or heavier than that house. No one played with me or smiled at me or sang to me. No one noticed when I walked or talked or began to smile. Maybe I didn't smile all that much. No one noticed or cared when I started to skip school, when I killed little animals with stones and then a BB gun, or when I held this kid down and broke his nose for saying my mother was drunk. I was a punk.

No one wanted to be friends with me. I was nasty, a liar, a thief, and a sneak. I hurt anyone who stayed long enough. I hurt anyone who trusted me.

Frank's mom had been three years younger than me when she gave birth. It was hard to understand. No one in Millstone had teenage babies. I mean, teenagers didn't have them. We were all on birth control, and if someone did get pregnant she was whisked away to a safe, clean holiday location like Palm Springs or Manhattan for a nontraumatic surgical procedure. I remember when we read "Hills Like White Elephants," the Hemingway story about the abortion. Most of the kids in my class couldn't believe it was even an issue. Why would they spend two pages discussing a dumb mistake?

A girl who had graduated the year before named Melissa Carmichael had returned from her senior project pregnant. She told everyone the father was a Basque separatist she met in Portugal, but her best friend said he was a bouncer in a Madrid nightclub who was married. "He's a total sleaze," Tara told us while we were smoking behind the hockey rink instead of running laps for outdoor ed. "He already has like three kids with three other women."

Melissa's Basque baby didn't go to Brown with her. When graduation rolled around she was driving a new BMW and had a tummy as flat as ever.

Eleven

THE BONES WERE SHIPPED TO MEXICO CITY. There were at least twenty skeletons found on the drug dealer's land, and each of them had a family, friends, and a history. I drew twenty circles on a piece of paper, lines radiating out from each. A person doesn't live without colliding into the lives of others. In seventeen years, Matt's web was tangled and extensive. He had kept secrets from me, secrets about my family and things he knew about the world. Maybe he wanted to protect me, but I think he wanted to have power. I think he wanted to have some kind of control over the world I lived in. This is love but it's also wrong. You have to let people discover their inner strength or someday they'll get knocked down so hard, they won't ever get up again.

Catherine Swan called and asked me to visit her in the new condominium. The old house had sold in about five minutes to a dot-com czar who had not lost his fortune in the crash. There had been a huge garage sale, advertised in the newspaper, that Alf attended by himself, returning empty-handed saying it was too weird and Matthew's sisters didn't know how much to charge for anything. People were walking down the street with antiques Samsara let them have for two dollars.

I wanted nothing. I felt clear and cold about my entire relationship to the Swan family. Matthew was dead and no one else mattered to me. I threw Catherine Swan's number in the trash, but my mother fished it out and handed it back.

"Go see her," she said. "She has things to give you."

"I don't want things," I replied.

My mother sat down on the edge of my badly made bed. "Look," she said, "when your uncle Adam died, I tried to throw out everything he owned. I was that angry at him for stepping on a land mine. But then I took it all and put it in the basement. A month later I went down and sort of sat with him. Things are important, Alice. Matt touched them all . . ." She paused and swallowed. "Catherine Swan has answers for you. She gave birth to that boy. When Adam died, I practically lived with Valerie Hardwood. We stayed up talking about Adam, just frantically discussing every stupid thing he ever said or did. No one knew him like she did. You need that to grieve."

"You look pretty." I rarely complimented my mother anymore, but she did look great. Her hair was longer, and the sun had turned strands reddish blond.

"I put on some lipstick," she said.

"You look like Susan Sarandon."

She blushed and ducked. "I need a haircut," she said.

"I like it long." I poked her in the ribs. "Daddy says you look like Greta Garbo with long hair."

She didn't smile. "He's full of fantasies," my mother said, staring at her hands. Because of gardening, she always had short nails, and her palm was callused. I love my mother's hands. "He should have married someone else," she said under her breath. "She looks like Greta Garbo!"

"Who?"

"Oh, forget it."

"No, she doesn't!" But she sort of did.

"Your father has really bad taste in women," my mother said. "Except for me and you."

"Like Matthew," I said. "He liked the grossest, neediest, most obvious creepy girls."

"Exactly," my mother said, pushing the hair off my face, "except for you. Your father is a dolt."

"Mom!"

When she looked up again, her eyes were full of tears. "Never mind," she said. "He's just an idiot, that's all."

"I hate him!"

She shook her head. "No," she said. "It would make life so much easier if we hated the people that hurt us. But they hurt us because we love them. And we love them so much, we have to forgive them completely."

"I'll never forgive him!" I was holding my mother's hand and my nails were digging right into her skin.

"Who, Alice?" She looked worried.

"Daddy." But I wasn't sure.

"Alice, your father and I are fine. I knew about what happened right away. He came home and told me. That's why we had those fights."

"Why did he do that to you?"

She shrugged. "It wasn't to me, sweetie. She's a smart, beautiful, unusual woman. He got a crush on her."

"You're smarter and more beautiful!"

My mother nodded. "Marriage is the long haul, honey. These speed bumps don't count for much."

"If my husband slept with another woman, I'd leave him," I said.

"You'd be wrong," my mother answered, leaning over and kissing me. "Sex is just the tip of the iceberg."

"So marriage is an iceberg?" I asked her.

"It's an iceberg, an earthquake, a hurricane, a blizzard, a drought, a tidal wave—just one long freaky weather pattern."

THE CARPET GUY WAS in love with my mother. Sometimes I still saw his truck in the neighborhood and wondered if he'd driven by our house just to see where she still lived. When I was in sixth grade, he made a job that should have lasted a week go on for a month and then he charged us half the estimate. He brought my mother presents—flowers and almond cookies from a special bakery in Hoboken, a crystal moon with a star embedded in its center, and then, finally, he gave her a tin of caviar that my father tossed into an omelet saying, "Here's to my wife, who's sexy enough to inspire beluga."

It was sort of sad and weird, but Matthew told me he totally understood why a young, nice-looking man would fall for my mother. "She's sweet and funny and smart and good-looking," he said one night when I asked the question how anyone, outside of my father, could be attracted to my mom.

The difference was, she never did anything. Not even flirt. I watched her every second that guy was in the house, and she behaved as if he were some friend of Alf's. She was polite and distant. My father would have tried to get someone like the carpet guy to like him more than anyone on earth. So would I. We need to feel like people want us more than the other person. This was why I seduced Morgan and why Sigrid didn't do anything but quietly go home. We walk into rooms expecting everyone to turn around and look at us. We're big, stupid show-offs.

"I'm disgusting," I told my mother, pushing my face into her shoulder. "I'm just like Daddy."

"Daddy's a wonderful person," my mother said, pushing me away slightly. "He just likes attention." She stood up. "Go see Catherine Swan," she said.

"I don't want to," I answered.

"There are things for you—"

"I don't want any things."

"Alice—"

I started to sob. "I hate him," I said. "He ruined everything with that stupid girl. We were going to have a wonderful life and now I'm alone and I can't manage—"

She sat down again and pulled me into her lap. "You don't have to manage, Allie. That's why we're still here." She stroked my head and made *shh* noises.

"What's going on?" Alf was standing in the doorway looking scared.

My mother held her arm out. "Come here, Alfred. Come and kiss your sister. No one will know."

And he did and it felt really good.

HER CONDOMINIUM WAS in the part of Millstone that had recently been developed so it looked older than the rest of town. While the oldest houses went back to the Civil War, these new houses were designed to look like old English cottages except they were huge instead of small. I locked my bike to a hitching post. This seemed like a dumb choice for a detail. Millstone had never been a town that had a lot of random horses looking for a place to get hitched.

Catherine Swan's unit was toward the end of a block of identical town houses. Matthew would have hated this change. He was born, like all the children, at home in the Swans' house. Born at the stroke of midnight, eyes open, no crying. A terrible pain knifed through my chest wall. It was like the worst stitch ever, worse than the one I had in eighth grade when I ran the eight-hundred-yard dash without warming up or drinking water. I stood gasping for air on the front path, wondering if I was going to faint.

I heard the door open and steps walking toward me. Catherine's shoes were always cool. These were gray suede boots with kitten heels. I could smell her also, the perfume she wore, Chanel 19 plus whatever else was layered over it. No matter how I tried, I would never be as sexy as Catherine Swan.

"I hate you," I gasped, talking to her shoes.

"That's fine," she said. I felt a hand on my back. "Breathe, Alice," she said.

"You did a terrible thing," I choked out, starting to straighten but changing my mind.

"Stop talking," she said.

I began to do the deep breathing exercise that Laura Youngblood had taught me. You imagined yourself as a tube and pulled the air right down to your feet.

"Better?"

"Leave me alone," I said. She patted my back lightly.

I watched her feet go back up the path, and I followed her into the house. Inside, I sat down on a chair and put my head between my knees. I felt like lying on the floor and screaming. I would not do such a thing in front of anyone who seduced my father.

She brought me a glass of water. "Dizzy?"

I shook my head and drank the water. My eyesight was still fuzzy, but everything else was pretty normal.

The place was basically a loft, much bigger than it looked from outside. She had finally done what she had often threatened, turned her living quarters into a zendo. There was almost no furniture, just huge expanses of polished wood, windows, sliding screens, pillows on the floor. There were altars set up all over, little tables with Buddha statues and incense burners and candles. Each contained a framed picture of Matthew. He would have hated this place. It was not a place for boys.

She had cut her hair. It was all gone, all the shining length of yellow gold, so that what came to just above her ears seemed nearly black in comparison, framing her face so all you saw were eyes and cheekbones. It would have taken me a minute to have recognized her on the street.

"Jesus," I said. "You look amazing."

Unlike my mother, she was easy with compliments.

"I needed a change."

"A makeover?"

Catherine Swan smiled slightly. "Right," she said. "A complete makeover. What do you think?"

I looked her in the eye. "Matt would hate it."

She nodded. "Of course. But that doesn't matter now. He's never coming back and his sisters don't care and Ivan likes no furniture and doesn't have any feelings whatsoever about how I look. It took him a week to notice the haircut."

"Has my father seen you? He prefers women with long hair. Like my mom."

"Your mother's a beautiful woman," Catherine Swan said.

"Did Matthew know?"

"Yes," she said.

"Is that why he was so angry at you?"

"Probably."

"Why didn't he tell me?" My voice cracked. I sounded five years old.

"He should have told you," she said quietly. "It wasn't right for you to hear it from his sister."

"Right? How can you say anything about what's right?"

"I haven't seen your father since Matthew went to Mexico," she said.

"I don't want to talk about it," I said.

She nodded.

"Aren't Buddhists supposed to be sexually responsible?" I asked, staring at the altar she had set up right in the hallway.

Catherine Swan sighed. "Yes," she said.

"Why didn't he tell me?" I said again.

"Because he loved you," she said. "He wanted you to love your father."

"I hate you," I said. "And I don't ever want to see you again after this."

Catherine Swan was standing in front of me. "Matthew's bones are in Mexico City," she said. "After they do some more tests, they'll give them back."

"I don't care."

"I want you to come with me to get them," she said, putting her hand against my face.

I stared into her eyes and I saw him. They had the exact shape and color and were set wide apart with the same shape of brow. Once I had loved her very much.

"I can't do that," I said.

"We would drive down and stop and do things." She took her hand away. "After you graduate. Before you leave for college." She was crying. Standing in front of me like a beautiful Zen nun, crying. "Please, Alice. I need you to come with me."

"My parents won't let me."

"Your mother said you could. She thought it would help both of us—"

My mother. She was like a saint, someone who looked beyond her own small needs to help the greater good. I wanted to smack her.

"How could it help me?"

"She said she never was able to get your uncle Adam's remains back from Vietnam and it felt wrong to visit the grave here because there was nothing in the coffin but his clothes. We need to finish, Alice."

"It's finished already," I said, not looking at her.

"No," she said. "You can't breathe and I can't sleep and both of us keep having nightmares about the place and the time and the way he died. If we know some things it will help." She shook her head. "Not all of it, of course. Not everything."

She was right about the truth. As terrible as it might be, it couldn't be worse than the horror I kept imagining. And Matthew was haunting me, in my dreams he kept walking around the house late at night, standing outside my window, standing next to my bed.

"What about the Swensons?" I made a face. "Do we have to bring back her bones?"

"They haven't found Hallie," Catherine said slowly. "I think they hope she's still alive."

And suddenly, I did too. Even though I blamed Hallie for nearly everything, I knew it wasn't her fault that something so evil existed in the world. She didn't deserve to be murdered, and if she'd survived, I'd be happy for her.

The thing on my chest moved slightly.

"You want something to eat?"

I nodded.

Mrs. Swan's cooking was so good kids always remembered meals at their house. Catherine made homemade egg rolls and puff pastry and deboned strange cuts of meat that hitherto vegetarian children consumed with passion. She taught me how to peel tomatoes, to char red pepper skin, to cut the bitter heart from garlic, and to render the juice from mushrooms. When she went to the University of Michigan in the late sixties, she had cooked for a communal kitchen and managed to feed twelve people on twenty-five dollars a week. "Mainly brown rice and tofu," she had told me, "but that's where I really started to study spices."

The Zen thing was all-pervasive. We sat cross-legged on hard pillows she called Zafus, and we ate out of small bowls, little piles of things that tasted delicious but didn't make me feel full. We finished with miso soup and sushi.

"Learning how to make sushi convinced me I needed to return to work," she said, laughing a little. "No one should have enough time to roll rice up in seaweed."

We both laughed and ate, but her eyes were dead, as dead as they had been when she drank a quart of vodka a day. This time it wasn't alcohol but sadness. Her darling, dimpled boy was gone forever.

"I don't hate you," I said, choking on a piece of wasabi-covered eel.

"I know."

"It doesn't matter that you were with my father."

"Alice," she said. "Your parents love each other and that's all that counts."

I nodded. "Do you have a boyfriend?"

Catherine smiled. "Right," she said. "It's a three-legged race between the gas station guy who calls me Cathy and asks if I want my tires rotated and the pierced teenager at Kinko's who keeps suggesting we get some brews."

"The one with the tattoo of the naked woman with horns?"

Catherine nodded. "How about you?"

"I'm the hottie of Rahway Prison," I said. "Oh, and Morgan Crawford wants to marry me."

"Now, Alice, Morgan's the dark horse. He's going to turn out incredible and successful and every high school reunion you'll wait for him to walk in but he never will because he's happily married and has four kids."

"Whatever," I said.

"I'd definitely consider him for the prom," Catherine said, laughing. But then she saw my face and she put down the chopsticks. "Jesus," she murmured, leaning forward to touch my face, "I can't believe I said that."

So we sat there and didn't eat any more raw fish and tried to think of anything other than what was not there—like the Neruda poem that names all the things death is. We were two women without their other half, their alpha male, their perfect love. The room grew darker and still we sat, breathing quietly, trying to let go, to empty, to be nothing but shapes on cushions. It didn't really work but it helped a little.

I saw it then. Her loneliness and her strength. She had been left by her husband, she had stopped drinking, her child was dead, but she wasn't giving up. Maybe the whole Zen thing was pretty exaggerated or contrived but really, so what? If it kept her from going back to being a drunk or from sleeping with the wrong people, it was a good idea. But it felt hard to leave her alone with all that polished wood and the pictures of Matthew.

"Where's Ivan?" I asked, as the room slowly turned dark lilac, our shadows on the wall like two space creatures without legs. One wall was completely glass, and the sunset was gorgeous.

"With his dad."

"Are the girls okay?"

Catherine sighed. "Well, no, but they can manage. They seem to have a real instinct for survival."

I slowly stood up. "I need to go home," I said.

Catherine smiled up at me. "Do you want a ride?"

I shook my head. "I have a lamp, and there's reflector tape on my wheels and stuff."

"Will you come to Mexico, Alice?"

"I don't know," I said. "Maybe."

She nodded. "Call me."

"Okay."

I let myself out, and before I rode away, I looked back. Catherine was still sitting on her pillow, the final light from the sun slicing across the room, shining around her so she seemed formed from something other than flesh.

I PUT THE BOX she had given me under my bed. I wasn't ready to look inside. I guessed what might be there, the totems we had exchanged over the years, the odd things that passed between us, and possibly some surprises. I felt him everywhere without his things, so I thought I'd wait until I felt alone again. I went out into the backyard and climbed into the tree house we had built together when we were in third grade. An entire summer had been devoted to the project, and when it was done, it was truly a feat of architecture; the platforms made several stories, and the rooms were large enough to furnish with small pieces of furniture. I hadn't been up there for years.

When I reached the top, I stood in the doorway and saw there was something blocking the light from the halogen bulb that burned so brightly it came through the tree house window.

Matthew was standing there in the shadows, his back to me, so tall he seemed like a grown-up. If I had any doubt, I could smell him. Just him.

"Oh," I said. "I knew you weren't dead."

"Look," he said, not turning around, "you have to get past this."

I didn't answer. If he was real, I was angry, and if I was having a hallucination, I didn't want to talk to a ghost.

"Alice," he said, turning to face me, "I'm never coming home again."

"Are those your bones?" I asked him.

He nodded.

It was impossible but there he was so beautiful, unhurt, young. Nothing was wrong. He looked the same.

"Can't you try?" I whispered. "Can't you just stop being dead and let me love you?"

He smiled at me. "You do love me, don't you?" he asked.

I nodded. There were so many tears coming out of my eyes I couldn't see very well. What do you ask someone who had to die?

"Is it bad now?"

He didn't say anything for a minute, but then he smiled. I was sure he was alive again but he wasn't. He wasn't really blocking the light. He wasn't a person anymore.

"No," he said. "I'm free, Alice, free of all the things that used to make me sad."

I squatted down on my feet, heels flat to the ground. Matthew had taught me how to do that. I put my head between my knees and stared at my toes. I felt his hand stroke my hair but I was afraid to look. He was dead and I was afraid.

"I don't want to go to the prom," I said.

He laughed and then he disappeared.

It was terrible when he left. Now I could feel how cold it must be to lie in the dark and the dirt without anyone there to hold your hand. I stayed in the squat until the muscles in my legs all started to shake. When I stood up, it was hard to move. I knew I would never go back to the tree house.

BEFORE I FELL ASLEEP, my father came into my room and sat down on the edge of my bed.

"How's the old tree house holding up?" he asked me after a long minute of silence.

"It's fine," I said turning on my side so he was facing my back. "You should tear it down," I said. "No one uses it anymore."

"Did you pick up your stuff at the Swans'?"

"Yeah," I said.

I waited for him to leave but he didn't. Finally, I looked over my shoulder. He was sitting on the floor cross-legged, his head bowed.

"Listen," he said. "If you can forgive me for what I did, I'll never ask you again. If something else ever happens, you don't have to give me another chance."

"What if I can't?"

He stared at me, his face shocked. "What?" he said. "You broke my favorite Jimi Hendrix album. You dented the new car. You gave Matthew my favorite sweater, a sweater my grandmother knitted, and you think it's possible not to forgive me?"

He was trying to be funny.

"Those don't compare," I mumbled into my pillow. "You cheated on Mom."

He looked down at the floor. "Right. But I'm not asking for anything else, Alice. You have twenty thousand future transgressions ahead of you. I screw up again and you can hate me forever." He looked up at me. "We have to be friends, honey. Nobody's dead. There's still hope."

I held my arms out and we hugged each other.

"Daddy," I said. "You have to let me go to Mexico."

He sighed. "Your mother said it would help."

"She's right. Catherine will take care of me."

He patted my face. "You don't need anyone to take care of you, Alice. You're the strongest person I know."

He kissed me on my forehead.

"I saw him," I whispered before he left my room. "He said good-bye."

My father paused. "Is he different?" he asked, his voice catching a bit. "Did he get taller, grow a beard, new earring?"

"No, Daddy, he's just the same. Not hurt or anything. He still loves me."

"Good," my father whispered. "Tell him I send my love the next time he drops in. Tell him we all miss him very much."

"He's not coming back," I said.

"Then tell him not to be a stranger," my father added as he shut the door. "Tell him he can always come back no matter how long it takes."

Twelve

"PEOPLE," MS. HARDWOOD SAID, "please pay attention!"

We stopped briefly, glanced in her direction, and then continued to talk, sipping our skim lattes and fizzy water, swallowing bagels, croissants, and fresh fruit. Someone's mother had decided to cater our breakfast in a misguided attempt to be an involved parent in the waning days of school. It was a disaster. Ms. Hardwood had been trying to announce ten crucial details about graduation for the last forty minutes, and no one was listening except Sigrid, who sat directly in front of her, impeccably dressed in ironed linen shorts, a button-down oxford shirt, and nice shoes. Most of us were in various parts of our pajamas. I had accused Sigrid of sleeping in her clothes, but she was too unwrinkled to have done such a thing.

Finally, Ms. Hardwood had had enough. She climbed on her desk, cupped her hands around her mouth, and yelled, "Listen up." She said. "You have just wasted twenty minutes of my valuable time.

This is a debt I will demand of each and every one of you before you leave me. Here are today's announcements. We will be having an assembly in ten days during which your various projects will be showcased. Sigrid's opera, Peter's play, the dance group will be performing a unique form of hoofing, which is only practiced in remote areas of the Jersey Pine Barrens." Ms. Hardwood shook her head. "Amazing," she said, "you are amazing children."

"Hillbilly dancing," Isabelle Folonari muttered. *"C'est stupide."*

Despite five months in Tuscany, Isabelle was still speaking snooty French.

Ms. Hardwood was squinting at a card she was holding. "What is this?" she finally asked Morgan.

"It's the name of my new Afro-Cuban-funk-ska group."

"But I can't say their name," Ms. Hardwood said. "It's obscene."

Morgan blushed. "No, it's not," he said, his voice squeaking a bit.

"Yes, it is," Ms. Hardwood said, glaring at him. "I recognize what this is, Morgan."

"What is it?" Sigrid asked.

"What's the band's name?" Wendy Henninger asked.

Ms. Hardwood glared at Morgan. "Go ahead," she said.

Morgan looked embarrassed. "Will I get in trouble?"

Ms. Hardwood looked exasperated. "If it isn't obscene, why would you get in trouble?"

"Maybe it means something I don't understand," he said. "It's called Long John and His Wet Pussycats."

Nobody said anything for a second. Then we all laughed.

"Alice?"

"The prison group is going to read some of their stuff."

"Isabelle?"

"I'm going to premiere part of my video on Raphael Visconti."

"And he is?"

"Her pimp," someone muttered from the back.

"Hello!" Ms. Hardwood glared toward the direction of the voice.

"Raphael Visconti is the new face of Italian cinema," Isabelle began. "He—"

"Fine." Ms. Hardwood put up her hand. "Sounds divine." She stared down at us. "Okay," she said. "Prom, commencement, and you're done. Try and not do anything truly hideous between now and then, and after that"—she smiled sweetly—"I don't give a damn!"

W E S T O O D in front of school starting to recognize that it was nearly over. We would soon be cast out, sent off to our new colleges, friendless and judged by professors who hadn't known us all our lives. People would criticize us and our parents wouldn't be there to dispute their opinions. No one would be filling our refrigerators with fresh fruit and changing the sheets on our dorm beds. We were momentarily stunned.

"Wow." Ben Jeffries shook his head. "I can't believe it's nearly over."

"Thank God," Isabelle said, sighing. "I can't wait to forget all this."

Morgan shrugged. "It isn't that bad," he said. "Maybe nothing will ever be so good again." He was staring at me with eyes like a cartoon character.

"You're freaked," Isabelle said, stalking off on her Italian sandals that appeared to be nothing but skinny straps and stiletto heels. I was in a pair of Alf's ancient Jack Purcell sneakers. They were bleached, stained, and two sizes too big. Sigrid had on spotless, dead white Keds. She had tiny feet.

"*Ciao*," Morgan bellowed after Isabelle's retreating back. "Don't be such a stranger!"

"Go back to Italy," Sigrid muttered.

Morgan and I stared at her.

"Wow," Morgan said. "In ten years that's like the meanest thing I ever heard you say."

"It's not even mean," I pointed out. "Isabelle wants to go back to Italy. America's too New World for her."

"Raphael Visconti." Morgan snorted. "How about the guy's real name is Vinnie?"

I shook my head. "I'm sure he is who she says he is but I don't care."

"What are the prisoners going to read?" Morgan asked. "I thought you hated their poetry."

"It's prose mainly." I avoided looking at Sigrid. She had never asked me if I'd seen Frank or whether he was in the literacy program. Probably she thought it was too crazy to believe I would betray her by tutoring the man who killed her baby-sitter.

"Have they written anything good?" Morgan asked. "Anything you can send to *The New Yorker*?" He started shimmying up the tow-away sign that was in front of the school. Boys always climb things. They should probably construct men's prisons with rope ladders and climbing walls and things they can attempt to scale. I think the women who actually ascended Mt. Everest had more male hormones or something.

"No," I said. "But there's this prison magazine that accepts all their work as long as the word *fuck* isn't in it."

Morgan made a face. "As long as nobody fucks or nobody says the word *fuck*?"

"Both."

Sigrid was staring at her perfect sneakers. "I've only said that word twice in my life," she whispered.

"What word?" Morgan looked amazed. "Fuck?"

Sigrid nodded.

"It's overused," I said defensively. "I hardly ever say it."

"You say it all the time," Morgan said, looking at me as if he had a right to make that kind of comment.

"No, I don't," I snapped. "Anyway, how would you know?"

"I've known you all my life," Morgan said, looking deeply hurt.

"What? I've been saying *fuck* since preschool?" It was annoying to speak to him while he was clinging to the side of the pole. The sun was shining in my eyes, and he looked ridiculous.

"Pretty much!"

"Get down," I said.

He dropped something from his pocket at my feet. It was a foil-wrapped candy Kiss. I picked it up and threw it back as hard as possible. It missed.

Sigrid was still staring at her sneaker.

"You want to say it, Sigrid?" I asked.

She shook her head.

"Is your dad okay?"

She shook her head again.

"What happened?"

Morgan slid down the pole.

"He's—" She choked on her words.

Morgan looked at me and I mouthed "Go away."

"Hey," he said, patting her back. "I'm going to let you talk to Alice but I'll call you tonight, okay?"

Sigrid nodded. There were tears landing in the grass near her sneakers.

I couldn't believe how dumb I felt, talking about nothing when Sigrid's father was getting sick again.

"Is he going back into the hospital?"

She shook her head.

"So it's really serious?"

She nodded.

"Too serious for the hospital?"

"He's not sick," she said. "He's getting married again." Sigrid pounded her fist into her leg. "To his doctor!"

"Wow," I said, without thinking. "That's really great."

Sigrid glared at me.

"I mean, well, it's normal."

Remarriage was normal. Divorce was totally assumed. I was one of the only kids in our school with original parents. Everyone else was divorced, separated, blended, step, extended, or adopted. Anyway, Mr. Anderson wasn't divorced. He was a widower, a tragic, lonely man without a wife. That was different from being divorced.

"And it's helpful," I added stupidly, "in case he needs a doctor."

"Normal doesn't mean anything," Sigrid said. "Normal can be totally horrendous."

I nodded. "Do you like her?"

"She's his doctor," Sigrid hissed.

"Is she nice to you?"

Sigrid looked really angry. "I don't know if she's nice to anyone," she said. "I've only met her during these horrible sessions when Dad's been getting chemo and I'm like the one who has to help at home . . ." She paused. "I just want to go to Juilliard," she said.

"Is she attractive?"

Sigrid sighed. It was unusual for her to be so unpleasant. "Alice, the woman wears a stethoscope, a white coat, and a pencil in her hair—"

"Well, does she have good bones, teeth, nice posture?" I poked Sigrid in the ribs. "Is she fat?"

"She's a doctor!" Sigrid said, laughing finally.

"There's lots of fat doctors," I said. "You still want to help me or do you need to pick out your flower girl outfit?"

I HAD ASKED Sigrid to be there when I opened the box full of Matthew's stuff. I didn't want to be alone. In fact, I didn't want to open it at all, but I remembered what my mother said about Uncle Adam's things.

It was in the backseat of my dad's car that he had more or less given me until I left for University of Wisconsin. The box wasn't too impressive: medium size with CAFÉ FILTRE #2 stamped on the outside.

"Where shall we open it?" I said finally.

"I don't know," Sigrid said, staring out the side window. "Here?"

"No," I said. "Let's go over to Amy's."

"Ms. Hardwood told us she didn't want to see a single senior until graduation."

I started the car. "She doesn't mean it. Anyway, she had something to do in New York, I think."

But Ms. Hardwood was home and seemed really glad to see us when she opened the door.

"Why, girls," she said in a fake, nice way. "It's been so long since I saw you. Two hours at least."

There was a terrible smell.

"I burned a bag of microwave popcorn," Ms. Hardwood said. "Damn thing practically exploded."

We nodded.

"Well, come in!" Ms. Hardwood's voice was weirdly nice. "Come in and we'll burn some more."

We followed her down the hall.

Suddenly Amy stomped down the stairs looking insane. Her face was all blotchy and red, and her eyes were puffy.

"Great," she said, glaring at me. "Why don't you just follow her home from work?"

Ms. Hardwood closed the door and turned to face Amy. "We have guests," she said in her most awesomely scary voice. "Now we must behave."

Amy didn't seem too scared. "No," she said, "now we must pretend to be perfect feminist fucking parents who are dying with goddamned happiness!"

"Amy!" Ms. Hardwood roared. "Lesbians are never perfect!"

I looked at Sigrid, who was as pale as the wall. I winked.

Amy caught me. "Winking?" she screamed. "You think this is funny?"

"No," I said, trying not to smile.

"Shut up, Amy," Ms. Hardwood said.

"Shut up? Shut up?" Amy opened the glass door and slammed it closed. The three of us watched her stalk across the yard, and when she nearly collided with a feed bucket she kicked it so hard it went at least twenty feet into the air.

"Spoiled brat," Ms. Hardwood muttered, opening the refrigerator and getting a beer. The kitchen was still full of burned popcorn smoke. Ms. Hardwood seemed to have forgotten we were there for a minute. She rummaged around in a drawer and took out a very flat cigarette. She turned on the stove and lit it. I had never seen her smoke. As far as we knew, no grown-ups smoked except Tucker Baker's mother, and she was always apologizing.

"You're fighting," I said.

"Shh," Sigrid hissed.

Ms. Hardwood just kept smoking and drinking her beer.

"What's wrong?" I asked.

"Shh," Sigrid hissed again.

"Stop shushing me," I said.

"It's rude to ask an adult a personal question," Sigrid said under her breath.

"I don't care," I said.

"She wants to get married," Ms. Hardwood finally spoke. "A wedding. White dress. Cake."

"To who?" I asked.

"Whom!" Ms. Hardwood snapped. "She wants to marry me."

"Why?"

"I don't know, Alice." Ms. Hardwood took a huge swig of beer. "Maybe she loves me."

"Can you do that?" Sigrid had finally exhaled.

"Yeah." Ms. Hardwood watched as Amy saddled Mockie. "In Norway and Hawaii, I think." She looked at both of us. "But I don't want to get married."

"Why not?" Sigrid asked. "If you love each other, why not?"

Ms. Hardwood opened the glass door and walked outside. We followed her. You could feel the humidity already, the slight wet weight of air on your face. Amy was galloping around the pasture without a riding helmet, her blond hair streaming behind her like a movie character that is about to have a nervous breakdown.

Ms. Hardwood looked at me. "I only wanted to marry one person and he's been dead for twenty-seven years," she said.

"Uncle Adam?"

She nodded. Amy started jumping Mockie over barrels like she was in a rodeo.

"But that was like forever ago," I said. "You can't still want that."

"Can't I?" Ms. Hardwood's eyes looked too bright. "I'm sorry,

Alice, but I do. If he were alive maybe we would be divorced by now, but I never got to the part where you could stop thinking about the person. Every day I woke up and smiled—" She stopped and shook her head. "I'm sorry, Alice," she said again.

"My dad still loves my mom," Sigrid said quietly.

Ms. Hardwood smiled at her. "Of course he does, honey."

"But he's marrying his doctor," I blurted out.

"Hey." Sigrid looked angry.

"Sorry," I muttered, glancing back at the box where it sat alone on the counter.

"When did this happen, Sigrid?" Ms. Hardwood asked softly, acting like a teacher again.

"He told us on Sunday." Sigrid shook her head. "Mother's Day," she whispered, tears rolling down her face.

Ms. Hardwood groaned. "Do you like her?" she asked.

"She's pregnant."

"That totally sucks!" I said.

Ms. Hardwood glared at me. "Maybe Sigrid is able to see another side to this," she commented, her voice flat and cold. "Possibly she's not totally self-absorbed."

"Yeah, well, maybe she can see the side that basically rules, which is she goes off to college and her dad starts a whole new family!" I wasn't being very helpful.

"He's so happy," Sigrid said, ignoring me and speaking only to Ms. Hardwood. "It's incredible."

"And when you come home from Juilliard, you can baby-sit," I interjected.

"We'll always be his children," Sigrid said, her lower lip trembling.

"Of course you will." Ms. Hardwood glared at me. "Older children don't get replaced."

"And stepmothers are famous for their ability to love their stepchildren," I said.

"Some do." Sigrid shook her head. "Why are you so negative?" she asked.

"Because everything isn't this little Disney cartoon with Cinderella singing to the tweetie birds."

"I know that, Alice," Sigrid said.

"Maybe your problem is that this is not about you," Ms. Hardwood said, sipping her beer and taking a deep drag on her cigarette.

"So what's it about? Two lesbians and a baby?"

Ms. Hardwood pointed her finger at me. "Listen, Alice," she said. "Grow up! Nothing stays the same. Everything erodes. Look at what happened to the beach last year—"

Jesus, I hate teachers! They use stupid metaphors when you just want to say something without comparing it to anything.

"Don't try to explain things to me," I shouted. "You think it's possible to survive getting your insides ripped out, but I don't! I'm never going to write an opera, or have a baby, or go anywhere interesting, or make my parents proud of me. I had sex with Morgan on his mother's lawn furniture because I feel dead! I want to take heroin!"

Ms. Hardwood's lip was twitching. "What kind of lawn furniture?" she asked.

Sigrid laughed first. Then Ms. Hardwood and then me. As we giggled, Amy suddenly appeared, covered in mud from head to foot, Mockie visible at the end of the pasture, bucking like a professional bronco.

"Stop laughing at me," Amy yelled. "I nearly broke my back!"

She was crying. Ms. Hardwood jumped up and ran over to her, hugged her, and said something into her neck. They fitted together like dancers. Sigrid and I looked at each other.

"I'm sorry," I said after a second. "I think it's really cool your dad isn't sick, and the baby will be great." I thought for a second. "Maybe after it's born she'll take off the stethoscope."

Sigrid smiled. "Thanks," she said. She reached out and took my hand. "Matthew will always know what you're doing," she whispered. "I feel my mother looking down at me, and I don't care how cheesy that sounds."

Amy and Ms. Hardwood came back onto the terrace looking pink and happy. Ms. Hardwood had muddy fingerprints all over her white shirt.

We went back inside the house and stared at the box. After a minute or so, I walked over and opened it. I started taking things out. There was a very small T-shirt, my T-shirt that had just disappeared one day. It had a picture of Pee-Wee Herman on it, which was our favorite after-school show.

"A T-shirt," Ms. Harwood whispered as if she were narrating a TV show. Amy and Sigrid nodded.

The next thing took a minute to understand. My mother used to cut my hair outside, where it would get left in these clumps on the ground until I made Alf pick it up or the wind blew it away. The envelope said "Alice's Hair, 1992–2000," and inside there was hair, curl after curl, each tied with a red ribbon, the last one containing evidence of my experimenting with pink hair dye. He had been saving my hair since we were eight.

"Her hair," Ms. Hardwood whispered, "he saved her hair."

Sigrid and Amy started to cry.

There was a homemade book. Inside the cover it said: "The Book of Alice: For Our Children, by Matthew Swan." It wasn't finished, but the book began with several artifacts, a playbill from when we were "Roaming Joe and Julie" in our second-grade play. A picture of me in a completely authentic cowboy outfit from when we visited

Rodeo Land in Delaware with his parents. My handprint from kindergarten done in a rainbow of clashing colors, pictures of me I never knew he had, old poems that I'd forgotten I'd written, every postcard I ever sent him, every dumb note I wrote when we were sitting in homeroom, ribbons that had been in my hair, old flowers pressed between Saran Wrap, pebbles I had given him, sea glass we collected on Cape Cod, poems and notes he had written to me but never let me read, love poems of such intensity and clarity I couldn't read them but just kept flipping the pages, tears rolling down my face, but I didn't let anything out, there was nothing to say.

Ms. Hardwood put her hand on my arm. "You should stop now," she said. "Look at the rest after graduation."

I nodded.

"You want to leave it here?"

I nodded again. "Let's go, Sigrid," I mumbled.

I picked up my car keys and we walked out the door. Amy and Ms. Hardwood were still standing there waving and crying, arms entwined.

WE WERE ALMOST at her house before I spoke.

"I never knew that he had all that hair." I paused. "Maybe he was stalking me," I said.

Sigrid glanced at me, her face shocked. "Oh no," she said. "I mean, I think you have to be famous to get stalked."

It wasn't funny but it made me laugh a little. The pain inside my chest was so intense it felt like something terrible had happened, like maybe I had been shot without noticing.

"You want me to come over?" Her face was anxious.

"No," I said. "I think you should be really happy for your father," I said.

Sigrid nodded. "And I can finally stop worrying about him," she added.

"I need to tell you something," I said, thinking of Frank.

"Okay," she said, turning her face to me.

"It's sort of complicated," I said. "Can we do it tomorrow?"

"Sure." Sigrid leaned sideways and kissed my cheek. "I really love you, Alice," she said, and then she blushed intensely and jumped out of the car.

Thirteen

MY MOTHER IS MUCH EASIER to discuss things with than my father. He doesn't listen to what you're telling him because he's so anxious to say something helpful. Our conversations mostly end with my storming upstairs and him standing at the bottom, arms outstretched, imitating Robert De Niro, asking: "Whatsa matter? How did I go wrong, Alice? Splain to me, please! For the love of God, talk to me!" At those times I hate him.

My mother on the other hand was an amazing listener. She focused all of her physical energy on what you were saying. My dad called it the mind suck. She rarely offered any advice, but she had this whole therapy thing where you validate the person's feelings mainly by repeating back what they said to you. This was sometimes irritating because you could feel manipulated. My father made fun of her by repeating back what she said after she had already repeated what I said.

I decided to run the whole Sigrid-baby-sitter-murder thing by her. I figured she'd be able to tell me whether I had done something evil. First I tried to make it all hypothetical and I asked her whether it was wrong to befriend someone who had done something terrible if someone else was going to be really, really betrayed by someone doing it.

"You better tell me what you've done," she said, looking up with a mouthful of pins from hemming a pair of Alf's jeans. "It can't be any worse than what I'm already imagining."

But after I told her about Frank Perone and how he had killed the Andersons' baby-sitter, she seemed stunned. I mean, actually shocked. She took each pin out of her mouth slowly, sticking them one by one into a pincushion shaped like a pig that I had made her in first grade.

"It's not that bad," I started to say, but she held her hand up to silence me.

"You have no idea how bad this is," she said, jumping to her feet so Alf's jeans and the scissors fell down in a heap. "I wonder if you ever pay attention to the truth."

I had almost never seen my mother lose it, so this was pretty intense. She started shouting about how I could never go back to that prison and what was the school thinking and how many innocent teenagers had to die before someone recognized the reality of our gun laws and something else about irresponsible yuppies and something else about innocence. She said I was having a fantasy life that contained the worst elements of self-deception, and she said she knew it was her fault because she was my mother and should have kept me from behaving so hideously.

"Young lady," she said finally, "I have never been so shocked and disappointed in my entire life."

She sounded like someone on a soap opera.

"Mom," I interjected, "why are you so upset?"

She stopped in midsentence and stared at me. "Oh, God," she said, "Alice— Oh Jesus Christ, tell me you think this is normal."

"Well, murder's not abnormal," I said slowly. "I mean, it happens a lot."

She shook her head. "But how has it become part of our lives?" she whispered.

"Matthew," I said. "And I guess the Andersons' baby-sitter. Plus, didn't Daddy's cousin kill someone?"

My mother's eyes widened. "How do you know about that?" she asked in a really pissed-off tone of voice.

I shrugged.

"Did you hear us talking about it?"

I nodded.

"Your father is such an idiot," she said. "I told him not to discuss it in front of you." She squinted at me. "Does Alf know?"

I shrugged again.

Of course Alf knew. The Cousin Benny stories were a staple of our childhood. I'd used them to terrify him when I was mad about baby-sitting. I told him Cousin Benny was a serial killer, that he rode the rails in search of innocent victims, mainly little boys, to drug and murder, chopping them into bits and grinding them up for sausage filling. A friend of my parents had given them a copy of *Sweeney Todd: The Demon Barber of Fleet Street,* and it provided enough gore to flesh out the snippets I'd gathered from my parents' whispered conversations. I'd turn off all the lights and put on *Sweeney Todd* and dance around with my underwear on my head until Alf was crying so hard he couldn't speak. Then I'd stop and he'd be so grateful, he'd dissolve into a puddle of perfect little brother and go to bed when I made him.

Cousin Benny had killed his neighbor because he believed the old lady was putting voodoo hexes on him and had stolen his pet ferret for a sacrificial ceremony. All of this took place in a small Pennsylvania town where people knew everybody and no one suspected their neighbors of secret blood rituals. He was supposed to take medicine for being bipolar, but he preferred being manic so he never took it.

My mother had an unrealistic idea of childhood. She believed children were given some sort of visa to exempt them from bad stuff until they were old enough to deserve it. I had already read enough books—*The Diary of a Young Girl, Oliver Twist, The Bluest Eye, The Bell Jar*—to know childhood was nothing but a concept and nothing guaranteed peace. I'd read articles about the kids in South America who lived in the mud and the kids in Northern Ireland who threw stones during riots, kids in Israel and Jordan with explosives strapped to their backs, and kids who lived close to us, kids in Brooklyn and Harlem and the East Village, who had seen people shot right in front of them.

Now, because of the prisoners, I understood that childhood could be the worst of all because you were too young to choose your fate and too powerless to protest against injustice. Maybe my mother's fairy-tale idea (and fairy tales are full of victimized children) was a response to how bad she had it growing up. I think when she looked at Alf and me she saw a chance to create perfection, to embroider our lives in brightly colored threads like the samplers she stitched and placed behind glass.

I think my mother wanted us to feel safe and happy all the time, which is lame, but I think you get lame when you give birth.

She finally stopped yelling and began to cry. I felt really, really bad. If there was one thing that was hard to see, it was my mother's pain. "I'm sorry," I said, "I'm sorry for being so weird and unhappy and angry and lonely and I'm sorry I'm a liar and I've done things I shouldn't have done because I wanted to disappear."

My mother stopped crying and dried her eyes on Alf's jeans. "Well," she said, "it's not like he can come out of prison and live here, is it?"

I shook my head.

"You'd better tell Sigrid as soon as possible."

I nodded.

THE SENIOR PROJECT ASSEMBLY was scheduled for the last week before final exams, which we didn't take anyway. There were so many details to take care of I was paralyzed. I did things like watch morning television, strange cable shows with people exercising on chairs or explaining complicated concepts on the cable access college station. I learned why there are tidal waves and earthquakes and how we are on this huge shifting plate which is the earth's crust. I'd learned that already in earth science but it didn't stick. Now it stuck. On the beautiful house channel, I learned how to hang sconces, and I watched several episodes of a show about the lives of supermodels.

Mainly, I lay on the floor of my room and tried to stop thinking about the future.

It felt like being ambushed. People kept asking how I felt about graduating, turning eighteen, and what was I wearing to the prom? Graduation seemed unreal, turning eighteen was inevitable, and I wasn't going to the prom. The last of these received the most response. People were convinced my refusal to attend the prom was a serious problem, right up there with global warming. Ms. Francis, my art teacher, gave me a ten-minute talking-to about how much I'd regret not dancing with someone in a long dress. This was hard to understand. Would the prom be my last chance to dress up?

"Did *you* go?" I asked her, trying to switch the focus.

"Yes, I certainly did," she said. "Everybody went to the prom! Even the losers!"

Most boomer parents had boycotted their proms, but then Ms. Francis grew up in Tyler, Texas, and thought high school was supposed to be all baton twirling and pep rallies. We didn't do much of that, so she was emotional about Millstone's few traditions.

"Now, Alice," she said, leaning over me, "I imagine this must be because of Matthew Swan. Was he your date?"

I nodded.

Her eyes suddenly filled with tears, and she hugged me. "I'm sorry, honey," she whispered into my ear. "He was a wonderful, wonderful boy."

WHEN MORGAN CALLED, we were finishing dinner. My mother had agreed not to tell my dad about the prisoner thing until I'd had a chance to explain to Sigrid. I took the call in the kitchen, but from the silence in the other room I could tell all three of them were listening.

"Listen," Morgan said, "will you go to the prom with me?"

"Hold on," I said. I put my head through the door and shouted: "Stop listening!"

"What?" my father asked. "I can't hear you over Alf's story about his biology test."

"Who's listening?" my mother asked.

"Talk to each other!" I shrieked.

"Shut up," Alf said.

"You shut up," I replied.

"But you said we should talk to each other." My father sighed.

I slammed the door.

"Sorry," I said.

"Well?"

"No," I said.

"Why not?"

I didn't say anything. I could hear my family whispering in the other room.

"Are you going with someone else?"

"Right. I'm going with one of the prisoners who just made parole."

"Maybe you could think about it."

"I'm not going to the prom."

"Okay," Morgan said. His voice cracked a bit. I felt terrible.

"Look, Morgan, it's not personal."

"How can you say that?" he asked, his voice rising. "Was it personal when we did it in the pool?"

I heard the extension slam down.

"I have to go," I said.

"Alice," he said. "Please come to the prom with me." He sounded desperate.

"Okay," I said.

He let out this huge breath as if he hadn't exhaled in about a week.

I pushed the door open, and there sat my parents looking really smug. Alf slipped back into his seat.

"I'm going to the prom," I said.

"Who's the lucky young man?" my father asked in a totally bizarre way.

"Morgan Crawford," I mumbled.

"She did it with him in his pool," Alf added helpfully.

I wrapped my arms around Alf and squeezed his head very hard.

"Don't be disgusting," I said, right into his ear. "Remember, receiving stolen property is a felony."

My parents looked puzzled.

"Let's go check my dress," I said, hauling Alf to his feet.

As we went up the stairs I punched him on his arm muscle, causing a huge goose egg. I held his face between my hands and squeezed.

"Listen, you little bastard," I said. "The next time I catch you listening on the phone, I'm telling everybody you're a hermaphrodite, understand?"

He nodded slowly.

"What's a hermaphrodite?" he asked as we went into the spare bedroom.

"Ask Daddy," I snapped.

There had been a fair amount of controversy about the theme for the year 2001's prom. The millennium had been such a bust, such a major antinonclimax, that no one wanted to use the Kubrick movie or even refer to the possibility of Armageddon. Several of the boys had planned on dressing as the Four Horsemen of the Apocalypse, so they were disappointed. In the end, the techno geeks won. They decorated the main gym with massive replicas of PalmPilots and cell phones, beepers, pagers, and Zip discs. It was sort of like a big computer convention. It was a pretty empty idea, but then we're an empty generation. The things that define us are all dependent on batteries and modems. My dad calls us the dial-up decadents.

In one way it was cool because we really were of a different species as far as the adults were concerned. Although they had largely mastered e-mail, they didn't understand most of what their computers could do. While we were watching one another in real time, my dad was still trying to figure out how to scan pictures. My personal organizer contained every single code required to make life successful. My mother could not, would not learn how to program the VCR. There's this story called "The Veldt" by Ray Bradbury where these two kids program a futuristic house to destroy their stupid parents. At the end they create a landscape of a jungle, and all that's left are several lions chewing on bloody clothing. If Alf and I wanted to mutiny, we could cause all sorts of malfunctions in my parents' lives. They had no idea of how most of the appliances in the house worked, and they were incapable of getting any information out of their cell phones or their personal organizers. I had to organize my father's video conferences with his clients in Paris and help my mother download anything that came over the Internet. They may have told us about sex, but we were truly the information suppliers in our family.

Despite its claims to being on the edge, the prom had lots of elements that were completely retro, too. Kids were hiring limousines and arranging to spend the night on the beach. The band was an eighties specialty group that played music by hair groups like REO Speedwagon and Poison. My father said it was the "creepiest era in music ever." He said it was tragic that we were choosing to end our high school years by celebrating the misery of Reaganomics.

"Whatever," I said. "It's just loud, stupid music."

When Morgan called to ask me what color my dress was, I hung up on him, but he found out from Alf and went out to buy a tuxedo that was an exact match. My dad said we looked like punk versions of Sonny and Cher.

The prisoners, obsessed with every detail of the occasion, provided the final piece of prom pressure. Their main focus was on me—how would I wear my hair, what color would I paint my nails, were my shoes matching my dress, and what about eye shadow? It turned out Lincoln had briefly attended beauty school on a scholarship, and while most of the women he'd worked on were "beautiful sisters," he still had a bunch of opinions about how badly I needed a makeover. He was surprisingly well-informed about current beauty trends and what colors were hot and what looks were being displayed on runways all over the world. He clearly had access to *Vogue*.

"And who's the lucky man?" asked Roger.

I rolled my eyes.

"Hey," Frank said. "Don't be waving off anyone brave enough to take you to the prom!"

All the men nodded.

"What's that supposed to mean?"

And then they started to walk—strut up and down the room like snarky models on the catwalk, doing that side-to-side, knee-knocking stroll that only the most anorexic, affected girls attempted. They sashayed around the room, noses stuck in the air, hands held out to indicate their lack of interest in anyone besides themselves. It was the attitude of a demented supermodel having a nervous breakdown.

"I don't look like that!" I said.

"Sure you do, girl," Curtis murmured.

"Who be 'fiending' after you?" Kenny asked, winking at Lincoln.

"Somebody dope, right?" Lincoln asked.

"No," I said. "And I don't walk like that!"

"Actually, you do," Hal said.

"How would you know?" I asked.

"I watch you," he said. "We all watch you."

But he smiled at me kindly and sort of squeezed my knee. And the prisoners were smiling too. Teasing me but really trying to help me appreciate how lucky I was to be young and healthy and going to the prom and not locked up for twenty years to life for doing something so bad you would have no life and be isolated from society, cast out like Macbeth or O. J. Simpson.

"It's Morgan—the guy who works for the studio—"

"Smoke Papa's pal?" Curtis made an impressed face. "Girl, you gonna be some kinda rock star honey—"

"He's a gofer," I snapped. "He gets their lunches."

"So what?" Roger asked. "People start out like that and they get to be the boss."

"Okay," I said, putting up my hand like a crossing guard. "What do I do with my hair?"

From there it got complicated. Lincoln's ex had been briefly married to a hairdresser in New Brunswick who now ran the hottest beauty salon in the tristate area as Lincoln put it.

"Lamont can do it all," Lincoln said, writing out his number. "Hair, makeup, feet—you gotta get yourself some less skanky-lookin' feet, girl! He'll wax away those caterpillar brows too! And it won't cost you nothin'."

"It's our graduation present," Roger said.

"We wanted to give you something interesting," Curtis said.

"A makeover," Howard added, clearing his throat. "Like the television program with the fat girl."

"She's not fat!" Curtis snapped.

"I didn't say unattractive, but she's definitely fat."

"Large. To be large is to be beautiful. Many countries in Africa believe large women are the most desirable."

"Well," said Howard, "in the USA to be large is to be fat and it's not so great."

"Do you think I'm fat?" I asked them.

They looked shocked. "No," said Curtis. "Girl, you got the thin thing down so it's pretty much nailed."

Howard cleared his throat. "We worry that you don't eat enough," he said.

"Not that it's none of our business," added Lincoln.

Frank put up his hand. "Maybe we could do a little writing," he said. "I imagine Snow White's a little sick of all the dwarfs."

I HAD ASKED Sigrid to go shoe shopping with me at the minimall they had recently dropped into the center of downtown Millstone. Until a few years earlier, there were no choices. You got your fall school clothes at Johnson's, your shoes at Franklin's Shoes, and your coats at Glenley's. Now we had retail heaven just a few miles outside of town, so the in-town stores were going bankrupt and disappearing. The minimall was an attempt to combine small store ownership with the concept of discount prices. It was failing and everything was always on sale.

Mr. Anderson answered their door. He looked really healthy.

"Congratulations," I said.

He smiled. It was the first time I didn't see the shadow of what he had endured. It was sort of amazing.

"Here's Sigrid," he said, moving to let her slip by him.

"See you later," she said to him, starting to go down the path.

"Sweetheart," he called, his voice breaking a bit. "Can you kiss your old man good-bye?"

She turned to look at him. "I'm just going to the mall, Daddy," she said.

He shook his head. "The mall is the beginning of the end. First the mall and then you're gone forever . . ."

We looked at one another. Our parents were behaving like idiots.

Before we checked the selection in Shoes R Hot, we visited The Nerve Center Coffee House and ordered lattes.

I began to talk about how people were basically good but unless we understood the possibility of sin and redemption, forgiveness and mercy, we were all animals. I had no idea how I was going to suddenly veer toward the topic of Frank Perone and how he didn't really mean to strangle her baby-sitter when Sigrid interrupted.

"You think it's okay to do something wrong if you say you're sorry?"

I nodded.

"So if Hitler wrote a really nice note, or called the families of the people he exterminated, maybe we could say he wasn't such a bad guy?"

This was too extreme an example.

"People can make amends, Sigrid."

"How hard is that? Anyone can apologize," Sigrid said.

I took a deep breath. "I've done something wrong."

"So you're apologizing?"

Sigrid's eyes looked cold. When she was happy, they seemed darker, a beautiful midnight blue. But now they had the strange light part to them like the eyes of a malamute.

"I guess so."

"What have you done, Alice?"

"Nothing. I just think I need to explain about something."

She smiled, but it was tight-lipped and creepy.

"I, well, you know how I went to Rahway to help—to be of service?"

Sigrid nodded.

"And how Frank—the poet prisoner guy—was gone?"

Of course she didn't know. I had kept the exact details of my service totally secret, and since her dad had started this engagement-baby thing, Sigrid wasn't asking me many questions.

"Frank? You mean Frank Perone? The murderer?"

I nodded.

"Did you see him?"

I nodded again.

"Actually, he came back. And he was in our group. I taught him and he wrote this stuff." She wasn't saying anything. I was afraid to look at her. "He had a really bad childhood, Sigrid—"

"What?"

"His mom couldn't take care of him." I looked up. Sigrid's face was totally white, like a mime's face.

"You like him?"

"No! I don't like him. It's different—I know him and I know how bad his life was and I can't hate him like you do—"

"But he killed my baby-sitter." Sigrid stood up. "He gave my father cancer!"

"No, he didn't. Come on, Sigrid. His boyfriend died of AIDS—"

"His boyfriend?" She looked stunned. "You care about his boyfriend? I hope he has AIDS. I hope that bastard dies in agony."

She was shaking, her whole body was trembling. I was afraid of her rage.

"Sigrid, that's so harsh—"

"You don't know him. I know him. I know what he did and how long he held her face and hurt her and made me so afraid I had to sleep with all the lights on and I had nightmares every single night, people chasing me and killing me and hurting me and killing Thor—"

"Sigrid—"

"I hate you, Alice."

"How can you say that?"

She looked down at me and shook her head. "You don't have a clue. How people die when they want to live. The way they struggle to escape, beg for mercy, the way they look so scared and sad. It doesn't happen fast like in the movies." She paused.

"He didn't mean to do it," I whispered, my face wet from tears I hadn't felt in my eyes.

"Says who?" Sigrid hissed. "Him?"

I nodded miserably.

"What about Matthew?" she asked. "Do you want to forgive the person who killed him?"

I nodded.

"Why?"

"There's nothing else to do, Sigrid. I can't stand this pain." I shook my head. "It won't bring him back to want the people who killed him dead."

She sort of smiled. "Hating is fine, Alice. How do you think I write such great opera?" She leaned down, whispering right into my ear. "Then pray for them, pray for all the fucking murderers in the entire world."

And then she left, her shoulders hunched as if to protect herself from a sudden attack.

Fourteen

PROM WASN'T AS BAD AS I'D FEARED. The best part was
going to Lamont's Beauty Emporium, which turned out to be in
Newark. My mom decided Alf better come to provide some protection since it was close to a run-down housing project. Of course Alf
didn't provide much of anything, but he came in handy for holding
various bits of beauty stuff. The girls who worked there wanted to
dye his hair, but I didn't think my mother would be happy if we
allowed them to turn him into Eminem, which was who they
thought he looked like. We took one tiny chunk at the back of his
head and bleached the color out. Then they dyed it bright blue. Alf
was thrilled.

Lamont specialized in black girls' hair, so he was devoted to tons
of braids, cornrows, swirls, and the use of a fixative that rendered
multiple pieces of hair into one solid mass, a wall of hair that stayed
wherever it was put. The idea was to decorate—shells, feathers,

beads, and jewels were woven in. After that, I received a complete set of Lee press-on nails decorated with diamonds. I looked like someone in a Lil' Kim video except for my lack of ethnic cred. My eyebrows were plucked thin and the hair on my upper lip ripped away with hot wax. Beauty was painful and time-consuming.

"You're a still life," my father said when I walked back into our house six hours later. "You're an objet d'art."

"She's like George Clinton," my brother said. "The Funkadelic guy with all the dreadlocks." He saw my face. "But prettier."

My mother just looked shocked. I think she ran upstairs and took out all my baby pictures to assure herself that the supervixen she was looking at had once been her bald and sweet baby. "It's temporary, right?" she asked several times, checking me for tattoos.

My dress was finished, ironed, and hanging in the upstairs guest room along with a pair of pink wedgie sandals my mom had worn out dancing at the Limelight, back in the day, during the disco seventies. I should have been excited but I felt something else. Sad and sort of sorry for being sad and sort of tired. I had this feeling inside my chest, near my ribs, a pain which was dull but still cruel. A pain that felt like you'd run too fast without eating.

Morgan rang the doorbell and I stood upstairs staring out into the night, wondering whether Matt might be out there, still waiting. We watched this movie once, a movie we weren't supposed to see but the baby-sitter fell asleep and we sneaked into my parents' room. The movie was about earth being invaded by giant crabs. In one part the husband's been eaten by a giant crab who uses his voice to call his wife.

The crab says: "Helen, Helen," and Helen goes to the door expecting her nice husband but instead she finds this giant, people-eating shellfish with clacking claws.

The wife starts screaming, "No! Go away! I hate you!" Of course, the crab eats her. This is my secret fear. I will find Matthew but he will be a rotting corpse and I won't be loyal enough to love him anyway. He'll run after me and I'll shoot him or something.

I could hear Morgan in the front hallway making small talk with my parents about the weather and if his mother had filled the pool yet. I didn't want Alf to make any lewd references to the Crawfords' pool so I ran downstairs.

Morgan's tuxedo was dusty pink, the exact shade of my dress. He had bought or borrowed a pair of frameless glasses that seemed to float on his face, and his hair had been highlighted and spiked. He looked like a record producer, which was somewhat strange. The corsage he handed me was pink, and I followed my father's pointing finger to see a pink limo parked at the curb.

"In the pink, eh, sis?" Alf asked, grinning like the Cheshire cat. I cuffed him across the ear, harder than a mere affectionate rap.

"Don't come outside," I begged them as they started to file out behind us.

As we approached the limo, I noticed Catherine Swan's ancient Mercedes parked across the street. I stopped and waved. She got out of the car and walked toward me holding a shawl in her hand. She held it up like a mother waiting to cuddle a clean child in a towel. I stepped forward into her arms and she hugged me, the shawl around my body. It was made from cashmere, finely spun, edged in velvet.

She stepped back and looked closely at my hair. Her lips twitched but she didn't laugh. "You are a thing of beauty and a joy forever."

I posed for her, my hand on my hip like a bad model.

"Gosh," she said, "wedgie shoes." There were tears streaming down her face she kept wiping with the edge of her shirt.

She stepped back to the car and reached into the open window, returning with a camera.

"For the girls," she said as she snapped.

It was June, but there was a chill in the air. I held the shawl close to me.

"Hi, Morgan," Catherine Swan said.

"Hi, Mrs. Swan."

"That's a great tux," she said.

"Thanks."

She took a picture of the two of us together, and I walked her back across the street to her car.

"Will you be okay?" I asked.

She stared into my eyes for a minute and I saw him there, inside Catherine Swan's eyes was the flame of Matthew's life.

"No," she said. She took my hand and kissed it.

"I want you to move on," she whispered, "but still love him just a bit."

Catherine climbed into her car and drove away, leaving me standing on the pavement, a pink limousine waiting. Morgan walked up behind me and put his hand on my shoulder. It didn't feel wrong. It felt like when we were little kids and hugged each other without thinking about it.

"I always wanted to be exactly like her," I said, inhaling the smell of all Swans from the shawl.

"I think your mother is much more beautiful," Morgan said. "And so are you. And you're normal," he added. "The Swans all need shock treatment."

"Oh, yeah," I said. "Tell that to the hair!"

And then I took his hand and we got into the limo. The inside was upholstered in leopard skin.

"Oh my God," I said. "This is totally ghetto."

The window rolled down, and a huge Hispanic man peered back at me.

"You mean good 'ghetto'?" he asked.

"Of course," I said. He was a very impressive-looking man with several visible tattoos, multiple piercings, and thick black hair pulled back into a ponytail. His muscles rippled beneath a silk shirt.

"You tell her who owns this fine car, Skippy?"

Morgan shook his head. "Smoke Papa," he said. "Raol, this is Alice. Alice, Raol."

Raol reached back a hand that held a huge gold ring on each finger. "In Wonderland, aren't you?" he asked, winking.

Raol reminded me of a pirate.

"You better keep close watch on this amigo," Raol said, pulling away from the curb. "He's gonna own his own record label soon and the bitches won't leave him alone."

I made a face at Morgan, who shrugged.

"What about Beloit?" I asked him.

"S.P. says college may not be the righteous choice at this point in time."

"S.P.? Has your mother met him, Morgan?"

"Excuse me for interjecting," Raol said. "But Smoke Papa and Ms. Mother Morgan are like this." Raol twisted two huge fingers together, winked at both of us, and disappeared behind a roll-up tinted screen.

"Wow," I said. "Is your mom dating Smoke Papa?"

Morgan shook his head. "She found some discrepancy in a performing contract he let me take home to study. She saved him two million dollars."

"So why doesn't she work for him while you go to Beloit?"

Morgan sighed. "It's not my fault I have a natural propensity for this business," he said. "Most creative types don't excel at statistics."

"Oh, shut up." I leaned over and pushed a button on the minifridge, which swung open to reveal many tiny bottles of champagne.

"Let's get drunk," I said.

"Okay," Morgan squeaked.

There were these gorgeous crystal glasses in a little cupboard under the seat. Morgan produced a jar of macadamia nuts, and we drank and threw nuts at one another. I thought it might not be so bad to be rich and decadent. I could be featured in *Vogue* as the wife of the newest recording honcho M. I would be incredibly thin, wear leather pants and black eyeliner.

"I love you," Morgan said, interrupting my fantasy.

"Shut up," I said, hitting him in the shoulder with a nut. I wasn't going to marry anyone. I was going to be alone for the rest of my life.

THE MILLSTONE INN WAS supposedly in existence when Washington crossed the Delaware and marched through Trenton to fight the British. Or something like that. When I was in first grade there was a portrait of Washington that hung right next to the clock with smoke where his neck was supposed to be. I thought he was God. I told Matthew that God was a middle-aged man who wore a wig, and he told his mother, who was always trying to encourage her kids to become Taoists or Buddhists or Quakers or something. She called our teacher, who then spent an inordinate amount of time trying to explain to a bunch of seven-year-olds that God might not be anything recognizable or familiar. I returned to my original idea that God was the Statue of Liberty, and Matthew continued to worship things like trees and stone walls. We were, in short, confused.

Parts of the Millstone Inn are ancient and parts were added last year. It's really ugly, overpriced, and the food is terrible, but people claim to love it and book weddings there years in advance. Every prom since our school was founded in 1902 had been held there. One year someone suggested a newer hotel with great food, but a petition was circulated to block the horror of rejecting tradition even if the tradition sucked.

WELCOME TO TUSCANY, said the sign outside what was usually the Presidential Ballroom.

"When did Isabelle get her claws into the prom?" asked Morgan.

Each of us had drunk a split of champagne. I felt pleasantly numb except my head itched.

"Smile! Oh look! It's Alice and Mini-Me Morgan!"

A video camera was an inch away from my face, and then I saw Isabelle standing to the side holding a mike. She had on an amazing dress, which appeared to include both fish heads and flying buttresses, which we had recently learned about in architecture class.

"Well, now," said Isabelle in her fake French-Italian accent. "What have we here? Are there birds nesting in that 'do, Alicia?"

"What's happened to your accent, Isabelle?" I asked pleasantly. "Are you suffering from the Madonna syndrome—I was born in the Midwest but now I talk like the Queen of England?"

Isabelle directed the lens at Morgan. "Let's hear the back story behind this tux, Morgan. How did you come to be pimpin' in pink?"

We left her with the minicam and walked forward into the main room. Everyone looked strangely grown-up. My school friends stood around in quiet groups holding cups of punch as if intimidated by their clothes. Boys I had known since preschool who were never seen in anything but jeans, T-shirts, and big shorts were oddly stiff, clean, and orderly. The girls were even more alien in tit-baring dresses, skirts cut up to their upper thighs, backless tops, and stiletto heels. It looked like a convention consisting of businessmen and whores.

"This is so weird," I whispered to Morgan, scanning the room for Sigrid, but she wasn't there.

Wendy Henninger teetered over in a pair of platforms so high she must have bought them in the transvestite store on Acorn Avenue. She looked very sexy but still in goth character, with a ripped slip dress, tattoos visible, a heavily spiked dog collar around her neck. Her date was a skinny girl in an old-fashioned man's suit, her hair slicked back behind her ears and a tiny mustache drawn above her lip.

"Alice," Wendy screeched, "who gave you that black girl's hair?"

"A brother," I said. "Lamont's Beauty Emporium in downtown Newark."

Wendy's date reached up and touched my hair. "It feels like papier-mâché. Will it wash out?"

Morgan put his arm around my waist. "You bake it," he said. "Then it just pops off like a big ole muffin."

Wendy watched Morgan's hand rest on my hip, and she raised a nonexistent eyebrow. "Hey," she said, "come powder something with me."

The bathroom was crowded with girls from our class drinking from small flasks and readjusting their boobs. Most people were afraid of Wendy, so no one said anything to us. She lit an unfiltered Sobranie Russian. Lamont had warned me not to get too close to an open flame, so I didn't have one. Anyway, my nails would have gotten in the way.

"So what's up with dating Harry Potter?" Wendy asked, sitting on the couch.

I sat next to her and checked my hair. It was like having a tight hat on your head.

"It's still there," Wendy said. "But some of the feathers are molting." She took a deep drag of the cigarette. "What does he have on you?" she asked. "Is his mother suing your parents or something?"

I shrugged.

"You're dating Morgan Crawford willingly?"

"I'm not dating him."

"Then why the fuck are you here?"

"The prisoners I'm tutoring got all excited about the prom. They bought me this day of beauty." I looked around the bathroom and felt really sad suddenly. "Morgan's not that bad—"

Wendy blew smoke at my hair. "Oh shut up!" she said. "Like this is what you need right now? You should be in black, screaming, beating your chest. I mean—goddamn it, Alice—he's fucking dead, a pile of bones."

The room was suddenly completely still and silent. Hands that held lipstick or mascara wands had frozen. We were being stared at, and one or two girls started to cry.

"What? You want us to pretend it's some fucking secret? It was in the *Millstonian* for God's sake, 'Local Boy's Remains Found in Mass Mexican Grave'—yeah, that's him, ladies. How does that compare to your latest cellulite trauma?"

Wendy was crying. Wendy didn't cry. Even when her tooth got knocked out in sixth grade or when her father left her mother, tears were not something she produced.

"Wendy—"

"What?" She was dabbing at her eyes with the bottom of her dress. Her underpants were so unlike what you'd expect, white, cotton, high-waisted. I smiled.

"Hey," she said, "so I wear old lady underpants! Who wants a thong up their crack?"

"What's the matter?" I asked.

"You think you're the only girl in school who loved him or something? I mean, I dreamed about Matthew Swan—we took karate classes in third grade. Remember when he brought Ms. DiSilvia that red rose? I was so jealous."

I nodded.

"He always asked me about my mom and the MS, and he came over and hung out when I felt bad." She looked at me. "You didn't know that, did you?"

I shook my head.

"He had a picture of you taped inside his locker at the dojo." She shook her head. "He was a fucking idiot," she said quietly. "Hallie just used him."

"I thought you were a lesbian."

Wendy glared at me. "Oh, who knows?" she snapped. "It's all stupid anyway. There's hundreds of people in the next room dressed exactly like their parents." She gestured at the mirror. "Except us! I mean, we're all idiots—children. Little, innocent children who never come home sometimes." She started to sob again. "Oh, God, Alice. He was only seventeen years old. Why would anyone kill him? How could they?"

Wendy's date came in looking worried.

"Is she okay?" she asked, her lower lip trembling.

"Yeah," I said. "Will you tell Morgan I'll be out in a second?"

She nodded.

I got a wad of paper towels and soaked them in cold water. I put them up against Wendy's eyes like I did when my mom got headaches.

"Alice?"

"Yeah?"

"Just remember, if no one ever loves you again, you had more than most people." She took the wet paper towels off her eyes. "He would have died for you," she said softly.

When we came out, Morgan was standing by a couch with a weird smile on his face.

"I thought you jumped out a window," he said. "Like in the movies."

"Let's dance," I said. "Let's dance until we're all sweaty and then I want to go home."

Morgan nodded.

DURING OUR SOPHOMORE YEAR at Millstone we had a physical education teacher who had been in the chorus of tons of Broadway shows. He said that table manners and dancing were the two indicators of a civilized society.

In class, we started out waltzing, two-stepping, lindy hopping, and then segued into the hustle, samba, and swing. We jitterbugged, tangoed, and cha-chaed. Mr. Keeley was a merciless critic, and dancing reduced social distinctions to one question—could you keep the beat? The white kids, on the whole, sucked. This meant the majority of us were tripping and stumbling and lacking anything you could describe as talent. There were some exceptions, and Morgan was one of them. I wasn't the worst. In fact, Matthew was one of the few who refused to dance at all but went off to the library instead. He didn't like being told how to move. He argued that raves had reduced all formal dance to antiquity. Mr. Keeley rolled his eyes and pointed at the few kids of color in our school who were gliding and dipping, transformed from awkward teenagers to graceful athletes.

"Tell me a bunch of drugged-out would-be hippies waving their stupid arms in the air compares to Darnell and Velma tangoing."

I loved those sessions. Life was disorderly, and dancing was all about responding to cues, feeling your partner's push and pull, sex without having to get naked.

Morgan was a good dancer, so I closed my eyes and let him hold me. As we moved, my hair began to unglue and unravel. Bits of beads and feathers dropped and rolled. It was an odd sensation but

I ignored it. We danced until the music stopped and they started to roll out dinner.

WHEN I OPENED the door to our house, I heard the television go off. It was just after midnight. My dad came out of the living room holding the remote. He looked tired.

"Did your hair turn into a pumpkin?" he asked.

"The mice came out," I said, slipping off my shoes.

"Want some food?"

I nodded and followed him into the kitchen.

As I tried to sit down in my too-tight dress, another part of my hair detached and fell down in a sort of dreadlock.

"I'm going to get out of this hair," I said. "I'll be back in a few minutes."

The tiles felt cool against my skin. I leaned against the side of the shower and let the water beat down on my head. I tried to identify what I could feel inside, and it was as close to hunger as anything. I wanted something I couldn't have. I had wanted this same thing for nearly a year. If I stopped wanting it, what would happen? Would the knife in my ribs disappear? Could I breathe again? What would it be like to open my eyes and not feel a gray veil of loss, a sadness so profound it felt heavier than anything in the world? I didn't want to wake up anymore, I realized. I was very, very tired and wanted to die.

"I don't want to wake up anymore," I told my father.

He didn't say anything.

"Maybe I should call Laura," I said.

He sat down across from me and smiled. Picked up my hand and kissed my fingers. "I'm so proud of you," he said softly. "You are a wonderful woman."

I tried to smile but it didn't work.

"Catherine Swan gave me a cashmere shawl," I said, slowly. "Did you give it to her?"

He nodded. "You don't have to be happy, Alice. You may not be happy for a long time."

I thought about this idea, that happiness wasn't necessary. It seemed like a good thing to remember. All those things people told you you'd love—clowns, holidays, s'mores, sex—many of them had turned out to be pretty disappointing. It was memory that was unfair. It wasn't so easy to love Matthew. He always demanded explanations for things I felt or needed, and he was critical of me, very, very critical. He thought I was spoiled and selfish, which is probably true but it's hard not to be when you're a teenager and your parents love you. He was impatient and judgmental and thought everything he did or felt was right. But my memory of him was that he was perfect.

"Your mother told me you've been teaching the person who killed the baby-sitter?"

My father never liked to warn you about a major shock to the system. He was all about get it out, get it over with. He was best at removing splinters because he went straight to the sliver of wood, no pussyfooting around, one sharp hurt and then kisses all around.

"Uh-huh."

"What are you going to do about Sigrid?"

"You think I did something wrong?"

"I think it was bad judgment to adopt her murderer."

I didn't look at him. "He was just there."

"Did you know he was part of the program?"

I didn't answer.

"Did you think you could help him?"

"I thought he could tell me why people kill each other," I said. "Like when you want to understand the government, you try and meet the mayor. I figured he'd understand murder."

"Nobody kills anyone for reasons that anyone else can understand. Even soldiers say that."

"Then why do we exist?" I asked him, starting to cry. "It's just so totally pointless— Daddy— Daddy— I can't—" I started to choke again. Something was closing my lungs, and this time it felt like I was letting go for good.

My father pulled me into his lap. He wrapped his arms around me and whispered into my ear. "Breathe, Alice. Just breathe and scream! You can't keep this away any longer. It will hit like that worst wave, the one that throws you down to the bottom, into the dark salt, but you can swim so well, so beautifully, my mermaid girl. Kick up to where you see the light on the surface and I'll pull you back from the cold."

I felt another pair of arms around me. It was my mother and she was crying, her face pale but her eyes as blue as anything, like the sky. And she looked terrified, like someone was destroying the thing she loved most in the world.

I exhaled.

I SLEPT BETWEEN THEM, holding each of their hands like I did when I was a little girl, before Alf was born and stole them away from me. We rolled close together and then far apart. My father snored and my mother whispered and sighed.

I dreamed about Mexico—or maybe it was hell. It was hot and dusty with skinny dogs and dead flowers and skinny children and broken cars and too much light, a white-hot, yellow light. I saw him on the horizon and he was dressed like a cowboy. I screamed and screamed and woke up and found both of them crouched over me, staring and saying my name over and over again.

I heard them talking about calling a doctor and I kept asking them to get me ice. I was burning up. I got sick and then I went back to sleep. When I woke up, I was alone in their bed. My old stuffed bunny was lying next to me. They had put me into clean pajamas.

"Are you okay?" Alf was standing half inside the door looking scared.

"Yeah."

"Did you get drunk or something?"

I shook my head.

"I'm sorry I'm such a bad brother," Alf said. "I'm sorry your heart's broken."

I pulled myself up and tossed the bunny at him. He didn't catch it. He was crying.

"Come here," I said.

He came and got into bed with me. I put my arms around him.

"Will you come visit me next year?" I asked.

He nodded but he was still crying. He was so sad and so was I that we couldn't do anything but lie there until I found the remote and turned on cartoons, which made things much better.

I think Matthew might have come back to steal me. I think if my parents hadn't fought hard, the morning might have brought the sight of me drifting down the river, covered with roses, a sacrificial maiden who finally died for love.

I NEEDED TO TALK to Ms. Hardwood about my senior project. It didn't seem like a good idea to have the prisoners read, but I wasn't sure what else to do and I had to do something in order to receive a grade. My parents were taking Alf to New York to see a musical about Bill Gates and to visit a famous cyber café. They were sure they could snag another ticket, but I didn't want to go.

I rode my bike to Ms. Hardwood's, and when I got there I saw that Amy's pickup was missing. I walked around the back, and there was Ms. Hardwood lying in the sun wearing a black sweater, jeans, and a pair of sunglasses. Her hair was short. It had been down to her shoulders, but now it was slightly longer than Sinéad O'Connor's. It seems like there's this hair thing middle-aged women do when they're pissed and want to make some kind of statement.

Grace was sitting at a little table surrounded by stuffed animals. The stuffed animals were all wearing very uncomfortable-looking dolls' clothes. Grace was giving them a lecture about their poor table manners.

"You cut your hair."

Ms. Hardwood didn't move for long enough that I thought she was asleep. Then she nodded slowly.

"How was the prom?" she asked after a minute.

"Fine," I said, sitting down across from Grace after obtaining her permission to remove a large stuffed kangaroo.

"Want some chai?" Grace asked.

"Yes, please," I said.

"Where's Matt?" she asked without any hope.

"I don't know, honey," I said.

"I hate him," Grace said without any real feeling.

"Me, too," Ms. Hardwood said.

"Me, three," I added.

"Mommy's gone," Grace said.

"What?" I looked over at Ms. Hardwood, who didn't react. "There's Mommy."

"My other mommy," Grace said. "My pretty mommy," she added, giving Ms. Hardwood a look from under her lowered eyelids.

"Ha." Ms. Hardwood snorted. "You got it there, Gracie. Pretty, young, rich Mommy's gone and left you with the Wicked Witch of the West."

Grace nodded serenely. "She's the witch," she whispered, handing me a brimming cup of invisible chai.

"Where did Amy go?" I asked after several sips of Grace's chai.

"To find herself someone who wants to reproduce in a manner more suitable to her taste."

"Huh?"

"Melissa Etheridge."

I decided not to say anything.

Ms. Hardwood opened one eye. "She and what's-her-face had a baby with David Crosby's sperm "

I knew who David Crosby was. My parents loved the song about the house, and he had been at the original Woodstock.

"Now they've broken up."

"I thought Melissa Etheridge was a lesbian."

Ms. Hardwood sighed. "Never mind, Alice. Amy wants me to get pregnant with someone's sperm. Like, hey, maybe your dad—"

I jumped to my feet. "Eww! I don't think so!"

Ms. Hardwood opened her eye again. "That's what I said."

"Why can't you adopt again?"

Ms. Hardwood smiled. "It's too easy and nice. Amy got infected with the same germs that all these twenty-somethings have been exposed to. They want to get married, have three children, be rich, selfish, and exactly like their grandparents, which is impossible since those same grandparents survived two world wars and their parents tried to change the world. They are just a bunch of ignorant, horrible, moneygrubbing twerps."

"Amy's not selfish or ignorant."

"Amen."

"You could get pregnant."

Ms. Hardwood opened her eye again and gave me a mean look. "I do know that, Alice. Menopause isn't a reality at the moment. But ask me if I'm prepared to spend nine months, have this baby, and hit fifty just when it begins junior kindergarten. I'm afraid the answer isn't yes."

"My father had an affair with Catherine Swan."

Ms. Hardwood sat up suddenly.

"Chai, Mommy?" Grace asked sweetly, holding out a tiny teacup.

"What?" Ms. Harwood gave me a smile full of concern. "Yes, sweetie. I would love some chai."

We both watched as Grace walked across the patio on tippy-toe, her high heels nearly eight sizes too large, a teacup trembling in her little hand.

"Oh, you wonderful girl," Ms. Hardwood said, giving her hug.

"My babies are very bad, Mommy," Grace said finally, untangling herself.

"Yes," Ms. Hardwood said, "but don't they deserve another chance to be more elegant?"

"No," Grace responded serenely, shuffling back to her chair.

"So." Ms. Hardwood looked at me. "How did you find out?"

"Nell Swan told me."

Ms. Hardwood nodded.

"At Matt's wake thing."

Ms. Hardwood winced.

"Thus the sex on the chaise longue scenario," she said, watching me closely.

"I guess so."

"Revenge against Daddy," she said. "Quite appropriate."

"Did you know?"

She looked at me. "Oh, dear," she said. "Maybe."

"You knew?"

"Matt told me."

I glared at her. "He told you?"

"He didn't know what to do."

"So he told you? Jesus Christ," I said, walking around in a circle. "This is totally fucked up!"

Ms. Hardwood gestured toward Grace and I nodded.

"Sorry," I said. "It's just I'm so stupid!"

"She's heard worse, but you have a great influence."

"I hate my life," I said melodramatically. "I mean, I don't even understand most of it."

"Join the party," Ms. Hardwood said. She suddenly looked much better. "Have you got any influence over Morgan Crawford?"

"He says he's in love with me but it's just sex."

"Well, what about this Smoke Papa thing?"

"Can't he delay Beloit a year?"

Ms. Hardwood sighed. "Do you honestly think he'll give up hip-hop heaven and go to college after a year?"

"Why do people keep asking me about Morgan?"

"He'll do anything for you."

"That's disgusting!"

Ms. Hardwood shook her head. "Blind devotion is a rare and wonderful thing."

I held my nose.

"How is the prisoner reading shaping up?"

"That's why I came over."

Ms. Hardwood sat up. "What's wrong?"

"Um, I— Remember the thing with Sigrid's baby-sitter?"

"The one who was murdered?"

"Uh-huh."

"Of course. It was the boyfriend, right?"

"Right. He got manslaughter and he was sent to Rahway Prison—"

Ms. Hardwood gave me a hard stare. "Don't bury the lead, Alice."

"Sigrid's murderer is in my literary group."

"What?"

"She saw him do it. No one knew, but she was in the closet when he strangled Antoinette—that's the baby-sitter's name. Sigrid says he did it on purpose, but I don't think a little kid would know the difference— I mean, kids think their parents are killing one another when they're having sex, right?"

"Right." Ms. Hardwood looked distressed.

"He told me it was an accident, and also he had this really terrible childhood—"

"This is the man who killed Sigrid's baby-sitter?"

I nodded.

"Is he supposed to read during the assembly?"

"Yes."

"Did you tell Sigrid?"

I nodded.

We both looked over to where Grace was sitting.

"I don't understand why but I thought it would help to meet some criminals."

"Help?" Ms. Hardwood looked confused. "Help what?"

"For me to accept what happened to Matt. But there isn't any logic. Curtis killed someone in a blackout. And Kenny had a gang thing, which means you don't question why you do something. Lincoln said he was a victim of racism and Howard embezzled money and Roger did terrible things in Macedonia." I paused.

"These are the prisoners?"

"Yes. And then there's Frank, who strangled Sigrid's baby-sitter."

"Ah." Ms. Hardwood frowned. "Just don't let them read."

"But that's wrong. If we put these people in prison, can't we believe they might have changed?"

"Has Frank changed?"

"Do you believe in the death penalty?" I asked her.

"No," Ms. Hardwood said.

"What if someone tried to hurt Grace?"

"I'd kill them."

"To protect her?"

"Yes."

"Why is that different than the state doing it?"

"It would be personal and unsanctioned. I'd have to be punished for what's essentially an act of revenge."

"That doesn't make sense."

"Of course it doesn't," she said.

"Adults don't know shit!" I said.

"We know what we don't know," she said. "What does Sigrid want?" she asked.

"I think she wants the victim to be able to speak. I think she wants me to understand that you can't forgive someone who kills a person you love."

"What if the victim is dead, Alice? Who speaks for them?"

"The rest of us, I guess."

"How would you show that?"

"I don't know." I shook my head. "It's not real, anyway. You can put buildings up or make statues or quilts or whatever—but nothing changes—"

"Maybe Sigrid has something to say. Maybe she needs to tell people about what happened to this person she loved."

"It won't help," I snapped. "It's stupid and pathetic. People won't listen and they don't really care. I saw this video with penguins pushing each other off an iceberg. As soon as one penguin died, another one took its place."

"Are people penguins, Alice? Isn't there a difference?"

I scowled at her. "People are worse. They hurt one another on purpose. Penguins are just trying to figure out whether there's an orca whale in the water. They aren't hateful."

"Let the prisoners read something or they'll feel cheated. Let Sigrid talk about her baby-sitter. And you talk about Matthew Swan. You and Sigrid can make something beautiful, Alice. That's why you found each other, and that's why you went to Rahway." Ms. Hardwood sighed. "I wish Amy would come back," she said.

"Where is she?"

Ms. Hardwood looked at Grace. "Hey," she said, "Gracie girl, let's go lie down for a little bit."

Grace frowned at both of us. "You didn't drink your chai!" she said.

"Yes, we did!" I drained the last drop and smiled at her. "It was the best chai in the world."

"Of course," Grace said. "My babies are very bad," she added.

"Well, give them all amnesty," Ms. Hardwood said. "We need a nap."

Grace walked around the table selecting certain stuffed animals, rejecting others. "Just these," she said, standing in front of her mother, barely able to carry the armful. "None of the rest."

"Have a good nap, Grace," I called.

"See you later, crocodile," she said, taking her mother's hand, dropping several animals.

"After a while, alligator," I replied, walking toward my bicycle.

Fifteen

NOW THAT SIGRID KNEW ABOUT FRANK, Frank needed to know about Sigrid. He'd probably be creeped out the same way I was when I found out other people knew about my dad's affair. It's hard enough to trust anyone in normal society, but it's really hard when you're in prison. Curtis told us information was like money inside. You had to know certain things to survive, and if you weren't in the loop you could be surprised, and surprise is a bad thing in jail.

I kept thinking Frank might ask me about Sigrid since we were the same age and we lived in the same town, but he never did. I think he didn't want to remember her or Thor or how he killed their baby-sitter. He wanted to be sorry and locked up and have deep insights into his past, but he didn't want to know anything real like how Mr. Anderson had cancer or that Sigrid could still remember every detail of the closet where she hid watching him strangle someone.

On the day of our last meeting before the senior assembly, Hal had jury duty so I had to go alone. I told him I wanted to change the format of our presentation and I was going to ask the prisoners to write letters to their victims instead of reading their poems.

"Christ," Hal said, "that's going to be really depressing."

"Yeah, well, murder isn't a lotta yucks," I snapped.

"Is this because of your boyfriend?"

"Frank killed a friend of mine's baby-sitter." I decided to let Hal in on the big secret.

"Frank? Our Frank?"

"Uh-huh."

"How'd you find that out?"

"He came to our school and she recognized him."

"You mean before we started teaching the class?"

"Yup."

"You're a scary person, Alice," Hal said.

"I'm the prisoners' poster child," I said.

"Right. Well, let me know how it goes with Howard. He was counting on reading a chapter of his novel."

"Yeah, that was really going to happen."

MY IDEA CAME from something Matthew had told me about his mother's recovery in AA. One of the steps asks you to make a list of people or institutions you had harmed and then another step tells you to tell those people or places that you're sorry. I already had a list of people, although I don't think I've done much to any institution except maybe Millstone Country Day School, and those were things like smoking behind the hockey rink or cutting class; not very impressive stuff.

I decided to go see Catherine Swan to make sure I had the idea

straight. Actually, I really wanted to make her feel bad about the cashmere scarf and to let her know I knew my father had given it to her
so her giving it to me was less like generosity and more like justice.

Samsara answered the door after I rang and pounded for ages.
There was new-age Irish music playing at top volume. Samsara
seemed more stoned than I had ever seen her. Her aura was the aura
of a person living in a parallel universe. An earthquake could have
occurred right in front of Samsara Swan and I doubt she would have
registered its shock.

Chloe and Nell wandered into the doorway, and I realized all three
girls were wearing Matthew's clothes—hats, scarves, and shirts with
monograms embroidered on the pockets. These were the special
clothes his father had given him, shirts handmade in Bali when he
was living an exotic poet's life with extra cash from a family trust
fund. Nell was in the bathrobe his father had bought him at Harrods.

"Who is it, girls?"

"Alice," they answered in unison.

"Oh-oh, Alice! Good! Come in."

I walked into the space that stood behind the Japanese screens
and saw Catherine sitting cross-legged on tatami mats sorting
through piles of clothing.

"I saved you some things," she said, smiling at me.

I couldn't look. All the things I saw there had a story, a word, a
taste, a night or day or something.

I glanced sideways at my pile. It was small but specific. Matthew's
dark green chamois shirt, worn and huge, bought at L.L. Bean's at
4:00 A.M. during a trip to Maine I took with his family. The leather
jacket his cousin the roadie gave him that had once belonged to Joan
Jett. His perfectly faded, soft blue jeans, too long but I had worn
them anyway, legs rolled like a geek. The raindeer sweater his Nor-
wegian grandmother had knit for him and he refused to wear

because it was a girly sweater with beautiful buttons and those rain-deer dancing across its back. On the first cold day of winter he'd throw it at me and say, "Here ya go, because, baby, it's cold outside!"

These things were so dumb they choked me. There is stuff between people that can't even be described without it sounding pathetic and corny. My mother still says "Good night, honey-bunny." I still hold my breath with Alf when we pass graveyards, and I still expect my father to look down at me and say, "Who's my peach pie?" and I will still answer, "Me." Alf wears my old Guns N' Roses T-shirt to bed every night. I wear my mother's faded blue jean skirt she had since college, and we all think these things will keep us safe and warm.

Laura Youngblood had once told me that ritual is essential to all human beings and that Native Americans recognize ritual as the essence of all their beliefs.

"Ritual freaks white people out," Matthew said when I told him. "It's like sex and singing."

"Here." Catherine indicated a paper bag.

I packed his clothes inside. The girls slowly removed their extra clothing, and one after another they kissed their mother.

"Where are you going?" Catherine asked.

"Work," Chloe said.

"Shrink," Nell said.

"Meeting," Samsara said.

"AA?" Catherine held on to Samsara's arm.

"NA," Samsara said, smiling while she gently shook free of her mother. "I have a week today," she told us, smiling dreamily.

"A week?" Catherine snapped. "A week of what?"

"A week of bliss," Samsara said. "Clean, okay?"

"In a pig's eye," Catherine muttered as the girls left, the smell of roses lingering in the air. "Maybe she only shot dope," she said to herself. "Instead of smoking crack as well." She looked at me. "I found all these new college clothes I bought for him to take to Wisconsin." She looked at me. "You want them, Alice?"

I shook my head.

"Of course you don't." She sighed. "What was I thinking?"

"My father gave you the cashmere shawl, right?"

Catherine nodded.

"You want it back?"

"No."

We stared at each other for a second.

"What would you do if you knew who killed Matthew?"

She looked surprised. "You mean who shot him in Mexico?"

I nodded.

"Maybe ask to see him."

"Why?"

"To be in the same room with the person who took away the life I gave, the life I grew inside my belly. To know the devil."

"Is the person the devil?" I asked.

Catherine looked at me. "I think so," she said. "I think it's the ultimate evil, so what else call it?"

"A mistake?"

She laughed. "No, honey, that's a pathetic word. Fender benders are mistakes. Murder is an atrocity." Her eyes were dark and the muscles in her face seemed to tighten.

"Do you remember Sigrid Anderson?"

Catherine frowned. "Matthew used to partner with her in bio— very blond?"

"Yes. She writes opera."

"Oh, yes. Shy and intense. Isn't her father sick?"

"He's better but her mother's dead."

Catherine nodded. "And her baby-sitter. Matthew told me her baby-sitter was murdered."

"I know the guy who did it."

"Isn't he in jail?"

"Rahway. He's one of the prisoners in the creative writing group."

Catherine shuddered. "Jesus, Alice! Do your parents know?"

"Yes."

"It isn't good for you to be close to someone like that."

"Why not?"

"Because . . . I mean—he killed someone."

"What about the eighth step?"

"You mean in AA?" Catherine looked horrified. "That's not the same thing."

"Why not?"

"Because you can't make amends to someone for killing another person." She shook her head. "It isn't forgivable. It just isn't."

"Didn't Jesus forgive the people who nailed him to the cross? I mean—what are we supposed to do? How can we exist if nothing ever gets forgiven? Is Matthew gonna hang around telling me to let him go until I'm so old I can't ever love anyone ever again!" I was shouting. Catherine looked totally freaked out. She dragged me into the kitchen and put cold water on my wrists.

"Alice," she said. "Are you religious? Have you been born again? Did the prisoners have you baptized or something?"

I shook my head.

"What do you mean about Matthew hanging around? Have you seen him?"

I nodded. I thought she would yell at me or tell me she was going to call my parents, but she smiled.

"Did he talk to you?"

"I feel what he's saying but he doesn't talk."

She pushed my hair off my forehead just like my mother.

"Is he tormented?"

"I don't think so."

She turned away. "Would you tell him we all want him to be where he is and that his sisters are fine and that his father loves him and that we think about him every day and that I'll never forget him?"

"I'm sorry," I said. I shouldn't have said anything.

Catherine Swan turned back to me. She was smiling. "Oh, Alice," she said. "It's so good to know you've seen him. Thank you, thank you, darling."

"What about the prisoner?" I asked.

"Which one?"

"The one who killed Sigrid's baby-sitter."

"Could you ask Matthew?" Catherine asked, grabbing my hand. "Maybe he could help you."

She was a bit mad, I realized.

"No, Catherine. It's not like he's this psychic guy on television. I can't call him up whenever I want to."

"Have you tried?"

"No!"

"We could have a séance."

This was too much, I thought. Catherine believed in things like spirit guides and channeling. Matthew thought it was bullshit.

"He hated all that stuff," I said. "He wouldn't show up."

She looked really sad.

"Can't I make them do the eighth step and apologize to their victims?"

Catherine considered this idea. "It's not really appropriate to enforce a step," she said. "But murder isn't very appropriate either."

*   *   *

SIGRID WASN'T HOME. The cleaning lady told me she was at the hospital, but when I asked if it was Sigrid's dad who was sick, she shook her head. "Thor," she said. "Poor Thor."

The Andersons were starting to be like the Kennedys I thought as I turned my bicycle in the direction of Millstone Hospital. When John John Kennedy's plane crashed on the way to Martha's Vineyard I was surprised by how emotional my parents were. I just thought he was a cute, rich guy from a famous family who married a really thin blonde who once worked for Calvin Klein. But my parents had a different interpretation of his death. They said it was the final chapter in an American tragedy that spanned nearly half a century.

When I got to the hospital I was sent to pediatrics, where a nurse told me which room Thor was in. A television was on without sound. Thor was lying on the bed looking perfectly fine except for a broken arm while Sigrid was reading a collection of essays by Calvino. I would have been reading a trashy magazine, but I don't hold that against her.

"Hey," she said.

"What happened?"

"Skateboard," Thor said, waving his arm.

"Can I sign it?"

"Sure." He gestured to the nightstand, where a number of Magic Markers were lying with their caps off. "Just don't use pink."

It took me forever to think of anything to write. The whole issue of yearbook signing was just as painful. Maybe I needed a book that suggested clever phrases to use to express empty emotions to people you don't really like. In Thor's case, I did quite like him, but little brothers just don't inspire brilliance. Finally I wrote, "You're an idiot!" and signed my name.

Sigrid had returned to reading.

"You didn't come to the prom." I waited for her to suggest I sit down but she didn't. So I sat down near Thor's feet, which seemed to make him happy.

"No," she said. "Was it fun?"

"Kind of. Wendy Henninger came with a girl."

"Paris?"

"Huh?"

"Was her name Paris?"

"I don't know." It was lame that I didn't even ask this girl what her name was.

"She was dressed like a boy."

"I've met her."

"Really?"

"Yes. At Wendy's."

I had never been to Wendy's house.

"She's kind of pathetic," I said.

Sigrid looked at me over the Calvino. "No, she's not," she said. "She has an IQ of nearly two hundred points."

"Oh, who gives a flying fuck," I said.

"What's Frank Perone's IQ?" she asked suddenly.

"I don't know," I said. "I have a feeling these guys haven't been tested all that much."

Sigrid got this really smug look on her face. "I read an article in the *Utne Reader* that said prisoners are given more psychological and intelligence tests than any other demographic."

"Well," I said, "Frank never mentioned his IQ, so maybe he's just a dumb ass."

Sigrid started reading the Calvino again.

"Look," I said. "I think you were right about how it isn't fair that murderers get to express how they feel about their lives and stuff and their victims can't and everyone else is just left hanging."

Sigrid lowered her book.

"I want you to bring something in, something about Antoinette, and read it during the assembly."

"Will he be there?" she asked.

"I don't know." I took a deep breath. "Did you ever hear the thing about praying for your enemies?"

She shook her head.

"Really?"

"I don't have any enemies," Sigrid said.

"That's impossible," I said. "Think."

"I guess I hate Isabelle," she finally said.

"Good." I nodded. "If you pray for Isabelle you'll feel better."

"And if I pray for Frank Perone?"

I shrugged.

"What else are you doing in the assembly?"

"They're writing letters to their victims."

"Letters?"

"Remember in sophomore year when we wrote letters to the characters in *Wuthering Heights*?"

Sigrid smiled. "You wrote an erotic love poem to Heathcliff."

"It was a poetic letter."

Sigrid rolled her eyes.

"Anyway, that's just the concept. This isn't fiction."

"How will you make them?"

"What do you mean?"

"Aren't they grown men? Hardened criminals?"

"They love me and they want to make me happy no matter what."

"That's disgusting, Alice."

"It's less creepy than Morgan Crawford—"

I felt Thor's foot nudging me.

"What?"

"Can I come?"

"Where?"

"To Rahway."

Sigrid glared at him. "If you don't stop being such a jerk you'll end up there anyway," she snapped.

"I love you, Sis," Thor said adoringly.

We both threw pillows right at his broken arm.

Sixteen

THAT LEFT THE PRISONERS. I knew they were going to be mad about what I was going to say. I had seen everything from *Birdman of Alcatraz* to *The Green Mile* and *The Shawshank Redemption*—enough to understand that many prisoners imagine themselves as better than normal people; not necessarily without sin but more aware of the essential truths about human nature. Maybe that's true, but it's terrible that you have to do something horrible to value people.

After I made my speech about victims' rights and how it was important to honor the people who were affected by the poor choices they had made in their lives, there was a long period of silence.

Finally Lincoln stood up. "Shit," he said. "If they don't want us to read nuthin' why don't they just say so?"

"Sit down, man," Curtis said. "You ain't listening to our teacher.

She's making the point about how we don't deserve to say lovey-dovey things about our moms or whatever when we're here to be punished. She's telling us we're still the bad men we always were and we still owe society more than just our bodies." Curtis looked at me. "That right, Alice?"

I nodded.

"So, you hate us?" Kenny was looking at me, his baby face sad, his brown eyes shiny. "You think we're dirt?"

"She don't hate us," Roger said, his Macedonian accent stronger than ever. "She's trying to be a powerful example! Why are Americans such little, whiny babies?"

"I ain't no baby," Lincoln said. "You better keep that shit to yourself, Dracula!"

I looked at Frank. He was staring down at the floor.

Howard raised his hand.

"Yes, Howard?"

"Does this mean I can't read the opening chapter of my novel?"

Kenny groaned. "You can't read that anyway, man! Thing's so boring those kids wouldn't keep their eyes open for a minute."

"Boredom is a defense, Kenneth. I'd be happy to help you improve your grasp of the English language."

"Fuck you, egghead! I was born right here in the US of A. Don't need some asswipe wanna-be professor telling me how to read."

Frank put his head up and stared at me. "Is this because of what happened to your boyfriend?"

I shook my head. I had the picture of Antoinette in my hand that I'd stolen from Sigrid's album. I handed it to him. He stared at it for a long time, and then he looked up at me. In my whole life I had never seen such a sad expression.

"Where'd you get this?" he asked.

"Sigrid Anderson goes to my school. We're friends."

Lincoln walked over and looked at the picture. "Who's that?" he asked.

"I killed her," Frank whispered, handing the picture to Curtis, who looked and then handed the picture so that it passed among all the men and back to Frank.

"It was an accident," Curtis said.

"You didn't know what you were doing," Kenny said. "Come on, man."

Roger looked at me. "You know this girl?" he asked.

I shook my head. "I know the girl who saw it happen. That woman was her baby-sitter."

The men all nodded. They all moved closer to Frank. They looked almost angry at me.

"What do you want us to do?" Lincoln asked.

"I thought you could write letters. Tell the people you hurt why you are sorry and maybe tell the survivors something."

Howard raised his hand. "I didn't kill anyone," he said.

"Apologize for your book," Kenny said.

Howard gave him a mean look but it wasn't very serious. "I stole from people who had no money," he said. "One old lady had a heart attack. I think I caused it. Is that bad enough?"

I nodded.

I handed out paper, and the prisoners started writing. They were focused and intent on choosing their words correctly. They crossed things out and rewrote parts and checked words in the thesaurus and the dictionary. They showed each other certain passages, and Kenny read a sentence or two aloud to Curtis, who nodded. No one asked me for any help at all. Usually they called me over and waited to hear something positive about their efforts. It was as if I didn't exist. I remembered Amy quoting a Buddhist teacher who said: "If you see the Buddha on the road, kill him." She said the idea was to move beyond your teachers. The prisoners had moved beyond me. They were writing together, and they didn't need someone to tell them whether they were any good. They were writing their letters and knew exactly what to say.

"Dear relatives of Carlos Alonso:

I didn't even know your son. My lawyer told me he was fifteen and went to a Catholic school in Elizabeth. He said you were very religious and you all felt Carlos went wrong because of something you did. Well, let me tell you something different. Carlos went wrong because of something I did. I went out with a loaded piece and I shot your kid, your nephew, your brother, your friend. I was the piece of scum that cut him down and it wasn't the streets neither. I wanted to be in this gang—the Outlaws—and they told me to kill somebody and I killed Carlos. Now my mother cries every day I'm in here, my daddy's like an old man, my sister Sonia don't talk to me and I don't even know her kids.

I am twenty-two years old. I been here in Rahway since five years. It isn't that bad and I am truly sorry for what I did.

If you can, pray for my mother. Her name is Agatha Martinez and she is a very good woman.

> I am sorry again.
> Kenny Martinez"

"Dear town of Gubchek,

I cannot apologize to you individually because I don't know who it is I killed. I am here in an American jail for something else, assault with a deadly weapon. I came to New Jersey on a stolen visa after the massacre and then a black man tried to take my things and I hit him with a tire iron.

No, I did not know you except that you are not Christians and you killed my friends and family and my ancestors hated your ancestors and when we started school it was nothing but fighting and calling names and making the other children feel ashamed for coming there. So it goes.

I don't remember much about it to be honest with you. Andrei brought vodka, the stuff his granny makes, and we drank. We went to the meeting and decisions were made. All of the men between sixteen and fifty they said. I kept wondering how or why we would do such a thing. Line up these men and shoot them. But the ones who went to the other places, Boris had been with the Ulster Defense League and those crazy Hamas guys and he thought these things were normal.

We shot them and it was something I will never forget. How we took away these lives, these people, and then there was silence. The bodies were taken to the old sausage factory and you should not know any more.

I think I hit this guy because he stole the money that comes from such a terrible thing. If I was an evil person it should not be for nothing.

I think God doesn't care what happens to me.

I am sorry.
Roger Slokick"

"Dear friends and relatives of Darnell Jackson and Taylor Wright:

This is me, Curtis Leonard Whiting III, the person you probably would like to think of as dead. I am here in Rahway jail and have learned to write things because of my fine teacher, a lovely young lady named Miss Alice McGuire. I am currently trying to study the Bible everyday and ask Jesus Christ for forgiveness. Miss Alice says victims don't get as much attention as the ones that make them victims so I would like to take this opportunity to say that I recall Darnell was somebody you could always have a good talk with and Taylor was just plain mean like a snake but he was a child of God and I wish I'd never saw them that night when I had about five too many Colt 45s.

Miss Alice always tells us to use details in things we write but I can't do that. I killed Darnell and Taylor in a blackout and the only detail I remember was waking up in jail with a bad headache and knowing somethin really bad had happened. The sheriff looked at me over the rim of his mug and he said, "Boy, you better hope you got a good lawyer 'cause you're in a heap of shit."

Sorry for the language but Miss Alice tells us it's okay to swear under certain circumstances.

Bless you all. Sorry from the bottom of my soul.

Curtis Leonard Whiting III"

"To whom it may concern:

I can't be more personal because the lawsuit was a class action suit and really, I didn't know any of the people I embezzled money from in any intimate way. There was one person, a Ms. Emma Keeling, that lost her pension and was left destitute, uninsured and homeless. After living in Cambridge all her life, she stayed and slept in alleyways. And she died of a heart condition that was brought on by what I did to her. Mrs. Keeling, I am very sorry.

My novel tells the story of an idealistic young man who goes to Harvard and becomes a thief, thus the title: *Harvard Made Me a Con Man*. While I understand the philosophy behind Ms. McGuire's decision to alter the format of our presentation to the young people of Millstone Country Day School, I do feel there is something to be learned by hearing a cogent and effective piece of fiction written by someone they must view as a hard-core loser.

Sincerely,

Howard Thorton Ashby III

Harvard 1951"

"Dear Children of George Young:

When your father called me a 'punk nigger' I thought about the teaching of Elijah Muhammad and I did not allow myself to become angry. The white man keeps the black man angry so the black man stays down and the white man rises up. You make a choice in this life. Doctor Martin Luther King made one choice, Malcolm X made another, Gandhi, Bobby Sands, Nat Turner—read your history, children, understand the way of the world if you press down on anything hard enough, it will, without warning, recoil and react.

Why did I kill your daddy? I killed him while robbing his store, Sip and Drive. I shot him because he disrespected me, he did not understand that I was serious and wanted him to open the safe and that I knew he could do so despite those stickers that said he couldn't.

What was I thinking? I was thinking that I hated your daddy. He was an ignorant cracker with a nasty way of talking. I saw your pictures stuck up there, four little blond kids smiling while their pretty mother held them tight. My mama was never home to be holding us on account of her working three jobs and in between taking dope and leaving us with my daddy's mother who didn't like little children and hit us so hard we got sent to foster care.

But I am still sorry. I am sorry that we live in a society that doesn't care what happens to poor children whether they are black or white.

And I am sorry that you had to know your daddy bled to death on the floor while I drove away. I am sorry that you had to know that someone could be so mean and bad as me. I am sorry that you still think I'm the devil when I'm nothin but an angry black man who never got given what he needed to start his life.

Sincerely yours,

Lincoln Jefferson"

After Lincoln finished reading there was a long silence. Frank hadn't moved. He was still holding the picture of Antoinette in his hand like it was something that he'd lose if didn't keep it close. When the prisoners looked at him, he shook his head.

"I'll write mine alone," he said. "I can't do it like this. I need to think." The rest put their letters down in front of me.

"Correct the grammar and stuff, Alice," Roger said.

"It's fine," I said. "They sound like you."

"We don't want those rich kids to think we're ignorant," Curtis said.

"Criminal is okay," Howard said, smiling a little. "But we need to sound smart."

"I'm not changing anything," I said. "Rewrite them if you think they need work."

Lincoln whistled. "Hey," he said, "Teach is getting tough."

The door opened and Officer Costa was standing there. "Last class, eh?" she asked.

"I guess so," I said.

"You leaving us?" Kenny looked upset. "Nobody said you were done."

"I'm graduating on Sunday," I said.

"Imagine that," Curtis said. "You wear gowns?"

"White dresses."

"Like brides," Roger said.

"You ever gonna come back and see us?" Lincoln asked.

"Of course I am," I said.

Then no one said anything. I knew I would never see them again after the assembly and they knew it too. They were prisoners and people left them. They never left anyone unless they died.

"We'll see you at school, right?" Curtis asked.

"Sure," I said.

And that was it, how it ended. Which is weird because I wanted to say something encouraging about their writing and maybe about their spending the rest of their lives in jail. I wanted to thank them for helping me. But I just walked out and I didn't look back once.

Seventeen

MY MOTHER ONLY MADE LUNCH when something bad happened. Pip's death was revealed over chicken noodle soup and bologna sandwiches. She told us my dad was moving to a condominium while grilling cheese on some special grill sold by an ex-boxer that my father bought her for a joke. And there was mushroom soup in the pot that she stirred, not looking at me, stirring and stirring, "They say he's missing, Alice, possibly presumed dead."

I had never liked the whole idea of lunch, anyway. Catherine Swan used to send Matthew to school with really weird things, leftover salmon wrapped in foil, cold baked potatoes, once she packed an entire half chicken as if we were little barbarians who ate hunks of meat with our fingers. Lunch annoyed me. I preferred being slightly hungry, alert and ready for anything. Breakfast was good and dinner was fine but lunch needed to be reconsidered.

When I returned from Rahway, she had made lunch and was lurking. I opened the front door, and before I could put my foot on the stairs she trilled out: "Lunch is ready!" And then she appeared wearing this stupid full-length apron my brother had brought her from marthastewart.com.

My mother has several jobs. She sells real estate, especially the older, expensive houses. A few years ago she won some contest and we all went to Paris. She buys houses, renovates them, and sells them again. She teaches tai chi at the retirement village where all the seniors are Nobel Prize–winning professors from Princeton who only want to be with elite senile people. She also counsels vets for jobs with a Vietnam vet organization and writes their monthly newsletter.

During the winter she shovels all the snow because she hates the gym. In the spring she plants, weeds, prunes, and digs. In the summer she mows, waters, and fertilizes. In the fall she plants bulbs, rakes leaves, and starts all over again. Other people like to occasionally sit around and do nothing but my mother hates it.

But when she's crazy, something else starts to happen. She makes lunch and she nags and she tries to change her children. She forgets you can't trim, prune, or protect people. You can't swathe them in burlap like she does her rosebushes to try and keep the frost away. If you really express anger or frustration or grief to my mother when she's in one of these moods, she will respond by saying something from a fortune cookie, something so stupid and pointless you just want to spit at her.

"I'll be down in a minute." I ran up the stairs as fast as I could, frightened by what I observed in the kitchen, the table set with place mats and napkins, goblets filled with sparkling mineral water. Her back was to me, but she was making a salad, listening to NPR's latest in-depth exploration of sea turtles.

Morgan had sent four e-mails. They would be about either his deferring Beloit or sleeping with me. I deleted all of them.

"How was your last day?" she asked me as she set down a plate containing a tomato half stuffed with tuna fish, my least favorite thing except for olives, which decorated the top of the mound.

"Yum," I said, "this looks great." I wondered whether this was a test to see if aliens had kidnapped her real daughter. But she didn't seem to remember my feelings about tuna fish. I began the familiar ritual of rearranging food so it looks like you've eaten some.

"Alice, Valerie Hardwood and I had a long talk—"

"Amy left her," I said.

She brushed my comment aside as if she were getting rid of cobwebs. "We don't think it's necessary—" My mother offered me a piece of bread. "Pita?" she asked.

"No."

"You love pita," she said.

I don't love pita. "Okay."

"Anyway, so it's not necessary." She smiled at me.

"I don't know what you're talking about."

"The prisoners reading. They shouldn't do that."

"That's my senior project, Mom."

"Valerie said you'd get an A anyway. The coordinator told her you had done a great job—" My mother paused. "What's his name?"

"Hal." I stopped myself from telling her he'd gone down on me in his car.

"She said he couldn't stop talking about what a natural teacher you are."

"I need the credit for graduation."

"You can write an essay."

"The prisoners wrote letters, Mom. They're going to read them. I promised."

She closed her eyes for a moment. "They are convicted murderers, Alice."

"They still understand what promises are."

"Animals."

"They aren't all murderers. Howard embezzled money."

"Mr. Anderson is very upset."

I wondered how he'd found out about Frank.

"Sigrid understands."

"How can she understand? Why won't you listen to me?" My mother was shouting. It was rare for her to raise her voice, but when she did it was pretty extreme.

"Mom—"

"No! A grown man strangles a grown woman and you understand? How? Do you know strangulation is the slowest, most painful, prolonged death there is? Do you know how long it takes to choke the life out of a person, that you actually watch them die as you do it?"

"Thanks for sharing, Mom."

"What is the matter with you people? Can you think or feel anything if it isn't on television, if the world isn't watching?"

This was another annoying habit of my mother's, bunching everything together. Last year some kids from Millstone made a tape about their families where they accused their parents of satanic worship and sexual abuse, and the police came and confiscated everything in the house including all the computers and sent the kids into protective custody.

"The real world?" She swept away my plate despite the amount of food that was still on it. "What do any of you know about reality?"

"Come on, Mom! It's not my fault we don't have a war to be in! Can't you just let me go—"

She turned to face me. "Like Catherine Swan? Look what letting go of Matthew did to him."

"That isn't fair," I said slowly. "It could have happened to him here."

"But it didn't, did it?"

"It isn't her fault."

"Then whose is it?"

"No one's. Maybe God just decided that was it for him—"

I stopped. My mother's expression was hard to recognize.

"God? Alice, this isn't about heaven and hell and God. It's about the absolute lie of existence. God's irrelevant."

"Don't you believe in God, Mom?"

She looked at me for a second, and then she slowly shook her head. "No," she said. "I tried but I can't."

"Yes you do—" I didn't really know whether she did or not. It was something we had never discussed. "What about Uncle Adam?"

"What about him?"

"Where did he go after they buried him?"

"They didn't bury any part of him, Alice. Those were all left scattered across some part of the Mekong Delta. They buried a gray suit and a flag."

"He's in heaven, isn't he?"

My mother smiled at me. It was a really sad smile. "I guess so, darling."

"You guess so? You have to believe in God, Mom."

"Why?"

I didn't know why. Except it seemed prudent to stay on good terms with something that was supposed to be running everything.

Sort of like not getting arrested and paying your taxes and parking tickets. If she didn't believe in God and there was one, what would happen to her?

"I think you should."

She smiled. "I didn't know you were so spiritual."

I shrugged.

"Bitterness is hard to avoid sometimes," she said.

"I'm sorry," I said.

"For what?"

"For your parents and the way they died and Uncle Adam and Aunt Barbara."

"But look how lucky I am. My children are the most wonderful human beings and I'm actually in love with my husband." She blushed.

"How can you be in love with Daddy?" I asked. "He's like been around forever."

"So?" she asked, laughing. "I'm used to him."

"I'm going to have the prisoners read, Mom."

"Valerie—"

"Screw Ms. Hardwood! You two just don't get it. I have a right to do this. The prisoners are sorry! They did bad things and they're sorry and that will help. It will help everyone. There's karma in the world and their karma will get better."

She shook her head. "Karma means future, Alice. They don't have futures."

"You can deny the existence of God if you want to, but that doesn't mean these men don't exist. They breathe and sleep and walk around like we do!"

"How dare they!" my mother actually screamed. "How dare they live?"

"It's really hard to die, Mom. You said that yourself."

She shook her head. "I never said that."

"Yes, you did. When we first found out that Matt was missing and I said I was going to die."

"Why do you know so much?"

"Because bad things have happened."

She looked upset. "Have you had a bad childhood?"

"No! I mean—some things—Daddy leaving, Matt."

She moved to touch me but I dodged her hand.

"Baby—"

"I'm not your baby anymore."

"I didn't say you were my baby."

"Well, I'm not."

We faced each other breathing hard. "I'm not a baby," I said, looking down at my size 9 feet.

"No," she said. "You'll be eighteen tomorrow. What do you want?"

"What do you mean?"

"You want a cake?"

I pouted.

"You still want a cake?"

I figured they were planning the blowout of the century complete with pony rides and a bouncy castle.

"You weren't going to make one?"

My mother made a face. "Of course I was going to make one. How about a big sheet cake with a clown on top?"

I hate clowns. "Maybe I should go to downtown Trenton and score some crack."

"You want to invite some friends to dinner?"

I thought about Wendy and Morgan and Sigrid. It didn't seem like the right crowd for a birthday.

"No. Can we go to Fargo's?"

"You want to?"

I nodded.

Fargo's was an all-you-can-eat restaurant named for the movie. Each table had a different theme, and the food was delicious. An entire refrigerated case was filled with flavored butters.

"We'll try and get a reservation, okay?"

"Okay."

"You still want a cake?"

I gave my mother a pained look.

"Homemade?"

I nodded.

"I think I'll invite Valerie." She looked at me. "You mind?"

I shook my head. "She's God's child even though she's a dyke," I said.

My mother looked annoyed. "Valerie Hardwood can sleep with small farm animals and still remain the finest human being I've ever known."

"Mother!" I raised an eyebrow. "I'm telling PETA."

WE HAD BEEN BOYCOTTING McHalligan's for as long as I could remember, preferring to remain loyal to Foodfest, with its ancient produce and its cashiers who were all collecting social security. Foodfest had nothing aside from staples—milk, eggs, meat, dry goods—like some kind of frontier store stuck in a time warp. McHalligan's had everything you could ever want: bagels, blenders, biscotti, baby clothes—and that was only the B's. I think my parents secretly shopped there and transferred their groceries into hoarded Foodfest bags, but I hadn't been able to prove this.

I didn't have the mental strength to wander the depressing aisles of the Foodfest searching for the cake ingredients required by my mother. Parking the car in a neutral zone occupied by the Manhattan Sports Club and First Run Videos, I sneaked into the brightly lit and well-stocked McHalligan's, where I managed to snag a working shopping cart and to locate half of the things on my list within a few minutes.

McHalligan's was famous for its food samples. Many of the people who had loudly denounced the new store for trying to destroy Foodfest, which unlike its competitor was unionized, were to be found in the aisles of McHalligan's sucking down free goodies. The gelato department had been forced to set a three-taste limit to discourage the browsing samplers who kept asking for teaspoons full of the different flavors.

By the time I reached the checkout line I had eaten several spinach pies, a miniature shrimp cocktail, chicken on a stick, a brownie, and strawberries dipped in milk chocolate. I wondered why the small population of Millstone homeless didn't just spend the day there, but then I noticed a security guard waving away a ragged-looking young man and saw that all the people shopping looked well-fed and wealthy.

Matthew hated McHalligan's. He had worked at Foodfest during junior high, and the employees there loved him. Until the news about the bones was published, the dusty windows had been hung with yellow ribbons and a huge picture of Matt standing next to a pile of crushed boxes was hung in the front window. The picture was taken right after he had shaven his head to look like the lead singer of a punk rock band called Black Jesus. He was trying to seem really hard and scary, but it didn't work. His ears stuck out and he looked geeky.

As I walked past the bulletin board hung with notices ranging from free kittens to free couches, someone called my name. It was Amy.

"Alice McGuire, aren't you ashamed of yourself?"

"You think it's okay for me to have meaningless sex on lawn furniture but it's a sin to shop in the decent supermarket?"

"Absolutely." She waved a three-by-five card at me. "I found myself a passenger to Seattle."

"Seattle? Seattle sucks."

"New Jersey sucks. You're confused."

I shook my head. "Seattle's so over, it was a 'not' in *Vogue* last month. Seattle is riots and fog."

Amy nodded. "Sounds perfect."

"You're leaving Grace?"

"No! I mean, for a bit." Amy shrugged. "She won't remember."

"Sigrid's mother died and she still can't forgive her. Wendy Henninger's mother has MS and it's like made her crazy—she's pierced and tattooed every inch of herself. And look at Morgan."

"Morgan Crawford has a mother."

"But his father left and now he's completely confused."

Amy snorted. "That's bullshit, Alice. If Morgan wants to defer Beloit, why shouldn't he?"

"Don't go to Seattle, Amy."

"Why not?"

"You'll break her heart."

"The Vietnam War broke her heart. I'm just something to get through middle age."

I shook my head. "She totally loves you. She's a wreck."

Amy rolled her eyes.

"It's my birthday, tomorrow," I said. "Come for dinner at Fargo's."

"I have to pack."

"It's my eighteenth birthday. I can get drafted."

Amy shook her head. "I won't promise anything."

I nodded.

We stopped outside the store to look at Matthew's box boy picture.

"Christ," Amy whispered, "look at that skull."

"He did it to look like a skinhead," I said. "He gave the hair to Catherine Swan, and she buried it in the backyard like it was a person or something."

"He looks like a baby."

"I never told him that. I told him he looked awesome and scary."

"You were his bright star, Alice."

"We were going to have sex on my eighteenth birthday," I whispered, staring at Matthew's stupid, dimpled face. "Even though we'd both had other things, it was like we were starting over again. Like morning."

Amy pulled me close to her. "Let time pass, Alice," she said. "It won't make it go away but it will hurt less."

"Ms. Hardwood needs you."

"She doesn't need anyone," Amy said. I could feel the hard muscles in her arm contract.

"That's stupid."

"I know."

"Why are you leaving?"

"I need a change."

"Geographics don't work," I said.

Amy exhaled loudly. "Are you sure you're eighteen? When I was eighteen I had this massive crush on Kurt Cobain and I thought I was a brilliant artist."

"You are a brilliant artist."

Amy smiled at me. "Thank you, but I'm just starting to understand what I'd like to do before I die."

"Matt used to say you reminded him of Georgia O'Keeffe."

"That old bag?" Amy smiled. "Well," she said, "I won't leave before tomorrow. You are a true gift to the world, Alice. Your birthday needs to be properly marked."

I didn't tell her Ms. Hardwood was coming.

Eighteen

WHEN I BROUGHT IN THE GROCERIES, my parents were making out in the kitchen. It was pretty gross, but I guess that's a healthy thing.

"You want to help me wash the car?" my dad asked me like I was five years old.

"No," I said.

"You won't write an essay?" he asked me as I began to leave again.

I turned to face him. "Would you?"

He looked to see if my mom was watching, but she was searching through the cupboards for a cake pan.

"No," he said. He lowered his voice even more. "And neither would she."

My mother whirled around. Sometimes she could hear you doing something wrong from miles away. "Don't assume anything," she said. "I am not who you think I am."

"Fine," I said. "You're Martha Stewart's aromatherapist." I looked at my father. "I'm going into downtown Manhattan to help Sigrid with her final project."

He nodded.

"Don't you want to lick the frosting bowl?" my mother asked.

I gave my father the she's-insane-and-you-married-her look and left the house before she could start screaming again.

Sigrid had agreed to meet me at Morgan's so the three of us could drive into Manhattan and put together Sigrid's tribute to Antoinette. Kids our age don't read much, and they don't get impressed by words without pictures. Our parents keep telling us we should appreciate things without needing them to be animated, but I think it's like what people said about television replacing radio. If we were presenting Sigrid's dead baby-sitter to the student body of Millstone Country Day, we needed to make a music video.

Morgan was so impressed with himself it was disgusting. He insisted we squish all the things we had brought in Sigrid's car into his yellow Spider because he said a Volvo sedan wasn't "an appropriate vehicle for a sought-after music producer."

"Who's seeking you?" I asked him as we entered the Holland Tunnel.

"Lots of new artists," he said, turning to face me instead of the road. It was bad enough he wore dark glasses on a day dark enough to be night, in the Holland Tunnel, but now he was looking at me while the car nearly hit the side wall.

"What's the pull, Morgan?" I asked. "Are we talking pedophiles here?"

"Morgan!" Sigrid shrieked from the boot.

I had a vision of the three of us incinerated beneath the Hudson, still on the Jersey side, a pathetic footnote to history. My parents would be totally bummed, Ms. Hardwood would have a nervous breakdown, Alf would briefly grieve and then blossom out from under my shadow; maybe Matthew and I would meet in the shadows of the netherworld, blending together in death into a perfect, pure force of love. I actually started to compose my own eulogy, but suddenly we were back in full daylight: New York City.

"You drive like an idiot," Sigrid said, "like someone who doesn't have a single bit of a brain."

I liked it when Sigrid was mean. It gave me a break.

The first thing I noticed about Funkatone Inc. was how no one was over thirty. Morgan was probably the youngest employee but only by a bit, and the receptionist was just a month or two older than us but she'd dropped out of high school when she was in eighth grade. She told us this while we were waiting for someone named Norman to open a studio up. She also told us she was getting married on New Year's Day to a hip-hop "genius" named Mr. Q and that she was going to wear a Vera Wang dress she had seen on the Style Network. Her name was Rochelle, and she had a fake French accent like the skunk Pepé Le Pew. She called Morgan, Michelle; Sigrid, Sigride; and me, Alicia. She was sort of annoying but also freaky enough to be interesting. Still, I could understand why Morgan's mom wasn't happy about his deferring Beloit. The place was like daytime television. You knew you needed to stop watching, but it was hard to turn the set off.

Rochelle's nails made it excruciating to sit in the reception area. They tapped on the keyboard with incredible speed, making a noise that sounded like a wild animal trapped in a Formica cage.

"You from Millstone, too, ladies?" she asked, looking at Sigrid and me.

"Uh-huh."

"It's pretty there," she said. "Not like Jersey at all."

We nodded.

"I grew up right next to the Elizabeth exit. You ever exit off that ramp?"

I shook my head.

"I have," Sigrid said. "My piano teacher lived in Elizabeth."

"You ever look through the window of the apartment building right there?"

Sigrid nodded.

"That was my bedroom," Rochelle said. "One time I flashed a trucker and he drove right off the ramp." She smiled at the memory. "Whole damn rig exploded."

Norman King was white, but he talked exactly like a ghetto rapper. He was about my parents' age, but his clothes were total FUBU. He was so yesterday, it was irrelevant.

"You must be Alice," he said to me.

"Duh no," I replied.

Norman winked. "Yeah, well, I know what I know," he said. "And this is the composer." He smiled at Sigrid, who didn't smile back.

"Listen, kids," he said. "Mi casa, su casa. Morgan knows all the codes except for one." He gave Sigrid a deep stare. "You got that one, babe," he said.

Sigrid looked sick. Norman was hitting on her.

"Shut up," I said. "So, Norm, when did you graduate from college? Before or after the Days of Rage?"

Morgan kicked me.

"Love the sweatshirt, Norm," I said. "Any chance we might get to see anyone famous today?"

Norman said, "Rochelle?"

"I think Al Green's in here tonight."

I nodded and tried to look impressed.

Morgan had told Norman we needed some video monitors, a CD player, a scanner, and a computer to start editing the film. All of those things were provided, along with a rolling cart that contained sandwiches, chips, and soft drinks.

"Morgan, this is amazing," I said, giving him a little pat.

Sigrid pulled out the CD of songs she had written about Antoinette. I couldn't believe she had been able to turn what happened to her and her family into art. I felt jealous of her. I had not touched art since Matthew had disappeared. I did my homework, but my imagination had nearly ceased. I didn't go to New York anymore to walk through the museums. I didn't listen to music that held any potential to inspire or move. I watched stupid movies and avoided anything that contained potential emotional truth. I began to understand what people meant when they said they just wanted to be entertained.

If the concrete and the real dominated my consciousness, I decided there would be no space for imagination, memories, or dreams. My father had been watching the movie *Elvira Madigan,* and I heard three minutes of the soundtrack and dissolved into hysterical tears, kneeling at the end of my bed crying for Matthew. There was a small boy lost in those places, a boy whose face I knew better than my own, a boy whose smell and touch and taste had been the smell of love and safety, my boy who would never be mine again.

"Flower gatherer," he had whispered into my skin the night we had stayed together on the camping trip, "sweet Alice who smells of roses. I will love you forever and ever."

No.

I would not do that. I would not try and bring him back. He had haunted me already, but I would remain in the actual, the gray lines of the real world. Matthew was chalk, dust, something lifeless. In earth science we learned there was living nature and then there was dirt and rocks. How sad, I thought. How sad to be without a soul.

We watched the home movies on the video monitors. Sigrid and

Thor: two blond, blue-eyed fairy children whose faces were always smiling. Despite their mother's departure, they seemed happy with the beautiful Antoinette. If I didn't know the little girl's identity, I would not have recognized Sigrid. The Sigrid who watched was dim, a shadow person whose whole self seemed to shrink from attention. The sunny Sigrid was exactly the opposite, energy radiating from her tiny, dancing body.

"Look at you," I whispered. "You're so beautiful."

"I was happy," Sigrid said. "My mother was up in heaven watching over us, and Antoinette would never go away."

"You must say that," I said.

"What?"

"What you just said. Start the audio with that." I glanced at Morgan. "Right?"

He nodded.

Sigrid frowned. "That's manipulative," she said. "I mean, it's like a commercial or something."

"Well, we're telling high school students not to grow up and murder someone because it causes pain. So maybe it is a commercial."

"Hey," Morgan said, "your mom told me that Beloit is right outside of Madison."

Sigrid giggled and I glared at her.

"So?" I asked.

"So"—Morgan pushed the pause button—"I'm thinking about not deferring."

"Because of me?" I asked.

"No." Morgan kept his face turned toward the video monitor. "Madison is really cool, and Norman thinks he can give me one of those campus-based jobs recruiting college students."

"Recruiting? For what? Your hip-hop dynasty?"

Sigrid was rolling around on the floor laughing. I kicked her.

The tape continued. It hurt to know the beautiful woman was dead. I could not imagine Frank Perone watching her die, but who knew what people did in their lives?

Sigrid and Thor reminded me of how easy it had been to feel happy when we were small. My father would rake up a huge leaf pile and after we jumped on it we would get potatoes, wrap them in foil, and light a bonfire. Later, when the flames died down, we would sit outside in sweaters and eat those mealy potatoes, my mom bringing out butter and salt and paper plates, and then we'd roast marshmallows on the embers. Huddled together in a circle of family, the smell of my father's lamb's-wool coat, my mother's shampoo, the food, all had the essence of sweetness.

I rarely considered my childhood as lost. Rather, it was simply back there, a past that I might easily return to or re-create for my children or describe to my future husband. But now it was forfeited for the sake of survival. I would never tell the truth to anyone so it might burn inside me until the end to be buried along with those things he had placed inside that box.

When Sigrid and Morgan started an argument about whether to use a Rage Against the Machine track or the Vivaldi music Sigrid had chosen, I walked outside. It was a little before midnight, and the sky above Manhattan was amazingly clear. I looked up to see nearly a perfect view of the Big Dipper.

"Wishin?"

Raol was leaning against the limousine, a big, unlit cigar in his hand.

"No," I said.

"No?" He touched his head. "What happened to the prom queen?"

"This is the real me," I said. "The hair had its own agenda."

"Any news?" he asked.

"You mean about me and Morgan?"

"Ha!" He laughed hard and sharp. "No, girlie! If that existed you betta believe yo little man would have told me. I meant your missing friend."

"He's dead. They matched the bones."

"That's tough." Raol looked at his limousine and rubbed at an invisible spot. "My brother got shot."

"I'm sorry."

"Yeah. Almost killed my mama. I wasn't so surprised."

"Who shot him?"

"His girlfriend."

I must have looked shocked.

"She was pissed! The man was double dipping, another crib, another woman, another baby."

"So she killed him?"

"Accident, I think. Meant to like fix him but it was too big a bullet." Raol gestured toward his crotch.

"How can you be so calm?" I asked. "Aren't you angry?"

"Whatsa point of that? She didn't have no way else to get him. My baby brother's dead so I can't get angry at him."

"What about God?"

Raol looked upset. "God? You can't be getting angry at the man, Alice. God don't like people mouthing off to him. You gotta love God."

"I don't love God," I said. "I don't even like him."

Raol frowned. "That's bad," he said, "real bad."

"What's he gonna do? Strike me dead?"

"Send you to hell. Turn you into salt. Bring a plague of snakes." Raol looked really upset. More upset than when he was discussing his brother. I couldn't believe my mother didn't think God existed and now Raol talked about him like he was the boss of everybody and had temper tantrums.

"Maybe hell's fun. It could be like Asbury Park."

Raol shook his head. "You have to accept the truth of God," he said.

"What's true about your brother getting killed by a crazy woman with a gun?" I asked.

"You have nothing if you don't have God's divine love!" Raol said, his voice loud.

"Then I have nothing!"

We stared at each other, both of us angry. But then we both exhaled.

"I am very sorry about your friend, Alice," Raol said.

I smiled at him. "Do you miss your brother?" I asked.

"All the time," Raol said. "He was my little pal. I taught him how to ride a bike and how to roll a doobie and how to do everything. He slept in my room for fifteen years."

As I went back into the studio I heard Vivaldi mixed with Rage Against the Machine. It sounded pretty good.

"DATING SUCKS." Catherine Swan looked at me and smiled. She was sitting at the kitchen table drinking coffee with my parents, a map of Mexico folded between them.

The only person who looked uncomfortable was my father, who immediately jumped up as if I'd caught him doing something wrong.

"What sucks about it?" I asked, sitting down in my father's chair with my coffee.

"It's so demanding! You have to be pleasant and charming or at least neutral. You can't be surly or irritable."

My mother shook her head. "I couldn't manage that for long."

"And you don't have to, darling," my father said.

I think he was trying to be witty but he sounded stupid. We all stared at him.

"You can't eat certain things."

My mom looked fascinated. "Like what?" she asked.

"There's different categories," Catherine Swan said. "Teeth: poppy seed bagels, spinach, licorice, salad."

"All salad?" my mother asked.

"Why do you care?" my father asked.

"Shut up," I said. "What else?"

"You can't eat things that seem disgusting—French fries, ice cream, fried anything."

"Anything?" my mother asked.

"Fried dough is a big turn-on," my dad said. "I like a woman munching on a corn dog."

We all glared at him silently.

"I'm going to go mulch," he said, walking toward the back door.

"Great idea," my mother said.

He walked outside, letting the screen door crash behind him. Alf was constructing something that looked explosive by the garage. My dad squatted down next to him.

"Look at that," Catherine said. "They are really adorable."

"Who are you dating?" I asked, not finding the sight of the male members of our household very endearing.

"Oh, you know, eligible divorced men who ask questions like Can you imagine living with a bipolar woman for thirty years? on the first date."

"Tell us about a good date," my mother said.

"Let me think." Catherine Swan wrinkled her forehead. "Okay," she said. "Dinner at Chop Louies, salsa dancing at this little club in the East Village, and then we stood in a doorway making out." She looked at me. "Sorry, Alice," she said.

"Yeah," I said. "You have five kids and I was sure you were still a virgin."

My mother gave me a look. "And then what?" she asked, her face all pink.

"Then he called two days later to tell me his real girlfriend doesn't like the idea of extra women."

"Extra women?" I asked.

"He was on some kind of serial dating slip."

I turned to my mother. "Did you know Beloit was near Madison, Mom?"

My mother looked at me. "What, honey?"

"Someone told Morgan Crawford that Beloit's right next to Madison."

"Oh," she said sweetly. "I told him that."

"Why?"

She frowned. "You wouldn't pick up the phone, so I told him you were trying to figure out the best driving route. I got the map out— Morgan always sounds so alone—"

"He *is* so alone! His mother travels about three hundred days a year."

"I was looking at the map and reading out all the towns close to Madison and then I said Beloit and he just started cheering—"

"He isn't deferring anymore, Mother. He's going to recruit hip-hop slaves on the campus."

"That is so adorable," Catherine Swan said, her voice like a purr. "That boy worships you!"

"Ick," I said.

"Alice," my mother said, "don't scoff at infatuation. You take these things for granted, but men change."

"And how," Catherine Swan said.

"You mean they get worse?" I asked.

We watched as my father and Alf consulted about something that appeared to be at ground zero with the lawn. Meanwhile, the mower was alone, mowing away on a bald patch of grass.

"What are they staring at?" I asked.

"Dirt," my mother said. "Men and dirt."

They straightened up at the same time and saw us looking at them. They waved in exactly the same way. We waved back.

"Holy Mother of God," my mother murmured. "Buddha give me strength."

Catherine gave her a worried look. "Are you all right?" she asked.

"Me? You're the one with the unbearable sorrow."

"Tragedy has many rewards." Catherine sighed.

"What are those?" I asked.

"Continuous sympathy both real and fake. Publicity. Discounted designer clothes. Free haircuts. Lowered social expectations. Casseroles."

"What kinds of casseroles? Tuna fish would be worse than nothing."

"Yes," Catherine said. "But this is Millstone, not some trailer park. I get exotic, delicious casseroles in nice earthenware with notes reminding me not to return the dish."

My mother sighed.

"What's the matter, Julia?" Catherine asked, glancing at me.

Julia. I never thought of her with that name. My dad used to sing the John Lennon song to her sometimes but still—she was Mom, Mommy, Mama, Mother on bad days.

"Alice is going to college," my mother said.

"You still have Alf," I snapped. "And Dad. And the dirt."

"I'll be outnumbered," my mother said.

"Come to my house," Catherine said. "It's your basic female coven."

"Mother," I said, "don't bum me out about going to college!"

Both women gave me really dirty looks.

"Remember how sweet she used to be?" my mother asked.

"Like a little bunny," Catherine said. "Just a chunky little bunny girl!"

I glared at them, but they were wiping their eyes. They'd known me for a very long time, my mother from before I was born.

"You spend nine months," my mother said.

"Nearly ten," Catherine murmured.

"Then you suffer the agony of the damned."

"Lose your figure."

"Acquire new, disgusting physical attributes."

I glared at both of them.

"Dear me," my mother said, "are we wrecking your groove?"

My father came through the door with a fistful of flowers. "Julia," he said, "don't give up on me!"

My mother and Catherine Swan stared at him. The thing Alf was building in the backyard suddenly flew into the sky.

"Houston," my mother said, "we have liftoff."

Nineteen

EVEN THOUGH IT WAS THE SECOND to last time we had to listen to Mr. Farley tell the history of Millstone Country Day, it was still an ordeal. We had heard the same speech for twelve years, five times a year. We had heard him explain how the school came to be coed sixty times. We had heard his feelings about education and sports and murals and ice hockey, his love for all of us and for the school and the state and the country and his stupid wife sixty times. We could recite his speech in unison, which would be a great idea except he took himself too seriously to see the humor and we'd all get suspended and then flunk and have to stay for another year of agony.

Isabelle Folonari sat in the front row and pretended to be entranced. Wendy Henninger was fast asleep, and no matter how many times Ms. Hardwood signaled for someone near her to wake her up, nothing worked. Morgan looked fascinated, but I could see the headphone wire extending from his ear. Smoke Papa had bought him some state-of-the-art CD deck with this microfilament wire that was almost invisible.

Sigrid was just the way she always was: composed, calm, and sort of robotic. I had once asked her if she took meds but she looked at me like I was nuts.

The prisoners came in a van. They were handcuffed until they were released on the sidewalk, which was sort of sad. At first I thought Frank hadn't come. When all the guys were standing on the sidewalk, the cop stuck his head back in the van and yelled, "Perone, get your slow ass out here!"

Frank didn't look at me as we walked into school. He just stared straight ahead and then sat down at the edge of the auditorium, where the cops had seated themselves on each end of a row. The assembly started with senior awards being handed out. This was always a touchy situation, as parents that contributed massive amounts of money to the school improvement fund weren't happy unless their children won things. Strangely enough, the largest contributors had the least talented kids. So awards that meant nothing were invented and bestowed on these students; these awards included things like "best overall member of the senior class," "most school spirit," "the foreign service award," and "the Millstone student of the year."

Once the meaningless part of the program was over, people became more interested in the winners. Sigrid won the art award; Wendy won the award they give people who agitate, a fund that was set up by an ex-member of the Weathermen who had lived underground in Millstone for a decade. Morgan won something sponsored by the local Chamber of Commerce. A girl who was perfect—sweet, pretty, smart, athletic, never absent, never mean, never anything but like a cutout paper doll teen—won the Millstone

Mothers' Award. No one knew which mothers gave this award or why there wasn't one for boys from the fathers.

Then Farley started to hrrmph and cough and stutter until we realized he was actually crying, something none of us had ever seen.

"Children," he said, "in all the years I have run this school, among all the students I taught, disciplined, counseled, or yes, disliked, several have remained so close to my heart, they might as well have been mine." Farley looked down and looked up again. He wasn't smiling.

"Matthew Swan came into junior kindergarten and immediately began to change the essence of our lives. Everyone who knew him loved him. The janitorial staff taught him how to pitch pennies, the cafeteria ladies let him bake cookies in their ovens, not a single teacher ever had a word to say against him even if he did poorly in their classes—calculus and Greek come to mind here."

Farley paused again to clear his throat.

"In short, he was a golden child. Last month it was confirmed that Matthew's DNA was a perfect match with the remains found in an unmarked Mexican grave, and last month the heart of this town broke."

There was this huge, terrible sigh. I looked around for somewhere to hide, but I saw that Catherine Swan was staring at me, her expression begging me not to run out.

"His father and mother are two of the finest people I have ever known, but this is finally about Matthew, who would have changed the world if he had lived but has left us to complete the task. Matthew had been awarded the highest honor of the Millstone senior class, an award that dates back to the founding of this school and carries with it a scholarship worth"—Farley looked down and shook his head— "This is really a great deal of money. Someone has been handling their stocks correctly."

Then he didn't say anything else. He just stood there looking older and sadder than I had ever seen him look. Finally, Ms. Hardwood leaned over and said something to Catherine Swan, who stood up, and the two women walked onto the stage. Catherine hugged Farley and then Ms. Hardwood hugged Farley and they all were crying. I looked over at the prisoners. They appeared uncomfortable, as if they were visitors at some sort of intimate family ritual.

Catherine Swan put on her reading glasses, which I had never seen her wear. She looked like a teacher suddenly.

"Thank you, Scooter," she said. Then she looked up at us. "I've known Mr. Farley for forty-three years," she said. "We went to kindergarten together. So I get to call him that, but you, children, do not."

She put down her paper and took off her glasses. "I have something I wrote but I'm not going to read it. You are all graduating on Sunday and people are going to be reading speeches to you and you'll start to wonder if it will ever end.

"You were Matthew's friends and maybe not. Some of you probably didn't like him that much because he was pretty bossy and show-offy and know-it-all." She stopped to wipe her eyes.

"Matthew wanted a family, a family that was his alone. He had to put up with an awful lot of bad stuff when his dad and I divorced, including his father's infidelity and my alcoholism. He was forced to take care of his sisters and his brother when he should have been having a proper childhood. But he was also in love, completely in love, with someone who is sitting here right now. And his dreams for the future all revolved around her and the life they would have together. I know this because I am his mother and he told me exactly what he wanted and nothing that happened can change the truth of that vision he had."

I could feel myself disappearing. The room was spinning and I felt myself circling with it. I looked down and there was a hand in mine, Sigrid's nail-bitten hand was holding mine very hard.

"My husband and I have decided to give Matt's award to his best friend, his childhood pal, and his intended partner for life. We don't need the money, and Alice deserves it. We can't bring him back to her, but maybe she can find a way to keep him alive for all of us."

There was applause, and then Morgan was standing at the end of the row of seats with his hand out, "What?" I whispered.

"You have to go up there," he said.

"I don't want to," I said.

"Come on."

"No."

Ms. Hardwood stepped up to the microphone. "Alice McGuire," she said. "Come up here immediately or we won't give you your diploma."

I didn't look at anyone but Catherine Swan, who was standing there holding an envelope. She hugged me.

"It's a payoff for sleeping with your dad," she murmured into my ear.

"Slut," I whispered back, slinking down the side stairs to be cheered by all the prisoners except Frank, who didn't look at me.

Isabelle's documentary was embarrassing. Basically, she filmed her annoying Italian boyfriend explaining why he was such a genius, why Italy was the source of all artistic inspiration, and why he was just a big stud. Well, he didn't explicitly state the stud part but he was clearly in love with himself. Isabelle kept murmuring questions that you couldn't hear and his answers revolved around the issue of his greatness. The applause was sporadic, and when the lights came on 95 percent of the school was fast asleep. Wendy's performance piece was interesting but unpleasant; the music was earsplitting and the visuals were hideous. It was hard to tell what the point was, and she didn't offer an explanation. There was a slide show of Peruvian clowns performing magic tricks presented by a boy who'd spent his five months in the circus outside of Lima. A girl who wrote a play read the first act, which was very bad, and several other students displayed ceramics thrown on handmade potter's wheels, and one girl showed a huge, gorgeous tapestry she'd woven while she was living with Coptic monks in Ethiopia.

Morgan's band was great, and we all got up and danced despite Mr. Farley asking us to remain in our seats.

Sigrid's opera played without anything to look at. It took a moment for people to realize how amazing it was, but then the entire assembly was silent, listening but silent. Sigrid was so far forward in her seat, her forehead was resting on the seat in front of us. I could feel she was criticizing things, but she was the only one. The cops on each end of the prisoners were wiping their eyes, the prisoners had their heads bowed as if they were praying in church.

When it was over, Morgan went up to the podium. "This is a tribute to someone who inspired Sigrid's opera," he said. "She was murdered."

I didn't look at Frank.

The video was projected on the huge screen above the stage. The audio started with those words she had spoken in the music studio: *I was happy. My mother was up in heaven watching over us, and Antoinette would never go away.* As Sigrid explained how she watched her babysitter get strangled, music from her opera was audible behind the words. It was very, very sad. Morgan had added news footage about the murder, and there were several shots of a younger Frank being led away in chains. The video also contained clips from the Andersons' home movies combined with still pictures of Antoinette growing up. It ended with a gorgeous black-and-white portrait of her reading a book to Sigrid and Thor sitting on her lap in a rocking chair with the dates of her birth and death under the image. They looked like angels. People were openly sobbing. It occurred to me that Morgan Crawford had a huge career in front of him since he knew exactly how to push people's buttons.

The prisoners had asked me to introduce them by telling the audience they would read letters they had written to apologize to their victims. One after another stood and read. It was surprisingly effective and dramatic. When Frank walked up onstage, several kids in the audience recognized him. There were scattered gasps; one kid applauded until Frank shot him such a mean look, he stopped.

"Hello," he said. "My name is Frank Perone and I killed your classmate's baby-sitter, Antoinette Warchowski. She was twenty-two years old, had two younger brothers, a horse named Harry, and a birthmark on her shoulder blade. If she had lived I'm sure she would have been a great doctor. She wanted to have three children and not let them eat sugar or watch television. She liked me to brush her hair. She was the most beautiful woman I have ever seen in my life." Frank stared at the far wall, "It would be good to be blind now," he said, like we weren't there, "better than this. Antoinette's mother called her Tiny and her father called her Elsa because when she was a baby she loved Elsa the cow. She cut her teeth at four and learned to read at three. Her parents are named Janet and Doug, and they hate me. Each time I have a parole hearing the whole family shows up and explains why I should rot in jail. I agree and welcome their insight into why I don't deserve to breathe the same air as the rest of the world."

Frank paused, searched the seats until he saw me, and then smiled. "Congratulations, Teach," he said softly.

"Thanks," I answered.

"How was that?" he asked. "Enough effective detail?"

I nodded.

"Here it is then," he said, "a letter to Antoinette Warchowski.

"Dear Antoinette,

I don't know what it's like to be dead but jail can't be all that different. In all this time I've accomplished nothing worth mentioning except I got a big tattoo on my arm and I learned what a bad childhood I had. You told me but I always thought you were just a spoiled girl who had it too easy. But now I know what happened to me was really bad and sad and maybe it is a reason why I lost my temper so long ago and kept hurting you until there was nothing left to hurt.

But it doesn't matter anymore why I did it. I wish I could give an explanation because there's another girl, a girl who reminds me of you who needs to understand how someone kills another person. The trouble is, everything is so damn different. Hitler killed the Jews because he hated them and was afraid of them and then some lady in Japan drowns her kids because she thinks it's a better life for them to be dead. Go figure, huh?

It comes down to this, like the bible says, an eye for an eye. It's never gonna make a difference to the people that want you back that I can't have a life but it's still the right thing.

Here are the things I want to thank you for. I thank you for telling me I was a good dancer and that I was funny. I thank you for showing me love and also that it's okay to feel sad sometimes. I thank you for thinking I had the capacity to change and wasn't the sad little asshole my grandmother thought I was.

When you told me you were going back to Poland to see your sister, I thought you weren't ever coming back. I thought your old boyfriend had probably asked you to marry him and you would disappear like all the other people I had loved in my life. I wanted you to stay or let me come with you but I was too proud to ask for that. And then you called me stupid and selfish which was true but it made me crazy to hear you say those things. I lost my temper and then I lost everything.

I'm sorry, Antoinette. And I'm sorry to the girl who is sitting in this room who watched me kill her friend.

Sincerely,
Frank Perone"

Frank bowed his head and everyone was quiet for a second. Nobody applauded. When we looked up, Sigrid was standing on the edge of the stage.

"Hi," she said.

"Hi," Frank answered. "Did you write that music?"

Sigrid nodded.

"It's great," he said. "Really great."

"Thanks," Sigrid said.

They stared at each other for a minute.

"Remember that time you braided my hair?" Sigrid suddenly asked.

I looked over and saw Farley looking upset. He was clearly about to move when Mr. Anderson gestured toward him and then he stayed where he was.

"It didn't look too good," Frank said softly.

"My mother always did that for me," Sigrid said.

"And you wouldn't let Antoinette do it," Frank added.

"I wanted my mother to do it," Sigrid said, her voice shaking a little.

"Of course you did," Frank said. "Who better?"

"It helped to hear your letter," she said. "And those other things as well. I wanted to know who you were but no one ever told me anything."

Frank nodded. "It's kind of hard to explain bad things to little kids," he said. "How's Thor?"

"He's fine." Sigrid gestured toward the audience. "He's here with my dad."

"Is your dad doing okay?"

Sigrid nodded.

"That's good," Frank said. "I don't ever expect to be forgiven for this. I just go to the parole hearings to make the state happy."

"You did a terrible thing," Sigrid said.

Frank nodded.

"I'm sorry you had such a bad childhood," Sigrid said.

Frank shook his head. "Doesn't mean anything," he said. "A person has to still do the right thing."

"Well, good-bye," Sigrid said.

"Good-bye, Sigrid." Frank waved. "Have a great life."

Sigrid nodded. "You should write a book," she said.

Frank shook his head. "There's nothing else," he said. "It's already the last page."

THE PRISONERS WERE EATING COOKIES and drinking the punch that marked every social occasion at our school. Mr. Farley was shaking everyone's hand and telling them how much he enjoyed their poetry. Maybe he'd been on some kind of drug during all the years of the readings.

Frank handed me a wrapped package before he followed the others out the door.

"Happy birthday," he said.

I opened it because I knew he wanted to see what I thought. It was a homemade book, the paper sort of mottled lilac and bound between two gorgeous covers with a watercolor picture of a phoenix rising out of the ashes. It was blank inside.

"Why didn't you write something?" I asked.

"That's your job," he said. "Tell your story."

"I was supposed to teach you," I said. "I was supposed to help you." I started to cry.

Frank laughed. "Oh yeah, how's that? Some rich high school cookie gonna teach me about the way of the world?"

I nodded.

"Well," he said, "it's like this—you let me teach you so I learned. We can't be just givers in this world and we can't just take. That's why we all came on your team, darlin'. It wasn't just how pretty you were but the way you let us show our real selves." Frank gestured toward Hal, who was standing with Farley. "Guy means well, but he'll go through this world with a mind like an Etch-A-Sketch; you shake it and everything disappears." He looked back at me. "Now you understand there are terrible people in this world, right?"

I nodded.

"And don't ever trust anyone until you know them. But maybe you see what is good and worth keeping too?"

I nodded.

"I'm proud of you. Is that okay?"

I nodded. If I said anything I'd start to cry again, and I knew he didn't want me doing that.

"Remember, you have a choice about how your life turns out, Alice. Matthew chose you, which was the best thing he could have ever done. He saw he had met perfection in kindergarten and he wasn't ever letting go."

"Then why did he let go?"

Frank shook his head. "Life let go of him, Alice. Maybe it was as

long as it was written. He was put on this earth to help all these people and to leave you with all them perfect memories. You gonna be
okay. Just don't take any shit."

He put his hand out and I took it. His fingers were strong but his
hand was soft. The prisoners were waving good-bye as they filed out
the door.

"I'll never see you again, will I?" I asked.

He smiled. "Not if you stay out of trouble," he said. "You just
have your life, blue-eyed girl, and we'll keep you right where you
belong, eighteen years old, sweet and smart."

He tapped his chest, gave me this two-fingered salute, and
strolled out the door.

Twenty

WHEN I WALKED INTO FARGO'S with my mom, there was a huge table full of people, wearing silly paper hats, waving tiny little banners from the University of Wisconsin. We had a private room to ourselves. On another side table was an enormous cake shaped like an open door. Through the door you could see a path lined with frosting flowers, leading to what appeared to be Fairyland.

"Who made the cake?"

My mother scowled. "Me!"

"Who decorated it?"

"Amy."

She was sitting at one end of the table, looking oddly incomplete without Ms. Hardwood and Gracie.

People were very excited. At first I thought maybe someone had slipped Ecstasy into the punch or maybe all the adults were drunk. Catherine Swan had brought Samsara, Nell, and Chloe, who were dressed in their usual way, scarves and lace and things that trailed. Waiters were hovering around them with water pitchers, trembling in their eagerness to be of help. Alf and Thor were sitting next to each other wearing ironed T-shirts which didn't appear to be advertising any death metal bands. Thor's cast was so decorated you couldn't see the plaster anymore.

My mother sat down next to my dad, and then everyone looked at me. Catherine Swan picked up her fork to tap her glass. Sigrid's dad was sitting next to her, and for a moment I thought he had cut his hair or bleached his teeth but then I realized he just looked happy, which made him handsome. I shook my head at Catherine Swan, but she tapped anyway.

"Speech!" Thor and Alf bellowed like they were at a concert.

"Freebird," Ms. Hardwood yelled, coming up behind me to give me a hug.

I hugged her back and whispered into her ear, "Don't get mad at me."

As soon as she saw Amy she ran her hand through her short hair and sort of smiled. Gracie ran down the length of the table screaming "Mama!" and threw herself into Amy's lap.

I gave Ms. Hardwood a little push. "Don't be too proud," I said. "Think of how long it took you to be this happy."

When Ms. Hardwood sat down next to Amy there was scattered applause, which stopped when she gave everybody really mean looks.

I started to sit down, but I was pushed back on my feet by my mother. "Give us something to ponder," she said.

I glared at her. "It's my birthday," I said. "Other people are supposed to make speeches."

Alf stood up. "I'll say a few words," he said, raising a glass of what appeared to be champagne.

"Sit down!" I jumped to my feet. "Okay," I said. "Here is a short speech that is unprepared and I'm only doing it because my mother made me."

"Damn the torpedoes," said Ms. Hardwood.

"Mommy swore!" Grace screamed.

"My parents are here and they should stay married. You're too weird and obvious to get divorced. Mom, stop pretending you want a new boyfriend, and Daddy, don't have any more affairs. Catherine, you were sort of a bad mother, but then you were a wonderful one and Matthew never cared about the bad part. Nell, stop being such a bitch. Chloe, go back to school. Samsara, go to rehab. Amy, she doesn't want to have a baby, you don't need another baby, and if you can't be happy with just Grace, get a dog."

"I want a dog, Mommys," Grace screamed.

"Alf, you are a wonderful, strange kid. Stay out of my room. Thor, don't break anything else. Morgan, I'm actually glad you'll be in Wisconsin, but I'm not going to be your girlfriend unless every boy in Madison is totally subpar. Wendy, that performance piece sucked, and you should major in journalism because you really write much better than anyone I know. Sigrid, you are going to be so famous you'll probably want a better best friend, but for now, I'm all you've got."

I sat down. Everyone looked a little shocked.

"Okay?" I asked my mother.

She nodded. "Plenty to ponder," she said.

After I blew out my candles, Laura Youngblood said a Native American prayer for the dead. She didn't say which dead, so everyone could imagine whomever it was they were missing. It was a really nice prayer about nature and weather and mountains. And then we got a little drunk and danced, and I kissed Morgan twice and I hugged my parents about thirty times and even told Alf he was wonderful. It was my birthday, and somehow I felt hope that we would all be better next year.

AND THEN WE GRADUATED.

Isabelle's dress was really unflattering. It made her look fat, which is weird because she's really skinny. She kept asking people if it made her look fat, and they took too long to say "No, of course not," so she was having this total meltdown. I think it was the cut because the fabric got all bunched up around the hips.

Wendy Henninger turned up in a gray dress, which didn't follow the all-white Ku Klux Klan effect we were going for. Mrs. Bennett, the coach for girls' hockey and lacrosse, said Wendy should not be allowed to commence because she lacked respect for Millstone's mission and traditions. No one wanted to tell her she had her head up her butt because there was never any tradition that demanded all-white dresses. It was a style thing, which I think is very shallow. And none of us knew Millstone had any particular mission except to charge our parents a ton of money and get us into as many Ivy League schools as possible so more parents would be willing to pay even more money.

But it was hot and humid, at least ninety-five degrees, most of us were hungover and just wanted to get our diplomas and go get drunk again and then leave home for good, so nobody said anything.

"It's a question of uniformity," Mrs. Bennett said, glaring at Wendy, who was wearing these Yoko Ono wraparound sunglasses.

"Exactly," Wendy said. "Uniforms totally suck."

"You wouldn't feel that way, Wendy, if you'd ever actually made it onto a real team."

I couldn't believe an adult would be so mean. Until last year Wendy had tried out for every sports team at school. She'd had an older sister who went to Yale on a lacrosse scholarship. The only time she was chosen was for intramural badminton, which was where all the burnouts ended up. Then she started piercing all available surfaces, which made her ineligible for anything more demanding than tetherball during gym.

"Look, Mitzie," Ms. Hardwood said, getting right in Mrs. Bennett's face, which made her back away. I mean, what if Ms. Hardwood suddenly had this mad butch moment and grabbed Mrs. Bennett's face and started French-kissing her? "What difference does it make? So we have ninety-seven all-white seniors and one who looks a little muddy?"

"It's not this specific transgression," Mrs. Bennett said, "it's the big picture."

"Well, big picture this, babe. These kids are all crossing the stage and graduating!"

I love Ms. Hardwood.

Morgan's car screeched up to the curb so fast that it shuddered on its front tires. When he got out he was wearing a lime green tux that looked like the tux John Travolta wore in *Pulp Fiction*.

"Oh my God," Isabelle Folonari said, forgetting her hips. "You look like a pimp."

Morgan beamed. "Smoke Papa gave me this," he said to Ms. Hardwood loud enough so we could all hear. "He had it made for the Essence Awards, but then he decided to wear something else."

"I can't imagine why," Ms. Hardwood said. "All right, Morgan, you come at the end with Wendy. We'll pretend you're foreign exchange students or something."

"He looks like a pimp," Isabelle said, her face red.

"And you look like a veal sausage," Sigrid said.

Isabelle began to answer, but the flowers were being distributed and they were all wrong. We were supposed to carry white roses and lilacs, but the florist had sent purple irises and great red flowers that looked like peonies. Isabelle got on her cell phone and started screaming at someone named Saul, who ran the flower shop. The florist delivery guy stood there holding a yellow paper, waiting for someone to sign.

Ms. Hardwood gave him a tip, signed the sheet, and he drove away. She walked over to Isabelle and held out her hand. "Give me the phone," she said. "You are graduating from high school. Flowers and dresses are meaningless. Do this when you get married. You'll never see these people again. You have your whole life to be a control freak. Give it a rest."

And then we graduated. Mr. Farley made this terrible speech that made no sense, and people started to shuffle and mumble. It was so hot several people fainted, and the boys loosened their collars or took their ties off and the girls started hiking up their dresses and kicking off their shoes. By the time we picked up our diplomas we were a mess, and then we ripped the heads off the peony flowers and threw them at the audience, which covered them in scarlet petals which was really pretty awesome.

WE ALL GOT UP for breakfast even though I didn't really go to bed. But Catherine Swan was coming to get me at ten so we could start our drive to Mexico to bring home the bones. My mother made this ridiculous amount of food: banana pancakes and waffles and homemade coffee cake and fruit salad and bacon and some kind of weird chutney. No one but Alf was eating anything. I could tell she was very upset by the way her skin was tight across her face and how she just kept heating things up. I'd never be home again to stay. I knew this had to be hard on my parents, but it made me feel wonderful, light and happy just to love the whole world because finally it was starting for me. I needed to go but she wanted me not to want to leave and I couldn't pretend that and it hurt her.

"Mom?" I said finally. "Come sit and eat with us."

She didn't answer me. She just stared out the window above the sink, which framed our old tree house. "We're going to take the tree house down," she said finally.

"Okay," I said.

"Alf is too big for it now and it's dangerous." She sounded like she had something stuck in her throat.

"Julia," my dad said, "come sit down with us."

"Can I have some more bacon, Mom?" Alf said. He had eaten an entire plate full of bacon.

"Holy shit," I said. "You're going to have a heart attack."

"Mom," Alf said, "Alice said shit."

"Shut up," I said. "Fat boy."

"Mom," Alf said.

My mother turned around and stared at me. She was crying. "Can't you even act like you're sad?" she asked. "Won't you miss us at all?"

"Julia," my father said, "don't do this to her."

But I got up and crossed to where she was and I hugged her close. I was as tall as she was, a bit taller, and she felt small and too bony in my arms. "I can't help it," I said, "this is what happens."

"Will you be careful?" she asked.

I nodded.

"Mom," Alf whined, "Alice called me fat boy."

"Tell your sister how much you're going to miss her," my mother said.

"Yeah," Alf said, "like a rash on my ass."

"Alfred," my father said, "no computer for a week."

My dad had burned a CD for us with traveling music on it: the

Allman Brothers ("Rambin' Man"); Simon and Garfunkel ("America"); Tom Waits (a bunch of songs, he was always leaving); Peter, Paul, and Mary ("Leaving on a Jet Plane"); and some others. He took me outside to give me a minitutorial on how to change a tire on the road, but we both knew we were just avoiding saying good-bye, so as we leaned over the wheel I cried and he patted my back.

"There, there," he said, "it's not like you're leaving home."

I straightened up. "Yes, it is," I said.

He looked surprised. "Oh," he said, "but. Madison's just down the road."

"It's eight hundred miles, Daddy."

"Yes," he said, "but you're here. You aren't out of reach, honey, you're close enough so we know we can see you if it becomes unbearable—"

"What becomes unbearable?"

"Not seeing you."

"You think that will happen?"

He nodded.

It's strange to be loved so well. Strange and wonderful. All my life I'll have to keep quiet about how destructive and bad my parents were. I won't be able to grow up and write a memoir about being left at a gas station or abused or neglected. I will start out by saying "My parents loved me," and no one will buy my book. It doesn't help either that I'm not a Chinese American lesbian with dyslexia.

THE BONES WERE ALREADY CREMATED, and the urn was in the house of the mayor of the town where Matthew's bones had been dug up. Catherine had provided my parents with a detailed itinerary and a map with our route highlighted in red. We would be gone for three weeks. She had friends in North Carolina we would visit on the way back, and I had a cousin in Texas who wanted us to spend the weekend with her.

I know it probably sounds sick, but I was really happy Matthew's ashes would be coming home with us. Catherine was going to give me a vial filled with them that I could keep forever. When you love someone so much your teeth ache when you are near them, nothing matters. If we had been able to grow old and sick with each other, I would have loved him the same way I love him now. I love him even though he's dead and I will love him until I die and it won't be cheesy like the end of *Titanic*.

It won't be two movie stars walking into the sunset but just me, Alice, and my boy who I knew my whole entire life except the little bit before kindergarten. And we'll walk into the garden like Hansel and Gretel or Heathcliff and Cathy, the garden of lost children who finally come home again. Our parents will be there also, and my mother's parents and Uncle Adam and the other people we thought were gone for good. But mostly it will be just me and Matthew, and we'll talk about the things that happened during the time he went away.

When it gets dark we'll lie down together and fall asleep holding hands. That's what you do when you love someone; you hold on tight and you don't forget anything. You say good night and you breathe each other's breath and you gradually go softly quiet and start to remember what it was like before you were born.